WADIA

"Heartwarming, eccentric, tender"

— Siddharth Dhanvant Shanghvi,
author, *Loss*

WADIA

Rohit Trilokekar

Copyright © Rohit Trilokekar 2023
All rights reserved
The moral rights of the author have been asserted.

Cover picture © 1889 books

www.1889books.co.uk
ISBN: 978-1-915045-17-1

To Arav
Never forget your roots

**Part One
Für Elise**

Chapter One
Für Elise

Something happened to seventy-one-year-old Rustom Wadia whenever he heard Beethoven's *Für Elise*. He placed his half-rimmed spectacles back on the desk in his study, because they served no purpose when it came to experiencing the marvellous composition that had enthralled his soul for ages (and undoubtedly millions of others over the passage of time). Only moments before, he had read (or tried to read) through a section of Homer's Iliad for the umpteenth time, without quite getting the gist of what the author was trying to say. A voice from a time forgotten. He had played Beethoven's magnum opus (at least to him there could be no other) on a vintage gramophone (for that matter, were they not all vintage in this day and age?) after placing Homer's masterpiece gingerly back in the bookcase that covered an entire wall in the study on the first floor of his large Bandra bungalow. The bungalow that was the envy of all the Christians in the neighbourhood. *Mansion*, they called it. There was a good reason for that envy, too. Bandra was their territory and if anyone should have the best looking house in it, it must be a 'Cattolic.' Or perhaps even a 'Protestant.' But they had never had a chance since the late 1800s, when this house seemingly arose out of nowhere (it was a barren plot of land no Christian had ever deemed fit to buy, and now just look at what had sprouted from it) and literally dwarfing Mr. Lobo's house (the one that used to have the most fancy decorations every Christmas) in both size as well as class. Needless to say, the best decorations at Christmas time in these here parts, were those in the Wadia household.

It had been Rustom's great grandfather, the late Jamshed Wadia, who had had this palatial structure erected, having migrated to Bombay from Surat and fallen in love with Bandra's idyllic existence. After all, the genteel Parsi was a bit accustomed to the *susegad* lifestyle that was, and is, pretty rampant in Goa. His several trips in Goa had fostered in him a deep love for the city; so much so that he almost considered giving up his business and moving there. But better sense prevailed (to him, that is) and in the end Bandra had been a great compromise. You could spend several hours at places like Bandstand and Carter Road, and feel like you were in Goa. Besides, he had set up a factory in the other part of town and his business had boomed ever since he set foot in Bombay soil. He had been a bachelor until the day an orphan showed up at his doorstep; that very orphan was the reason Rustom existed in the first place.

Nights in the Wadia household in the present era, were like this: a glass of whisky (or two) followed by dinner in the living room, followed by a splash of Cognac (or two), then off to the study on the first floor, Wadia's most cherished room. It was here that he had been introduced to the greats in literature, from Shakespeare to Dostoevsky, by his father, the erstwhile Percy Wadia. It was also the room where he would come to cry every night. It was a ritual, just like any of the several other rituals he indulged in on a daily basis. He would play Für Elise on the record player. And he would cry.

He stared at the photograph of his father, the late Percy Wadia, a distinguished-looking gentleman wearing a stylish black hat, fitted in what appeared to be a striking bespoke suit. Old-fashioned, of course. Like his whisky. Not the cocktail, mind you; he believed anyone who mixed anything with their alcohol was sheer nuts. Not *daru*, as Wadia would refer to it every now and then, but *alcohol*. In that sense, Percy Wadia was very much like a Britisher. After all, he had been married to a fine British lady for the better part of his life, until she passed away in the most sordid fashion on the lawns of the Willingdon club in Haji Ali at a tea party the Wadias had been invited to by some British magnate who was just settling down in Mumbai with his Chinese wife.

The late Elizabeth Wadia just crumbled, like a cookie would in a cup of chai if it is kept in the hot liquid for a second too long, while the Chinese woman jumped out of her chair and started screaming hysterically. And just like that, Percy Wadia's world crumbled. His Lizzie had gone. Gone as in 'goodbye,' not 'bye.' What would he tell his son Rustom? After all, he was the apple of his mother's eye.

These thoughts, coupled with the still rampant effect of the rather generous splash of Remy Martin he had indulged in just a few minutes earlier, had him crying even harder. He remembered a conversation he had had with his father a long time ago; perhaps when he was around fourteen years of age.

'Rustom, dikra, I want you to know that I have no expectations from you.' Uttered nonchalantly as he buttered his bread, first on one side, then the other (how else to enjoy that *akuri*, no?)

For many years Rustom had pondered the gravity of those words. Was this a father's way of telling his son that he had given up on him? Or was he simply a loving dada who didn't want his son to get embroiled in the proverbial 'rat race,' and instead simply enjoy life (the way he had ended up doing)?

Truth be told, there was but one man that was truly responsible for this legacy having been passed down to Percy. His father, Rustom's grandfather, had been a menial slave somewhere in the last part of the nineteenth century (before he had found himself tossed around in several foster homes), until he finally arrived at the house of a Mr. Jamshed Wadia, a Parsi bachelor who kept mostly to himself. *Jammy*, as Jamshed was affectionately (or perhaps not) called by his *Cattolic* (as Jammy called his Catholic neighbours, affectionately or not) neighbours, hardly made an appearance, except to go to the Caledonian Co-operative bank on the other side of the street once a week (first thing every Monday morning, to be precise).

Jamshed took an instant liking towards the little boy, who must have been around fifteen years or so when he arrived at the former's home, hungry and in search of work. He would later find that the boy's earlier employer of the last couple of years, a Gujju gentleman, a certain Mr. Kenny Shah, had kicked him out (literally, with his prized leather boots; the boy would remember those boots till the end of his time because he never saw boots so beautiful in all his life) on account of his having innocently gawked at his beautiful eldest daughter Petunia (she really was every bit as pretty as a petunia, thought the boy several years later after he discovered that the word petunia was also used to describe a flower), freshly returned from London after her higher studies.

No amount of education in schools can teach you to be kind, is what Mr. Wadia had told the boy a couple of years later, after the latter had revealed to him the exact fashion in which he had found himself at the doorstep of this home that was filled with the *warmth of a hundred thousand candles* (these were the actual words he used, which made the old man's heart swell with joy). To the others, Mr. Jamshed Wadia might be crazy, but to the little boy he was no less than God himself. After all, he had changed his life forever.

As a matter of sheer coincidence, the boy had all the features of a Parsi child. It was as though he was *meant* to show up at Jamshed's doorstep. But the one thing Mr. Wadia could not understand was this: how could a Parsi be a slave? He had never heard of a Parsi slave, let alone a Parsi who was poor. Where were his parents? That was something the little boy could not answer. All he remembered was a few foster homes he had spent time in, and those memories were not too kind. The topic was never broached again. Needless to say, the boy never lifted a finger to do menial labour thereafter. In due course, Jammy legally adopted Dhunji (which was the name he gave the young child) and provided him with all the comforts money could buy.

Everything seemed to be going just fine in the Wadia household, until one fine day Mr. Wadia had a massive stroke in the middle of the night. There was nobody at his funeral, except for little Dhunji. Well, by then, he was not so little any more. Popularly known in Bandra circles as the *Prince of Perry Cross Road*, the thirty-year-old was the eligible young bachelor all the Christian ladies wanted for their daughters. The Prince who was now King.

In the later years of his life, Dhunji Wadia would think, as he sat in the balcony outside his study sipping his cup of masala chai at 5 a.m. in the morning, without having to worry about his Cattolic neighbours spying on him, 'Would I have still been adopted if I hadn't been Parsi? What is the *Parsi-ness* in me? Is it because of the way I look? He would tell his son, Percy, several times over in his dying years, 'The one regret I have is not knowing who my mama and dada were. Luckily for Rustom, he knew his parents very well. He was, after all, the apple of his mother's eye. The beautiful 'Lizzie,' as she was popularly known to her friends, and simply 'Mama' to him, most unfortunately had her heart attack when Rustom was the tender age of nine. Old enough to have the most beautiful memories of his mother, old enough to suffer the ravages of loss (even though he kept his sadness inside him for way too long). It was only years later, when his father died, that he *really* cried. In one deft swoop of fate, he had been rendered an orphan.

Rustom was tired. His pets of fifteen-odd years, Polly and Fluffy, had peacefully passed away a decade ago, leaving him all alone in a palatial home. As he stared at his father's portrait again, a thought struck him. Perhaps this pain he felt stemmed from a lack of identity. Maybe it was time to find out more about himself; to *know where he came from*, so to speak. With a renewed sense of energy, he got up and trod slowly across the wooden floor of the study (this was the only room in the house with wooden flooring) towards the door. And then the lights went off.

The next morning, Wadia watched the tea flow into his saucer as his wiry servant poured it nimbly, his hands trembling for fear he might create a splash. This was the way his dada had had his chai, and before that, his dada's dada. It was on account of his grandfather's humble upbringing (in the years before he had been adopted, that is), that he drank his chai in a fashion usually reserved for society's lower crust. Most servants he had seen, drank their tea in this fashion. Like they could never envision using a Western toilet.

"Thanks, Ramukaka," he said and the old man's face lit up like a million light bulbs. *He* certainly seems happy today, thought Rustom. Ramukaka had been the help in the Wadia household for years; and before that, he had been Rustom's best friend. They were of the exact same age, although Ramukaka was certainly in better physical shape than Rustom, on account of the manual labour he did, undoubtedly. After Lizzie Wadia's death, though, something changed in Ramu. He kept his distance from Rustom, and the latter couldn't understand why he had been abandoned in a moment of crisis by his best friend. It was only later on, when he was much older and he reflected on how his best friend had literally turned into a servant overnight, that he came to the realization he should have arrived at years ago. With his mama gone, Ramu felt it was his responsibility to take care of the little prince. And take good care he did; whilst earlier he would be lost in a game of Monopoly with Rustom, now he ensured his master got all his meals on time and that the house was spotlessly clean. It would still be a while before Rustom called him Ramukaka, of course.

And it was right then, in the midst of being lost in the past, that Wadia remembered what he needed to do today. He had to get some clarity about 'his roots'; to gain a better appreciation of where he came from. And there was only one person that came to his mind. His Maharashtrian friend, Anil Velkar.

"Hello. Anil? Can you hear me?"

"I can always hear you, bawa. You're always full volume."

"I have something of great significance to discuss with you. Could I come over for a cup of chai?"

Velkar was silent for a few moments.

"I can do better than chai. My wife has cooked the most amazing kolambiche khadkhadle and we are having it for lunch. Would you like to join us?"

Wadia could never say no to a lunch invite. Why, even the slightest mention of the words *vada* and *pav* uttered in unison, or perhaps even separately, could get him excited. Anil stayed on Linking Road in the adjoining suburb of Khar. The reason he had called Anil, was because he was the head of an association of the Pathare Prabhus, a community of Maharashtrians that numbered only seven thousand in the world. If there was anyone who could help him retrace his roots, it was he. But first things first. Lunch, to be precise.

"What time? And do I need to eat a hearty breakfast?"

"12 o'clock. Tiger prawns. Starve."

The phone clicked off. It was just what Wadia needed. He always liked the fattest steaks, the largest ox tongues, and yes, tiger prawns were just about the biggest prawns you could ever get in the market. He waltzed his way to the bathroom, after telling Ramukaka he would be skipping breakfast that day. Vidya's home cooked lunches were the best. Vidya was Velkar's wife. 'Love is blind' was her favourite phrase in the entire English language.

One look at her husband, and it made perfect sense.

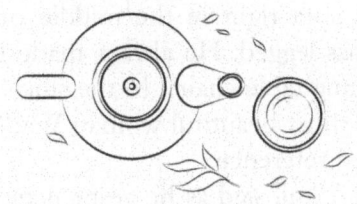

Chapter Two
Kolombiche Khadkhadle

Like Wadia, Anil Velkar also lived in a bungalow, except it was covered in moss. Wadia wondered what the actual colour of the building might be, as he rang the bell and stepped back, waiting for someone to open the door. After several moments had passed and there was no answer, he felt as though he should press the button again. Just when he was about to do so, the door opened. It was Vidya.

"Rustom? What a pleasant surprise. How nice to see you."

"Tiger."

"What?"

"I–I'm sorry. Didn't Anil tell you he invited me over for lunch?"

"Why, that wily fox," she said with a wink. Please, come in."

'The cheek of that fool!' thought Wadia as he walked into the interior of the house that was far more resplendent than its outside. And there, on the sofa right in the middle of the living room, his friend Anil sat, cross-legged. He always made it a habit to sit cross-legged, even on dining table chairs. In the single seater to his left on a sofa chair, was the most beautiful woman Wadia had seen in his life. Hence, the 'wily fox' reference.

"Meet Manjiri," Anil said as he gesticulated towards the vixen in the armchair. She gave Wadia a smile, but seemed nowhere as besotted at the sight of the rotund Parsi gentleman as he had been, by a mere glance at her.

"Beer?" Vidya chimed in.

"I'll have two." Everyone burst into laughter.

At the dining table, Wadia felt it inappropriate to bring up the subject matter of his roots. Right now, in any case, what mattered more was this lovely flower he had just been introduced to. He had gleaned over the course of drinks, that Manjiri Prabhu was Anil Velkar's cousin. Unlike Anil, however, she was a Brahmin. She had made a point of stressing that, for reasons she knew best.

Wadia tucked into the first tiger prawn he had carefully selected from the large stainless steel vessel the prawns had been cooked in (he had selected the largest one of course, because it would undoubtedly be the juiciest) and closed his eyes right after he took that first bite.

"Don't like it, kaay?" Anil asked, but Wadia knew it would be Vidya who would be more worried. After all, it was she who had cooked it. If Wadia could have put his fork down for dramatic effect right then, he would have done it. Except, there was no fork. In this house, you ate with your hands. In gorgeous stainless steel plates. Just like most Maharashtrians did.

"This is by far the most amazing prawn curry I have eaten in my life, thank you, Vidya," he remarked, and Vidya's face lit up. Velkar, seeming a bit distraught all of a sudden, intervened.

"I go to the market and get the prawns, and *thanks* only to Vidya?"

"The prawns are indeed fresh and juicy, Velkar Saheb," Wadia said, and paused for effect before continuing, "But this *khad* gravy – what do you call it – absolutely *makes* the dish."

"The name is khadkhadle. Kolambiche khadkhadle." Spoken just like one might utter the words James and Bond, in that particular order.

"This dish is reminiscent of our roots," said Vidya proudly. Rustom noticed that Manjiri hadn't touched the prawns. Might she be vegan? But – wait a minute – had someone just uttered the word 'roots'? He forgot about Manjiri as quickly as the thought of her had entered his mind.

"I see," said Wadia, lifting his beer glass and finishing the remnants of that second Kingfisher pint, before tucking into another gargantuan bite of the *kolambi*, which was what the Maharashtrians called *prawns*. He laughed then, as a thought entered his mind. The *prawns* could very well be a sub-community that belonged to the larger *fish community*.

"It's very important to know your roots, you see," Vidya continued. "This dish you are eating here, kolambiche khadkhadle, as Anil rightly pointed out, is highly representative of our Pathare Prabhu roots. How on earth can you get a feeling of being a part of the community you belong to, if you don't sample and relish its local fare?" Why the hell had he called Anil? Rustom thought. He should have called Vidya instead. But no, then his dear friend Anil would think he was *line maraoing* his wife, and that would be the end of their friendship. In retrospect, not such a bad idea.

"That's exactly what I wanted to talk to Anil about," Wadia said excitedly, confused as to whether he should finish the remainder of the half-eaten tiger prawn in his right hand, or tell the others at the table the real reason for him being here. At least, conversations at the dining table in the Velkar household weren't frowned upon. His late mother Lizzie had ensured that nobody spoke while they had their meals at the table. It was the 'proper' thing to do, she said. After all, she was a Britisher and she ensured that Wadia was raised with the best possible manners. Little did she know her only son would turn out to be the kind who would scratch their bottom on the way to the bank across the street in their later years, while the Braganza children next door squealed in laughter.

"Oh really? And what makes you think Anil knows anything about his roots? He doesn't even know which vegetables *are* roots," said Vidya, and both women laughed. Anil was stone-faced. First, the fish thing, and now this. It wasn't even a great joke. No, he was being deliberately outed here. He turned to his mad bawa friend for support. As if reading his friend's mind in Marathi (*Aata mi kay karu?* It seemed to say), Wadia spoke.

"He *is* the President of the Pathare Prabhu Association, isn't he?"

"All humbug," Vidya said, dismissing what Wadia had just said with a wave of her hand. "The actual origins of one's roots lie in one's household; certainly not in a small organization that procures large funds seemingly from nowhere."

Wadia looked at the fancy artefacts in the wooden cupboard with the glass front, right opposite to where he sat at the dining table. So *that's* where the money for these came from, he thought. Perhaps I should organise an I-T raid.

"I wish I knew my roots." He sighed.

Vidya's harsh exterior seemed to soften all of a sudden. She knew all about Wadia's ancestry – that his grandfather had been a slave, and that she might be treading in precarious territory here. Nevertheless, she went on.

"Well, why don't you find out more about him, then?"

"Who?"

"Dhunji Wadia. Your grandfather, you know. For instance, where he was before he came to your place." She said *where he was* instead of *where he worked*, to perhaps soften the blow.

"What a brilliant idea!" Wadia almost screamed, leaving three terrified Maharashtrians, out of which one was a Brahmin. A few moments later, he seemed to have come down from that sudden high. There was absolutely nothing he knew of the old man, who had passed long before he came into this world, except for some fragments of conversation at the dinner table. How was he to find out anything of relevance about him?

"What's the matter?" Manjiri said, and Vidya gestured to her with her right hand, to leave it be.

"I will help you," Anil said.

"You will? But how?"

"For that you have to invite me over for Parsi chai."

The ladies looked at Anil, clearly flabbergasted.

"Anil? Kay kartos? Can't you see that your friend is in pain?" Vidya said.

Anil squirmed in his seat, before appearing to gain some semblance of confidence.

"Well, it certainly didn't seem that way when he was relishing that tiger prawn."

Even dirtier stares from the women.

"It's perfectly all right. You can come over this evening itself for a nice piping hot cup of Parsi chai, Anil. In fact, I would love it if all of you would come."

"I can't come. I have my primetime show on Sony TV. Please take Anil with you." Wadia knew there were no primetime shows in the evening (because four o clock in the evening was not prime time); however, that was Vidya Velkar's way of getting her much-needed space from her husband.

"I have a flight to catch," said Manjiri.

And Rustom looked at Manjiri and thought, 'never mind. It would never have worked out anyway.'

She was vegetarian.

Chapter Three
A Cup of Chai

"The great thing about chai," said Wadia, after taking a long, slurpy sip from his white china saucer that blended perfectly with the white exteriors of his home, "is it's a great humbler. There are emperors who drink in the company of peasants, and I can tell you this: the peasant feels none the lesser in the company of the grand emperor when he is sharing tea that has been brewed in the same pot. Neither does the emperor feel any more magnificent than the peasant."

They were seated in the large balcony that was an extension of Wadia's first floor study. This is where he would come whenever he was feeling low; staring at the birds and enjoying the openness of the place for fifteen minutes, he would be energised again.

Anil Velkar stared at the man he undoubtedly thought of as crazy – Parsi stereotype notwithstanding. *What does he think I am? A peasant?* That being said, the chai or *choi* (as some Parsis like to call it), had been a pleasant treat. Infused with cardamom, it was a pretty nice change to the garma garam *chaha* his mother used to make for him when he was in his late twenties, struggling to find a job. In fact, he loved that daily morning cup of chaha so much, he actually credited it to his finding the job to which he would devote forty long years of his life, until he retired a few years ago. Not that he would ever admit it to Vidya, of course. She would skin him alive.

Unlike Wadia, Velkar drank his chai straight from the teacup. Wadia scoffed whenever he saw someone do that. As though they were too 'proper' to drink it the way it should be: from the saucer, of course. And Velkar thought, 'Only peasants drink in the manner that Rustom does.' The Maharashtrian couldn't stand the sight of someone bringing a saucer filled with chai to their lips, and making those loud slurping noises. Had Rustom's parents not taught him any sense of etiquette? The truth was, Wadia dared not do something like that in front of his parents. It was only after his father's demise, that he dared break convention and drink like his best friend from childhood, Ramu, did. As a child he had not been allowed a cup of tea; yet they allowed Ramu to have it. He wondered why. His parents had told him caffeine was not good for children; why would they let that poor boy have it then? They did care for him dearly and even took care of his basic education; why that one slip? He had always wondered.

"Arre, what happened to your best friend? That other bawa – what's his name – yes – Jimmy Mistry?"

"He migrated to Canada," Wadia said wistfully. Jimmy had been his best friend for many years. In fact, he *was* his best friend. Just because you couldn't meet someone who was dear to you, did not imply that there might be any change in the relationship, did it? The last ten years or so had not been as kind to Jimmy Mistry as they had been to Rustom, though. He spent most of his time in bed, and doctors had been clueless as to why he was afflicted by such excruciating weakness. All of his organs seemed to be working perfectly, after all. In the end, his eldest daughter, Delna, had intervened and taken her parents to live with her in her home in Quebec. All Wadia had left was this dolt, Velkar. The backup plan, so to speak, where having a friend was concerned. He wondered many a time what it would be like to tell Ramukaka to stop working and simply 'be his friend.' No, that would never work. The gap had become too large.

"So Mistry is gone, huh? So now… *we* are best friends?" He said this with an impish smile on his face, before holding up his cup of chai to Wadia as though to say 'Cheers!'

Wadia chose not to answer the question. He diverted the subject, with a question he had been meaning to ask somebody – *anyone*, for that matter – for the longest time.

"Velkar, do you think I'm Parsi?"

For a moment Velkar seemed baffled. Then he said, "Why, of course you are. Everything about you suggests you are Parsi. Why do you ask?"

Wadia shook uneasily in his large wicker chair, while kites wheeled in the sky overhead. It was 5 p.m. in early December, and there was that proverbial 'nip in the air.'

"But there remains the possibility that I might not be, right? I mean, there was this girl I had a crush on in a bookstore at Kala Ghoda I would frequent, before I got married. She was the cashier there, and she had the most amazing smile. *Rahila* was her name. Many a time I bought books I didn't even want, just so I could talk to her, although after a few times she realized it wasn't books I was after. I always thought that she might be Gujju, but she turned out to be Muslim."

"What are you trying to say, bawa? You don't like Muslims? I thought as much, given your political inclinations."

"Why– I would never. And political inclinations? I don't support any of these parties. They are all corrupt. I just mean, she turned out to be Muslim, but in my mind's eye I would have never thought her to be one."

"So, what happened to this Rahila of yours?"

"What happened? One day I asked her if she would like to come and eat vada pav with me."

"And then? Then what happened, bawa?"

"She said no."

"Oh."

"You're not getting it, Velkar. The same mistake could happen with me. After all, my grandfather could never quite prove his identity. What if he were indeed not Parsi, after all?"

"That's about the silliest thing I've heard, bawa. If that were the case, at least one person would have thought you were not a bawa. Am I right or what?"

Wadia took another long sip from his saucer, before pouring the remains of the Parsi chai that had been brewed by a Bihari, into the saucer again, for a much needed refill. The Maharashtrian did have a point. However, he didn't seem quite convinced.

"Do you know what the definition of a poor Parsi is, Velkar?"

Velkar looked long and hard at Wadia. What kind of questions was this bugger asking him?

"Well, you most certainly aren't one."

"According to the Bombay Parsi Punchayet, a poor Parsi is one who makes up to 90000 rupees a month."

"Really? That's almost a lakh!" Velkar was shocked. A Maharashtrian making 90000 rupees a month would be considered to be doing rather well for himself. He had been earning that exact same salary at Larsen and Toubro after working there for years. Luckily he was a rich Maharashtrian and not a poor Parsi.

"Yes. And my grandfather was a menial slave who earned nothing. What are the odds of his having been Parsi?"

"I'm sure there must be plenty of poor Parsis out there," said Velkar, draining the last of his Parsi chai.

"Hmmm." Wadia just stared at the kites overhead. For a moment there wasn't even a noise on the street, which normally abounded with the sound of cars honking.

"You said you were going to help me, Velkar. How can you?" It was then that Velkar seemed to assume an air of seriousness.

"We start by finding out the name of your grandfather's employer. Do you have any idea who the man was?"

"All I know was he was a rich Gujju gentleman who lived somewhere in Juhu."

"That's all you know? Didn't he keep a diary or something?"

"I doubt it. Although he did have a great love for literature. Most of the books in my study, belonged to him. Imagine, a boy who was illiterate at the age of fifteen, growing up to read the Iliad. And there are parts of it even *I* can't understand. And I had a good education in Bombay Scottish School, mind you. One of the finest schools in all of Mumbai."

Velkar knew this was a silent taunt to him, as he had gone to a school that was not much better than a municipal school, back in the day. But then, only one of them had gone on to become an engineer, from the Indian Institute of Technology, to boot. So, he let the comment slide.

"The matter of your schooling is indeed most commendable. But let's get on to more important things. Is there anything else you remember about your grandfather?"

"The reason he got kicked out of that household. Apparently, the Gujju gentleman who had enslaved him, well, his daughter had just come home from college in London. Petunia was her name."

"Like the flower?"

"Like the flower. My grandfather never forgot her name, even though he didn't quite know at the time he heard it, what it meant. He told my father her name was as beautiful as the way she looked."

"And therein lies the beauty of our expedition, dear Wadia; the ability to make inferences with even the slightest details."

"What?"

Anil Velkar seemed to have assumed the air of the great detective Sherlock Holmes, after he has thrown light on something *elementary*.

"Wadia, how many girls do you know by the name Jane? I mean, not know personally, but how many times have you heard of a girl who goes by the name Jane?"

"Why, plenty, of course! It's such a common..." And then Wadia got it. Petunia was a name he had never heard before, and it was most possible that if he asked the first hundred people he met at random, none of them would have heard of a girl named Petunia, either. But then, that's what narrowed down the search even further, didn't it? The Maharashtrian was indeed onto something here, or so it seemed.

"So, what do you suggest? We break into a Government office in the middle of the night after scaling its walls, and search through the records with a flashlight?"

"You see too many movies. Of course not, you dimwit. We live in a digital age. Now, while this Petunia would most certainly be long gone by now, there could very well be a mention of her somewhere. All we have to do, is find a reference to her somewhere in some digital archives."

"And how do you propose we do that?"

"You have an internet connection, right?"

"Yes, of course."

"Where is it?"

"In my study."

"Let's go."

That Parsi chai had been quite fine indeed, thought Velkar Saheb as he glanced at Wadia's large *Apple* computer (the one with the big monitor you see in some rich people's houses) come alive. Show-off! It was a little weird to be sitting in a chair reminiscent of a throne, while the actual emperor sat on the edge of his bed right behind him. Weird, but nice. Everyone knew who the real king was, after all. As for the emperor, well, he looked like he had been defeated by the brave warrior Velkar.

'The emperor of delusions!' he thought, as he gesticulated towards his friend with a couple of his fingers, to key in the password. The username was autosaved and displayed on the screen: 'Wadia1111.'

"Fur Elise, all small, no spaces."

"Fur Elise? What kind of password is that?"

"*My* password. That's what kind it is." Velkar could get on your nerves after a few minutes. It was surprising he had tolerated him thus far.

"Okay, okay. Fur Elise. All small, no spaces." Velkar keyed in the word 'furelise' in the password box, pressed the 'Enter' key, and voila! The computer came to life. Rather, the desktop background came alive to the picture of a cat and a parrot, seemingly in meditation together.

"Aah. Fluffy and Polly, the loves of my life," said Wadia, and his eyes seemed to moisten. As though expecting Velkar Saheb to want to know more, he went on, "It's been ten long, lonely years that they have been buried in my back yard. On the way out, I can show you their crosses."

"Spare me the morbidity. Anyways, let's get down to it," said Velkar, who seemed to be in some sort of hurry. I give him the finest Parsi chai and he wants to leave as fast as he can? And Wadia was thinking, it's close to happy hours. He couldn't have this Maharashtrian here for way too long, risking the *sad hours* that might follow thereafter.

"Wait a minute. Did you just say *crosses*?" Velkar had literally turned ninety degrees in his chair, to face Wadia.

"Yes. Why?"

"Don't you guys hang the bodies of your dead in some kind of large well, for the vultures to pluck their entrails out?"

"You mean the 'Tower of Silence'? That practice is now defunct. We use the electric crematorium, much like you people do."

"But why *crosses*?"

Wadia reflected. "It was a conscious decision. You see, I always thought I should give something back to the larger Christian community in Bandra. Respecting the way they bury their dead would be a nice way to start."

"You really are one crazy bawa. Now, about that girl. What was her name? Let's see… Petunia." And he carefully entered the letters that spelt the word Petunia in the Google search bar, as though he were plucking out individual petals of the flower in question. Then, he added the word *Shah* and pressed the *Enter* key.

"Shah? Where did that come from, Velkar?"

"Shhh. Every second Gujju is named Shah. Now, let's see what we have here."

Apparently, nothing. Plenty of references to flowers, some companies even; not a person.

"Velkar, why don't you remove the word 'Shah'? Maybe then you will find something." But there was no response from Velkar.

"This is useless," said Wadia. "There's no way we–"

"Relax bawa, we've just started. Patience is the key. Now, do you have a Facebook account?"

"No."

"Really useless. Never mind. I'll use mine."

"But – why *Facebook*?"

"You will find even Ramukaka there. Want to bet on it?"

"No."

"Very well then." Velkar opened the Facebook website, keyed in his details and signed in. The page opened to a picture of a plate of eggs Benedict, sans bacon but with a rather generous dollop of salmon underneath the perfectly poached egg.

"My niece, in Australia. She loves her eggs Benny with salmon."

Uttered with the greatest sense of relish; as though he had got the salmon from the market himself. No wonder she had her eggs Benny with salmon, thought Wadia. These Maharashtrians and their eternal love of fish. And then, Velkar clicked somewhere and a list titled 'Friends' appeared on the screen.

"See? Five hundred and fifty friends. How many friends do you have, Wadia?" Velkar said this with the greatest sense of pride; like he had won a gold medal for an individual event in the Olympics. Unlike Velkar, Wadia knew that most friendships on platforms like Facebook were unreal. Besides, what did one need friends for?

"I'm not famous like you, Velkar Saheb. Now, can we please proceed to the search?"

"The *search*? What search? Ah! The search, yes!"

And in a small box alongside what appeared to be a small magnifying glass, Velkar Saheb keyed in the word 'Petunia.'

"Wonder of wonders," he said as the screen displayed what appeared to be ten odd results.

"Have you found her? Have you found Petunia Shah?" Wadia strained to see; he had left his reading spectacles downstairs in the living room, as he always did. He only got them upstairs at night, so that he could indulge in his reading ritual.

"*Shah*? What makes you think she's a Shah?" Said the man who had insinuated that she would in all probability be a Shah only moments ago. Then he continued,

"Wait a minute. Let me look at the search results."

"Mightn't she not be on Facebook at all? Considering she lived in the last part of the nineteenth century?"

But Velkar seemed unperturbed, as though he might have tunnel vision; and there was a sparkle in his eyes, as he added the word 'Shah' after the word 'Petunia.'

"But she won't be on Facebook–"

"Sssshh!" said Velkar, effectively silencing the mad bawa. There were zero results. This was turning out to be a lost cause. Then Velkar clicked on a button (if that was what they called the things you clicked on Internet pages, Wadia was not quite sure) titled *Posts*, and what followed was something Wadia would be ever grateful to Velkar for. Velkar clicked on the post. It revealed the picture of a beautiful girl with a charming smile, sitting in what seemed to be the patio of a heritage home. The kind of picture a writer might use for their author page. There was a caption on top of it. Velkar read it out loud for Wadia's benefit.

"In my ancestral home. The legacy my great-grandmother Petunia Shah passed down to me. I have big plans for this place. Stay tuned." He told Wadia the post was dated a mere three months ago. What's better was, there was even a location. 404 Gulmohur Road, Juhu. Juhu! Wadia's ears perked at the very mention of the word. His grandfather had worked in Juhu; he knew that well. Velkar made a note of jotting down the address on a notepad next to the bulky monitor, along with the girl's name, *Toral Shah*.

"Now you can go and meet this Toral Shah and find out all about her great grandmother, Petunia. My job is done."

"Hey! Where are you going?" Velkar had already got up to leave.

"Arre, baba, I have to give Vidya her medicine for diabetes. Then she will give me my medicine also."

"*Your* medicine? What medicine do you take?"

"Old Monk Rum. 60 ml. Two cups, with water."

"I have plenty of better, stronger medicine for you. Come, let's have a drink together." Wadia surprised himself. Only moments earlier the mere thought of having a drink with Velkar, had made him squirm.

"But – who will give my wife her medicine? Sorry, I'm off!"

And without further ado, Velkar ran down the stairs. Wadia shook his head. That severely henpecked Maharashtrian.

Chapter Four
Toral Shah

"Can't get a bloody rickshaw anywhere," thought Wadia as he tried to hail down one of those black and yellow contraptions that could take him to his destination, 404 Gulmohur Road, Juhu, for fewer rupees than taking a taxi would entail. Most of the rickshaws he had stopped, or tried to stop, had either simply whizzed past him without a glance, or shaken their heads and speeded away after he had mentioned the word 'Juhu.' He remembered the time he had a shiny black vintage car that was the envy of one and all on Perry Cross Road. When he drove, everyone would stare. At the car.

Finally, a rickshaw stopped.
"Juhu, please."
"Aa jao, uncle." The word 'please' had done the trick. People were nice to you if you were nice to them. It was really that simple. But 'uncle'?

As the rickshaw sped through the bylanes of Khar on its way to its beachside destination, Wadia was shocked to see how much of the city's landscape had changed in the last ten odd years. Ever since the death of his pets, he hadn't moved out of his bungalow, and now, as he looked at the buildings en route to his destination, every fifth building seemed to be a work in progress, every sixth a high-rise. He thought of all those greedy builders who would harass him every now and then, each of them trying to outdo the other; telling him they would build the fanciest building in all of Bandra in place of his magnificent bungalow (they never mentioned the word 'magnificent,' of course). It would be the *Queen of The Suburbs*, one builder had told him, before Wadia had chased him out of the house, chappal in hand. He already had a magnificent bungalow; why on earth would he want to give it up for a penthouse (no matter how plush the bathroom fittings might be)?

Not long after, the rickshaw had made its way onto Gulmohur Road, Juhu, and Wadia was only a few moments away from 404. Wasn't that number reminiscent of a computer error that flashed on your screen when you didn't get what you were looking for? Was that an indication that he was not going to find anything in this place?

"Rickshawallah, please stop. Let us ask someone or you will end up extorting me." He could converse with this rickshaw driver in English, which was certainly welcome because his Hindi was not up to the mark. He had even learned in the few snippets he had exchanged with the driver along the ride, that this rickshawallah had been a mechanical engineer who had quit everything because he had been disillusioned by the fabric of modern society. Now he drove a rickshaw, and was happy. He had married a Muslim girl against his parent's wishes, but he was happy. He had moved out from his 3BHK[1] in Matunga and was living in a chawl with his new bride. Still, he was happy. "Was anything more important than happiness?" He had asked Wadia, and the bawa had said "No! Certainly not." That was the exact mantra by which he lived his life, after all.

They stopped at the first shop they could find. Wadia asked him, "Bhaisahab, can you please tell me where 404 Gulmohur Road is?" The man appeared to be a paanwallah. He gestured with his finger to the building behind him, and Wadia suddenly felt like a fool.

After having tried unsuccessfully to haggle with the rickshaw driver for the amount of money that had to be paid for the ride, Wadia reluctantly paid him the sum of twenty-three rupees. Next time I will come here walking," he told the mechanical engineer-turned rickshaw driver, who merely laughed it off and said, "Uncle, what are you holding onto? Everything goes away in the end."

"That's right," thought Wadia. He had met Kafka in a rickshaw this fine morning. He looked then at the paanwallah, who seemed to be studying him as though he might be some exotic creature that had just crawled out of the Amazon rainforest.

The place in front of him looked like a restaurant. Could he have been mistaken about the number? Right then the latter part of the girl's Facebook caption rang loud in his ears; the part where she said that she was going to do something great with this place. How dare she convert what undoubtedly looked like a heritage home, into a restaurant? He stormed into the bright blue gates, dismissing the doorkeeper's salute with an angry wave of his hand.

Wadia found himself in a tastefully done up *restobar* (the ones that cannot decide whether they are restaurants or bars). Not that Wadia even frequented restobars; the only restaurants he ever went to

---

[1] 3BHK is a term used by estate agents in the sub-continent: 3 bedrooms, a hall and a single kitchen in the property

were those at The Willingdon Club in Haji Ali, and he hadn't even gone to those in the last ten odd years, on account of the recluse he had become. This part of the restaurant (that seemed like an outside section) had several large coolers that didn't seem to be turned on. And why should they? It was smack in the middle of December. The furniture was chic, tones of beige and white, and he found himself walking on pebbles. He had to ensure he trod carefully, or he was sure to lose his footing and have a nasty fall. He had to sit down. And sit down he did, at the nearest table he could find. There was nobody here except for a couple of waiters, who regarded him with highly curious eyes. Finally one of them, a slim chap with an upturned moustache that deserved to be shaved off with immediate effect, came up to him. He seemed a bit tentative as he spoke.

"Sir, I'm sorry but we open at one o'clock. If you have some work to attend to, then you can finish it and come back?" Wadia had left his home at noon sharp, and he estimated the time must now be around twenty minutes past twelve. He had an internal clock that worked like magic; sometimes he felt like he didn't need his phone at all, to tell him what time it was.

"Some work? I'm of independent means!" Then his voice assumed a deep baritone as he boomed, "Young man, my name is Rustom Wadia. I want to speak to Toral Shah. Is she here?"

Waiter One looked towards Waiter Two, who seemed to be averting his gaze. What an incompetent fool! Couldn't he answer a simple question himself? Where was the maitre d', for crying out loud?

"I'm sorry, sir, but Toral ma'am only comes here at night. You too should come here tonight, Sir. It's karaoke night."

"Are you implying that I leave?"

"N–never, sir! I only meant, you should come here at night, too."

"And you didn't think to add the word 'too' in the appropriate place, in your previous sentence? Don't you realize you said 'You *too* should come here tonight,' instead of saying, 'You should come here tonight, *too*?' Listen to me, young man, and listen to me well. I will not leave until your Toral ma'am comes here, you understand?"

"Just a minute, Sir." Waiter One left him and went towards Waiter Two, who seemed to be standing to attention now, knowing something had gone wrong. The two of them conversed briefly. Then Waiter Two went inside and returned a few minutes later with a third gentleman who seemed to be wearing all-black. Finally, someone in charge. Looking like he were all set to go to a funeral. Perhaps his own.

The man who stood before him seemed to assume an air of importance; as though he might be the manager of this place. He seemed apologetic in tone when he spoke to Wadia. "How can I help you, dear Sir?"

Had the message not been conveyed to him by the nincompoop waiter? Might they think he suffered from Alzheimer's and would forget the very reason he had come here in a mere few moments?"

"Thanks to your incompetence, I am forced to repeat my request. I need to meet with Toral Shah. I know she's your boss, and that you have her mobile number. Give it to me, will you? If you people cannot call her, *I* will!"

The maitre d' shook his head. He knew there was no point in arguing with this man. He fished out his cell phone and quickly pressed a few buttons.

"Ma'am? This is Vinod. What? No, no, nothing's wrong. It's just, there's a gentleman sitting here, who insists on staying until he meets you. What? Does he – wait, I will ask him."

"Toral Madam is asking if you know her?"

"Tell her I haven't had the pleasure."

The message was aptly conveyed to Toral Shah. The manager kept listening to her as she spoke, nodding his head and muttering the word 'Yes,' several times over. Was she calling the cops? Wadia didn't mind. He had once heard someone great say that you haven't lived a complete life unless you've gone to prison. Now, just who might that person have been?

"Madam says she is coming here in fifteen minutes. In the meantime, can I get you something? A glass of water?"

"A Nescafe will be fine, thank you." Wadia had the satisfied look of a man used to getting his way in life.

"I'm sorry, Sir. Our kitchen is closed."

"Then why the bloody hell did you ask me if I would like something?" Wadia snapped, and it seemed to the manager as though the old man in the neatly pressed white shirt and grey trousers, might be a feral dog in disguise. He jumped back in alarm. He almost stuttered as he spoke. "I– I will make an exception of opening the kitchen especially for you, Sir. I will get you your coffee, but I have to inform you that we have beans imported from Nairobi. They will make a far better coffee than your Nescafe, I assure you. Also, I can serve you some butter cookies on the side. Delish."

Delish? What had the world come to? He nodded his head. After all, he could surely use a cup of coffee. Not so much the cookies, though. He was trying to cut back on his sugar.

A few moments later, halfway through his coffee, Wadia sensed a flurry of activity behind him. It didn't take a genius to figure out that the grande dame of the establishment, Toral Shah, had made her presence felt, what with the staff scurrying in all directions around him. Where had these mosquitoes been all this while? Moments later, she was standing in front of him. She appeared to be in her early twenties and, just like her Facebook picture, clearly very attractive.

"Please, take a seat," said Wadia. Despite his being difficult at times, he was always chivalrous. Never mind this restaurant belonged to the girl he had just offered a seat to. She let out a laugh and sat down, facing him.

"How can I help you?" She hadn't offered him her hand, he noticed.

"I'm sorry to have made you come all the way here on such short notice."

"It's okay, Sir. Anything for our customers. And I didn't really come 'all the way.' I live right here, on the second floor. Pointing upstairs. The first thing Wadia noticed was white windows very much like the windows in his own home.

"What have you done with this place? Don't you think your grandmother must be squirming in her grave right now?"

"Excuse me?"

"You heard me. This is your inheritance, right? Don't you think your grandmother would have wanted it to remain largely untouched? And – you've converted a third of it into a restaurant!"

"Why excuse me! What I do with this place is none of your business. And you speak of my grandmother as though you knew her well. Did you know her at all?"

"No, but my grandfather did. I mean, he knew your great grandfather."

"How did he know him?"

"He was his slave." And Wadia's shoulders slumped, as the girl stared at him like he was a lunatic.

"You mean his *servant*."

"No. His slave. If I had meant servant then I would have used the word *servant*. I said *slave*."

"What era are you living in? My family would never keep a slave."

"Oh, but they did. And my grandfather, he was just a boy when he was kicked out by your great-great grandfather, literally speaking. All because he looked at your great-grandmother with eyes infused with love."

The girl laughed again, and this time it was a rather hearty one.

"Eyes infused with love? Do you even know how cheesy that sounds?" Now she assumed a serious tone, as her face hardened. "What do you want, mister? Are you after my money? I can assure you, you won't get a dime from me."

Wadia shook his head. He seemed weary as he spoke.

"I'm not after your money. I don't even want your complementary coffee. I will pay for this coffee and those butter cookies, even though I haven't touched them."

"Coffee's not an issue. And cookies are complementary with all our hot beverages. I will only ask you this once again, dear Sir. What is it you want?"

Wadia sighed. "I thought that if I came here, I might find out somehow how my grandfather might have landed in your home. Some clue that might help me trace my ancestry. Even though your great-grandmother, Petunia Shah, must have barely met my grandfather, when she came back from her studies in London."

"Wait a minute. Did you say *London*? And you're sure you're talking about a certain *Petunia Shah*?"

"Aah! I wouldn't be here otherwise."

Toral Shah seemed to soften right about then. She glanced at the watch on the elderly gentleman's wrist.

"I see your watch has stopped. Might that be the reason you landed here early?"

Wadia shook his head. "No, no. That's my lucky charm. The time 11:11, that is. They say if you make a wish…"

"I know all about it, never mind," said the girl with a dismissive wave. Wadia sighed. This generation. No patience. And then the girl's eyes suddenly lit up, as though she had suddenly had some kind of revelation.

"I think I have something for you. Would you like to come over to my place?"

"No." Toral was surprisingly amused by the old man's bluntness.

"As you wish. Wait here a minute, please?"

Wadia had no idea what he was doing, or what the young girl might be up to, but then, he thought to himself, what choice did he even have?

Moments later Toral reappeared, with what seemed to be a black notebook of some kind. She plopped it on the table before sitting across Wadia once again.

"My grandmother's diary. When you said 'London,' I knew your story must have an element of truth in it. Besides, this was the diary that my great-grandmother brought back with her from London. Just so you know, I haven't read it."

"And you're just – giving it to me?"

"Yeah, sure. Take it. Don't give it back to me, either."

Wadia took that latter statement of the girl's to mean, 'Don't you ever dare come back here, you crazy old man.' And then she spoke again, her voice shaky this time round.

"My great-great-grandfather was a wicked man. He tortured my great-great grandmother, and I think my great-grandmother, Petunia, never forgot the horror that unfolded every single day during her childhood years. It wasn't a happy family, you know?" She paused to take a sip of water, before continuing, "She readily accepted going to school in London just so she could be spared the drama that unfolded every single day in our home. If you could even call it that. And in case you're wondering why she left this house to me, well, she was there to see the birth of her great-grandchild, something she had thought would never happen in her lifetime." She paused to take a sip of water before she went on, "You know, she had a soft spot for me. She told my grandmother when she was drafting her will for the final time, that this house would belong to me when I grew up; that I could do whatever I pleased with it. There was a clause, though. In the eventuality that I sold it, it would have to be to a woman only. She hated all men, of course. Sigh. Times were different then. Women didn't have the guts to leave their husbands. Even if they weren't dependent on them."

"Where is your mother, child?"

"She died young. A crazy man slit her throat on Carter Road when she was taking a walk. I was only two years old. Luckily my father was like both parents to me. He let me do whatever I wanted. He died last year. He had a heart attack while he was taking his morning walk on the beach. A perfectly healthy man, gone in a second. And I didn't even have the chance to say goodbye." She seemed to be fighting her tears with a sense of fierceness. "My father's death didn't come too long after the deaths of my great-grandmother, grandmother and even mother. Four people who meant the most to me gone in a flash. You might think that life is cruel, but I have come to accept that what is ordained to be, will be."

"You poor child." Wadia reached out and took Toral's right hand in his, lightly squeezing it. She didn't object. He released it after a few moments, waiting for her to speak again. She was clearly overwhelmed.

"It's okay. You see, when I heard your story, I thought you might be looking to gain a part of my inheritance, skewed as it might sound."

"It doesn't sound skewed at all, trust me," said Wadia. "Once I thought Queen Elizabeth was after my money."

The girl laughed. That reference to the queen had softened the painful blow of her mother's memory. Come to think of it, might he actually be serious? That would be even funnier.

"Where do you stay, anyways?" She asked Wadia.

"You know the Caledonian Co-operative Bank on Perry Cross Road in Bandra?"

"Of course. I'm in Bandra every other day. Do you stay in that building?"

"No. In the bungalow opposite it."

"You mean, *The White House*?"

Wadia laughed. 'The White House'? He had certainly not thought of his house by that name. It did seem to lend a regal sort of air to it. However, he was never one to make a show of his wealth. After all, he was well aware of its humble origins.

"Well, it *is* most certainly white." And they both laughed.

"Dude. That bungalow is the loveliest bungalow in all of Bandra. The Christmas decorations every year... wow! All my friends wonder who the lucky Catholic is. And now, wonder of wonders, I've met him. How cool is that, uncle?"

Wadia seemed miffed.

"Did I – say something wrong?"

"Not one, but two things, my dear. Whatever you do, don't call me uncle again, ever. Please. Also, my name is Rustom and I'm Parsi, not *Cattolic*."

"That's what I thought when I first sat across from you! I mean, you look one hundred percent Parsi. But aren't the bungalows there, all Catholic-owned? At least that's what I thought. What all my friends think, too."

"You thought wrong, child, and so did your friends. You see, in the very beginning, the bungalow belonged to the great Jamshed Wadia, my grandfather's father. My grandfather, the slave, remember? He left it all to him – the money he had in the bank and his bungalow. Needless to say, the bungalow was passed down to my father, Percival Wadia, who then passed it down to me."

Wadia looked around, to see if he could perhaps locate the door through which his grandfather had been so unceremoniously kicked out, long ago. However, the structure of the place had changed dramatically, thanks to the restaurant popping up. Such a shame.

"Wait a minute, we're talking about the late nineteenth century here. If I'm not mistaken, I think slavery was abolished by the British by that time."

"And we have people breaking traffic signals every second. You think people would have listened to the rules?"

Toral nodded. Knowing her great-great grandfather, he was most capable of keeping a slave. After all, he treated his own wife worse than one. Not forgetting to mention his daughter, who he thought he could control like she were putty in his hands.

"Here's my number, in case you need to call me for anything." The young girl deftly fished out a fancy card-holder from her bag, and handed her business card to Wadia. 'Toral Shah,' it read. Below it, in a stylish and larger font, was '404 Juhu.'

"Thank you for this, said Wadia, as he carefully placed the girl's card in his wallet. "And ever so much for this," he added, alluding to the diary he held tightly in his hand.

"Just one question, though," he said, just before he was getting into the rickshaw that had been waiting for him outside the restaurant for the last minute or so. (Toral had insisted her driver drop Wadia back home, but he had refused. He had even paid for his cup of coffee, despite the young girl's several protests. He never took favours from anyone. That had been his policy, after all, for years now. It was nice of her to walk him all the way to the rickshaw, though.)

"Yes?"

"Why did you never read this diary?"

Toral fidgeted nervously with her lovely tresses before answering,

"It was something we found hidden behind a brick in her bedroom wall, while we were renovating her room. I think she wouldn't have wanted anyone to read it. If she had passed it down to me along with the rest of my inheritance, of course, it would have been an entirely different matter."

"Why *me?*"

Toral paused then, before saying, "I think it was waiting for the right moment; the right person."

"Thank you, dear. That means a lot to me. One more thing."

"Yes, Rustom?"

He liked the sound of his name from her lips, without the word 'uncle' coming after it.

"You don't need an invite to come to my place. It would be lovely to have a meal with you."

"Thanks so much. Of course I will. See you." And a few moments later, she was waving out to him as the rickshawallah who had been waiting impatiently for him for several minutes, sped away.

Sped away was an understatement, really. Wadia clutched onto the diary for dear life as this new, *not-a-mechanical-engineer* rickshaw driver took his flying machine through all the potholes there could possibly exist from Juhu to Bandra. It was as though he had an affinity towards them; like he might be living out his longstanding dream to go to Disneyland.

Chapter Five
Petunia Shah

Wadia stared long and hard at the diary on the large mahogany desk in his study, all the while with a sense of trepidation. What might he find, contained in the pages inside it? Was it right to be opening the diary of a woman who obviously wanted to keep her life a secret? Does the statue of limitations for the 'secret' bit expire when we die? He had just consumed his standard two large pegs (small was only for wimps) of Scotch whisky, followed by his dinner of dal chawal that was topped off with some delectable lagannu custard prepared by his Gujarati cook Hemali (she made it better than most Parsis did, without a doubt). After that he had enjoyed his postmeal Cognac, thinking of nothing in particular. Rather, thinking of nothing at all. He thought that it was an art to do completely nothing, especially in today's fast-paced world.

Now, of course, he was in his study as of habit (needless to say, he couldn't envision himself doing anything else). This was the time of evening when he would indulge in a good book; preferably something that would stimulate the intellect. Sometimes he would lose track of time, whilst he were engrossed in a really great book. Like that book by Robert M. Pirsig, *Zen and the Art of Motorcycle Maintenance*. That was his all-time favourite book. It wasn't a very easy read, mind you; sometimes he had to read a couple of lines over and over again, just to get a gist of what the author was really trying to say. Looking at the diary, though, he felt that this one would probably be his hardest read.

He ran his fingers across its black leather cover that hadn't lost as much of its sheen as one might have expected, on account of it being more than a century old. The pages inside were pretty brittle and discoloured, though, and Wadia struggled to read, even though he had his reading glasses on.

A couple of blank pages into the book and he found the first entry.

January 1st, 1857

A *new year, a new beginning. We had so much fun bringing in the New Year. Carol and Lydia and me sang till the wee hours of the morning. It was delightful to read from my favourite play, A Midsummer Night's Dream, to my dear friends, until we simply couldn't keep awake any longer and escaped into dreams of our own. I have blocked the events of the last year out of my mind, and I don't intend to excavate those memories anytime soon. All I can say is that it is great to be here in London, far from the clutches of The Beast.*

What had happened that last year, that had made Petunia Shah desperately wish to forget all about it? Who was *The Beast*? Surely it must be a living person and not some mythical character the young Gujarati lass had conjured up? In his mind, he already knew who it was. Her father. It had to be. After all, it was he who had given the unceremonious boot (literally speaking) to his grandfather.

The next few entries were all about hanging with 'friends of friends,' and visits to cathedrals and other places, just outside London. It was the outskirts of the city that seemed to interest the young lass most. Clearly a country girl at heart. She must have been a sweet sixteen when she came home and my uncle caught a glimpse of her, Wadia thought then. He read on. An entry dated around a couple of months later.

March 23rd, 1857

It's getting really lonely. Everyone has going-home plans. While there is a general sense of excitement in the air, my sadness stifles me. I have to go back and face The Beast. The only thing that keeps me going is the thought of meeting my lovely mama. In any case, it will only be a couple of months. No more sneakily meeting Phillip in the few hours before curfew. Bye, my sweet prince. I shall see you soon. I wonder what you will do without me. I only hope that you will be a good boy and not kiss other girls.

So Petunia had been having an affair with some British chump. Oh, little Dhunji was far better for her than sweet prince Phillip, didn't she know that? On second thoughts, give the poor girl a break, Wadia. She hasn't met Dhunji yet, after all.

The next several pages were blank, yet dated meticulously with a different pen from those used to create the earlier entries. No wonder, thought Wadia. There were no airline flights back then. Of course the poor lass would have had to come back via ship. It could very well be that the diary might have been stowed away safely in her luggage, and opened after she came back; which would be when she dated those pages, of course. And then a worrisome thought crept into his mind. Had that entry been her last? He flipped through the pages frantically. And then, as though by magic, he found what he had been looking for. After several blank pages (towards the end of which he was about to close the diary for good), was an entry dated ten weeks later.

June 3rd, 1857

I am finally home. Just when I thought that terrible seasickness was going to get the better of me. Today is the first day I get to write in my diary again, after the longest time. I tried my best to avoid being hugged by The Beast, but avoiding it would not have served my cause any better than making a scene at the dinner table. I am so happy to be with my mama. The very first thing I did was get changed and have a long chat with her in her room. Then it was down to the living room where everyone was waiting to hear what I had learned in music school. I think I played a pretty good version of Für Elise.

Für Elise. Wadia had goosebumps. This composition was haunting him in an entirely different way now. He read on.

I couldn't help but notice a young boy standing in the corner of the hallway. He was seemingly enraptured with what I was playing, or so it seemed. I wish I knew his name. His eyes were blue and they shone like the sun. I have to admit he was rather handsome. Something happened shortly thereafter, that I couldn't quite understand. The Beast caught that boy by the scruff of his neck after I had finished playing, almost like a mother cat will her children on occasion, and led the helpless lad out of the house. In all my life I have never seen someone quite as enamoured by my music as that boy had been in those brief moments.

That was the absolute last entry in the diary. Wadia checked the last few pages over and over again, but they were empty. There was nothing left to read. He stared at the closed diary, still in a state of shock. Might this girl's playing Für Elise have anything to do with him being haunted by it? What was the connection, really? Could she have passed on the love for that musical piece to Dhunji Wadia? How had it found its way to him? If there was ever a time he wanted to listen to Für Elise (like really, really wanted to), then it was now.

He went up to his record player and set his favourite record to play. As the haunting music filled the study, his mind drifted to his father telling him he was *not good enough* to play the piano, to the sight of himself lying in bed for days (as though he might be having an out of body experience and seeing himself as he really was back in the day), severely depressed either because his long-time dream of becoming a world class pianist had been shattered, or he had realised that his father had given up hope in him, or both. Tears streamed down his cheeks. He looked at the picture on the wall; the one that had been specially commissioned by his father, who had once sat in the very chair he now sat in, while the artist worked his magic.

"*Why*, Daddy?" he cried. "I loved you. Isn't love enough?"

That night Wadia did not sleep. Rather, *could not sleep*. Thoughts of his grandfather kept coming back to him. Poor little Dhunji. What a terrible tragedy to befall a child. He must have wandered hungry on the streets for a few days before he landed at Jamshed Wadia's home, all the time thinking of how his life had been torn apart in a matter of a few seconds. Come to think of it, it might just have been a blessing in disguise. He would have undoubtedly been mistreated by The Beast all his life, if he had continued living there. Yes, it was perhaps on account of this terrible travesty that he finally got what he truly deserved.

He must get some sleep now, he thought. He had already decided what he would do first thing in the morning. He would go next door to Mr. Fernandes' home. Mr. Fernandes, who lived in the dilapidated bungalow next door with a caretaker. A gentleman everyone thought was mad. Not mad like Wadia, but *bat shit crazy* mad, or *stark raving lunatic* mad. If anyone knew Dhunji at all, it would have to be him. After all, they had been thick as thieves in their youth. The only real trouble would be gaining access to a mind that had been lost for ages.

Chapter Six
Mr. Fernandes

Wadia stood outside the gates to the Fernandes home. It was literally the most dilapidated bungalow on all of Perry Cross Road. He glanced at his cell phone for the time. It was a quarter past eleven in the morning. He stared long and hard at the front yard and the tall grass that clearly hadn't been trimmed in years, trying to muster the courage to set foot in a place he hadn't visited in ages. Finally he pushed the squeaky little gate of the building compound open and walked in. Mr. Fernandes's children had left him a long time ago for the 'picket fence dream' in the United States of America. Wadia remembered them well. Sandra Fernandes, the eldest of the children, had been besotted by Wadia when he was fifty and she in her late thirties. In any case, he had felt absolutely nothing for Sandra Fernandes and had even made it a point to succinctly convey that to her by telling her 'I don't like you,' when she had sent a bouquet of flowers to his house one day. He had walked over to the property he was on now (thank God Mr. Fernandes was not there that day) and told her that. She never looked at him again.

Thank God I don't have children of my own. They leave you in the end. His mind flashed to the time when his father had told him that he was sending him to the London School of Economics instead of letting him stay back in Bombay and pursue his silly *hobby* of playing the piano. Here he was, telling his father that he didn't want to leave him and instead practice playing the piano, and his father wanted to send him off to the UK, to be miles away from him. Wasn't it normally the other way around? Children wanting to leave and parents seeking desperately to hold onto them? In the end, all said and done, Percival Wadia had been a good father. In Wadia's own words: the best dada in the world.

Shrugging those thoughts aside, Wadia climbed up a couple of steps and found himself standing in front of a large wooden door in the middle of a crumbling, creaking patio; a door that seemed to be falling apart. This was clearly not the door he had walked into quite a few times in his youth. It was almost completely covered with fungus. He rang the bell but didn't hear the sound of it ringing inside. After several moments had passed without any response, he knocked on the door a couple of times. No response yet again. He knocked harder. No luck this time round, either. Just when he was about to make his way back, the door opened, slowly, making the most awful creaking sound.

"What the hell do you want?" Almost a holler. A lady who seemed as though she might have to go sideways through the door in order to fit through it, stood before him. She didn't seem all that pleased to see him.

"Can't you see the sign outside, the one that says 'No Salesmen and any other people allowed'?"

What sign? Thought Wadia. He had clearly seen no such sign outside.

"I'm sorry. I didn't see any sign. Could you please tell Mr. Fernandes that I only need a few minutes of his time?"

"Mr. Fernandes? Why that bugger died a few years ago. Didn't you know?" This was said so nonchalantly, like it meant nothing at all to her. Why would it? She wasn't family.

"I–no. How? I'm so sorry." Wadia was distraught. And how would he know? He hadn't left his house for the last ten odd years, and the blinds in his home were down practically all the time. Perhaps his very last hope of finding someone who knew his grandfather well, had been dashed.

"How did he die?"

"Like people do," she said, and then broke into a manic laughter. As though she might have murdered him while he slept.

"I'm so sorry. And you're his – carer?"

All of a sudden the woman's demeanour changed. A mixture of fright and anger had crept into her visage.

"Why? Are you going to call the police? Fifty years I took care of that man full-time. Fifty years, baba. Do you even have any idea how long that is? That's half a lifetime. His children left him all alone. Never visited even once in all these years. Not even wrote a single letter. And now, you want me to give up my inheritance? He never made a will, but he told me, Caroline, this house and everything in it is yours. And so, I request you, kindly let me live the last few years of my life with dignity."

"Look. All I want is to know about my late grandfather, Dhunji Wadia. That's all. If you have even the slightest bit of information about him, that will be a great help. I know you must have met him, because my father, Percival Wadia, would come here often. Even I did, but that was before you came along." Caroline's demeanour had changed considerably now. Even her voice had softened. She looked Wadia, from the bottom up.

"So *you're* Rustom? Why didn't you say that earlier? Percival Saheb was the only one who ever treated me with some kind of respect. Please, come on in. And she led the way in, all the way to a sofa that had most certainly been half-eaten by vermin. What's worse was, there was no light in this place. As though sensing Wadia's unease, she said,

"Sorry, but I prefer to keep the windows shut. Please, sit down."

Wadia sat down, or rather, did as instructed. The sofa squeaked loudly as his bum pressed into it.

"Chai?" She asked, although in a manner that seemed to implore that it was best he say no.

"Yes, please." An angry look.

"Just to be clear, I'm not the help any more. Not that I ever had any shame being the same, of course. I just want you to know that I'm the lady of the house now, and I'd like you to treat me as an equal."

Wadia nodded. This woman clearly knew what she wanted in life. A few minutes later he was having a cup of chai with 'the lady of the house.' Rustom took a generous sip from the saucer, as the lady gawked.

"You always drink tea like a bhikari?" Wadia almost spewed the chai out of his mouth.

"This is how my father would drink his chai, and this is how my grandfather would drink it too," he said rather proudly, before proceeding to take another large sip, as though in complete defiance of a proper lady.

"Ah, yes. I noticed that about your father."

"What else did you notice?"

"Certainly not his figure," she said and laughed. Alone.

"Did you know my father well?"

"Not *that* well. I would leave Mr. Fernandes and your father to chitchat whenever your father would come along. Boy talk, you know. Ah! That time was different. The house was also in far better condition than it is today. Agh!. What can I do? I'm all alone here." Wadia fought off the urge to tell her that perhaps she could employ a maidservant. Now that she was the woman of the house. Surely Mr. Fernandes had left some money for her, too? Of course, he dared not ask her that. He placed the saucer gingerly on the side table, next to the cup.

"Thank you for this cup of tea. I really must be going now."

"Going? But you haven't even met Mr. Fernandes yet."

Wadia stared, shell-shocked. "But you told me he was—"

"Dead. Yes, to the world he is most certainly gone. Especially to his children and people who are after his money. But, you sat and had a cup of tea with me. Your father did that once, you know, a long time ago, while he waited for Mr. Fernandes to come home from Bandra Gymkhana. Ah! The years I was acquainted with your father, they were lovely. What a fine man he was. He looked up to Mr. Fernandes as though he might be a father figure to him. Not that your grandfather was any less of a father himself. From what I heard of him, he was a doting dad and great human being. So, shall we?"

Caroline got up and Wadia rose slowly, not believing his luck. Fernandes had gone from alive to dead to alive again in a matter of mere minutes. Caroline seemed to sense his bafflement.

"Let's just say you passed the test. Even if you weren't connected to Mr. Fernandes in some way, you're a good human being, and that is the most important thing."

A few moments later, as they were ascending the stairs, Caroline added, "There's something I must warn you about. Please, never bring up the topic of his children. All it does is get his blood pressure up. And he's not in the best of health, either."

"Got it," Wadia said, and soon they were at the top of the stairs.

It was the last bedroom down the passage. The other rooms must have belonged to the children. What a cruel fate to have befallen Mr. Fernandes. His father always spoke of him fondly, and even though Rustom had hardly interacted with Mr. Fernandes, what he did remember about the Catholic legend was that he had been larger than life. One day he had come to his home, inviting Percy for a ride in his new vintage car. He was going to take his dada for a drive to Malabar Hill, he told Rustom while waiting in the garden for his Parsi friend. Rustom had been out playing in the garden and had been completely bowled over by the fancy car that now stood in his building compound. Reflecting on this, Wadia thought it was this precise moment that inculcated in him the love for cars.

Seeing him lying in bed all these years later, Mr. Fernandes looked but a shadow of his former glorious self. His body seemed almost entirely shrivelled, like a grape left to dry out in the sun.

Rustom slipped into a chair Caroline pulled up for him, next to the bed.

"This is Rustom Wadia," she said. She looked at Rustom, then back at Mr. Fernandes and then back at Rustom again and said, "I'll be downstairs. There's a bell here in case you need to call me for any reason." She gesticulated towards a bell on the wall slightly above the bed, with her index finger. Wadia nodded. "Thank you," he said.

Mr. Fernandes stared at Wadia long and hard, as though to ascertain that he was indeed his late best friend's son. Then he dismissed him with a wave and said, "Okay, this must be really important. Nobody ever comes to see me otherwise." The last sentence was uttered sadly, and Wadia felt a twinge of guilt. After all, it had been close to thirty years since his father had passed away, and he had not bothered to visit this gentleman even once. That is, until now, when he wanted something from him.

"I'm sorry, Mr. Fernandes. I really should have visited you a lot sooner."

"Ah, never mind. You didn't even know me well. But I know everything about you."

Wadia just stared at Mr. Fernandes. What could he have possibly meant by that statement? As though reading his mind, the old man went on.

"I know, for instance, that you did nothing after your piano days." Uttered like a doctor would: clinical and detached. To the world he was a failure; however, in his eyes, he thought he had done pretty well for himself. After all, why was it necessary to do anything at all? If you had the money, that is. And he had plenty. Nonetheless, he did have a dream at one point in his life. Did Mr. Fernandes know that?

"Well yes, after my dream was shattered—"

"By your father," the old man cut in. He knew. He continued. "That is something he regretted until his dying day, though, mind you."

"But you must know why he did that." Was he really going to know the reason he had gone through all that trauma? Was there even a valid reason for what his father had done?

"Don't you see, child? Your father wanted to protect you, that's all."

"From *what*?" A trifle angry now. Wadia didn't know if the old man had sensed his anger, but he felt the need to apologize. "I'm sorry. I didn't mean to lose my temper. I don't mean to take up too much of your time."

"*Time?*" Mr. Fernandes laughed. "I have all the time in the world. I always dreamt I would be having this conversation with you.... I didn't even know if you were alive. Shame on me. I've lived too much. And the young die every day. But I'm getting ahead of myself here. I hope Caroline offered you something?" And he reached for the bell.

"Please, Mr. Fernandes. I had a very nice cup of chai downstairs. Caroline was very courteous, I can assure you."

"Isn't she the best?" Mr. Fernandes said dreamily. "She's all I have, you know."

"You have *me*."

The old man's eyes brimmed with emotion. It was as though something in him had thawed; something that had been ice cold for a long, long time."

"I'm glad you had my Caroline's chai. Oh, but it hasn't a patch on that fine Parsi chai your father would invite me over for, at times. I didn't see much of you though, Rustom. Why was that?"

Rustom shrugged. "Maybe I was in school."

"Ah, yes. I do remember you taking those piano classes with that wonderful teacher I met once – I even had a crush on her – what was her name?"

The thought of Mr. Fernandes having a crush on his piano teacher was ludicrous. After all, Mrs. Braganza had only been thirty or so back then, and Mr. Fernandes would have been old enough to be her father. Besides, she had been married at that point in time. And so had Mr. Fernandes. That cheeky old... better not think the word.

"Mrs. Braganza was her name. Mr. Fernandes, I'm really sorry to have to cut in here but what was my father trying to protect me from, exactly?"

"It's not you who should be sorry, it's me. You really want to know? All right. I will tell you. You see, your grandfather Dhunji Wadia, one of the finest gentlemen I have had the good fortune of having met, had only one ambition in his life. It was to become the best pianist ever. Now, the man who adopted him, Jamshed Wadia, that is, took great pains to ensure that he had only the best tutor possible. He even got him a piano from Germany, that fancy one, Steinway and Sons, I think. You still have it?" And as soon as the old man had uttered that last sentence, he regretted it.

"I'm so sorry. I hope you can understand. I'm ninety-five years old and I tend to forget a lot of things. I knew your dada threw that piano away and—"

"It's okay, Uncle, really."

"Whatever you do, please don't call me Uncle."

"Yes, Mr. Fernandes."

For an instant Wadia saw the young Mr. Fernandes again. And then his thoughts turned to his beloved piano. It had been a Steinway and Sons, indeed. The name that had been inscribed on it came back to him now, after all these years. It's amazing how memories just creep in from seemingly nowhere, he thought. His most cherished possession, the grand piano had been placed in a corner of the living room next to a window outside which you could see the wonderfully white bougainvillea flowers running wild on vines that climbed the walls of the bungalow. Ah, it had really been the perfect setting for a pianist. The bougainvillea flowers were long gone. And so was the piano.

"Now, where were we? Ah, yes. You see, the piano transformed that fifteen-year-old boy's life. It was the very first thing the senior Jamshed gave him, when he asked him what he would like. Percy told me that he would regale one and all with his magnificent renditions of Beethoven's masterpieces. By the age of twenty-three, his tutor told Jamshed Wadia that his son was ready to take on the world. That's when they went to London, to take part in a competition. Tickets were expensive but clearly not a problem for Jammy. He and his talented son were gone for a very long time. I never knew what happened in that competition, and neither did Percy. All he knew was that his father had taken part in a piano competition in London, and that he never played the piano again. When he asked his dada why, he heatedly told him that he should never ask him the question again, and neither should he ever play the piano in his lifetime."

Wadia sighed. That seemed to explain a lot. But then, why had his father allowed him to play the piano, when it hadn't been touched in years on account of a secret that couldn't be revealed at all costs? Why had he let him believe that he could do something beautiful with his life by playing that magical instrument, only to cruelly snatch his dreams from him a few years later?

As if reading Rustom's mind, the old man went on. "You see, this is what I think. Your father loved you far too much to deny you anything. That is why he let you play your heart out on that piano.

And like your grandfather, you were exemplary. I saw you play the piano once, so I can tell you that with absolute certainty."

"Thank you. It's nice to know my grandfather shared the same love for playing the piano. What I can't seem to understand, is why he stopped. I doubt it was for the very same reason. If it were, my great-grandfather wouldn't have taken him to London for that competition."

"That's true. It's a mystery that beats me too. All I know was that Dhunji was never the same again. Well, at least that's what Percy told me about his dada. It's like he went into some kind of shell. And he never laid hands on the piano again. It just sat there for all those years, waiting for someone worthy to come along and create magic with it. And you did."

Wadia was tired. This was a lot to take in. Right then Caroline appeared, as though sensing that the conversation between the two men had run its course.

"I'm sorry, but it's time for Mr. Fernandes to have his lunch."

Lunch? It's barely noon, thought Wadia. He rose to his feet then, to bid adieu to the grand old man. He shook his hand, and then Mr. Fernandes said, "I'm sorry I couldn't be of more help."

"Oh no, please, Mr. Fernandes! You have helped me plenty enough."

"Oh, and one more thing, Rustom."

"Yes?"

"I know this sounds impossible, but do try and find out what happened in that competition. I think that will help you find what you are looking for, even though I'm not quite sure what it is." Wadia nodded, even though he himself wasn't sure about what he was looking for.

"I will, Sir. And I will make it a point of telling you, too."

"Please do. I will be happy to know."

And thus, it was with a sense of newfound knowledge, that Rustom Wadia left the Fernandes home. For a moment he didn't quite know what to do. His mind racing with thoughts, he couldn't go back home. He fished out his cell phone and stared long and hard at it, before dialling a number and holding it, hand trembling, to his left ear.

"Is that Mrs. Braganza?"

Chapter Seven
Mrs. Braganza

Wadia glanced around the living room of the modest one-bedroom flat in Andheri where Mrs. Braganza lived. It had taken him a good forty-five minutes to get here, after having hailed a rickshaw from right outside his home. Luckily for him, he didn't have to wait all that long (after all, he knew the 'magic word'). He glanced at the time on his cell phone display. It was past one in the afternoon, and he had several missed calls from his man Friday already. This was not like his master at all – undoubtedly what Ramukaka would be thinking right now, he mused. After all, he would always make it a point to inform Ramukaka in those rare instances when he would be late for lunch. But today, Rustom Wadia's world had been turned upside down, and as such, *the world must be topsy-turvy*. He didn't feel the hunger that was normally associated with his lunchtime (that was at 1 p.m. sharp every day, no matter what day of the week it was). Needless to say, his bum would only kiss the dining room chair at 1 p.m., no later. If the time were 12.59 he would actually wait for it to become 1.00, before resting his bum on the chair's soft cushion.

It was actually in the elevator of this rather decrepit building in Vile Parle, that Wadia had finally met his dear Mrs. Braganza after all these years; she was carrying a bag of groceries, and in an instant the both of them went back to a time they had each fiercely kept under lock and key, silently hoping there wouldn't be some kind of cataclysmic event that would somehow unlock those memories.

"I can't believe it. Is that the little Rustom Wadia?"

"Only the child whose life you changed, ma'am." Rustom's head was bowed in respect. He didn't notice the solitary tear that trickled down Mrs. Braganza's cheek; the one she quickly dabbed with the handkerchief in her bag, as though it were sinful to cry. By the time they reached the eleventh floor, he had looked up again and she was beaming, like she always did when she would come to the Wadia bungalow to teach little Rustom to play the piano. For a moment he forgot all about his current setting; it was as though he were right there, in that living room in his house in Bandra, sitting alongside Mrs. Braganza, doing his best to live up to the unwavering faith she had in him.

Now, as Wadia sat in the cobweb-infested living room, he couldn't help but wonder what had happened to his teacher. Quite clearly a contradiction of her earlier self. It was as though the world around her were crumbling, both literally as well as figuratively speaking.

"Sorry about the mess," she said, as though reading his mind. Wadia had insisted she not bother getting him anything to eat or drink, before apologising profusely for having arrived at lunchtime. Well, at least it was lunchtime for him. She had dismissed him then with a wave of her hand, saying the mere sight of him was all she needed.

"Your father made it a point to serve me the finest Parsi chai with those delectable *nankhatai* biscuits whenever we had our sessions together, remember?" she told him, looking out the window into the distance as though the memory might be playing on a projector somewhere in the blue sky overhead. "I was very sorry to hear about him. He was a good man."

There was silence for a few moments. Wadia took a sip of water before asking her the question that had been playing on his mind ever since he left Mr. Fernandes' home.

"Do you still teach, Mrs. Braganza? The piano, I mean?"

Mrs. Braganza laughed, before turning wistful again. When she spoke, she looked out the window once again, as though it might be too painful to say it to Wadia's face.

"I stopped teaching right after you quit. You were my first student, if you must know. Not forgetting to mention, my last as well."

"But – why? You were so amazing, ma'am. You could have gone on to create a legendary pianist."

"Ah! That was what I wanted to do with you. I really tried, Rustom, I'm sorry." Crying now, her face in her hands. This poor woman had been affected to such a great extent by what his father had done, she had stopped teaching altogether. Not one, but two lives had been altered by his father's harsh decision. Not that there was any certainty that he would have become that 'legendary pianist,' but not even letting his son try – that had been the biggest injustice of all.

"Are you okay, ma'am? Do you need a handkerchief?" He reached for the unused handkerchief in his pocket but Mrs. Braganza waved to indicate she was perfectly fine. She took a few moments to compose herself. Then she looked straight at Wadia. She was beaming once more; as though there might exist a switch inside her that she could flick, on demand. In his case, well, he didn't quite have such good control over his emotions. Which was the very reason that he didn't allow himself to be so weak as to cry at the drop of a hat.

"I'm okay now, child." *Child.* Another vivid memory from his past. She was the only one who ever called him that. All of a sudden he was twenty-one again, his fingers flying across the piano keys, creating magic.

"If you don't mind me asking, what have you been doing all these years, ma'am?"

"Oh, I worked in a government bank. As a cashier. For close to thirty years. What can I say? It paid the bills." She laughed. "Someone's got to pay the bills, right? After Mr. Braganza passed away because of that heart attack that came out of seemingly nowhere, I had to do something. I was so young, you know. Who would have thought that my husband would have a heart attack at the age of thirty? Not that we had a luxurious lifestyle; on the contrary, we were all for frugal living. But even living frugally in a place like Bombay comes with a price tag, you know."

Wadia nodded. He sometimes forgot exactly how difficult it was for a lot of 'Mumbaikars' (because there was no such word as Bombaykars) to make ends meet in the metropolis they lived in. He needed a reminder like this every now and then just to remind himself of how lucky he was to be living a life of luxury without having to lift a finger.

Talking about working in a bank, that was probably what Rustom himself would have ended up doing, had he gone on to enrol in the London School of Economics. Or perhaps he would have been stuck in a mundane business like his father (who ran a plastic bottle cap manufacturing business that his grandfather Jammy Wadia had passed on to him – until his late fifties, when he sold the plant for a decent sum of money). Most people are stuck in jobs they don't like, and he was glad he was not one of them, even if that meant he spent his time doing nothing at all. Doing nothing, on the other hand, was what the people who supposedly did 'plenty,' craved to do at the end of their days. And they called it retirement. Unluckily for them, they couldn't cope with doing nothing, conditioned that they were to doing something all the time.

"Forget about all that. Tell me how you found me. And why you have come here." Mrs. Braganza's tone had suddenly turned authoritative, like it used to in the midst of their erstwhile piano lessons. Behind that beaming countenance there was a strict disciplinarian, albeit not a very harsh one; nevertheless, someone you could not afford to take lightly. It was this disciplinarian streak that he credited with making him the piano player he had been right at the very end – before his father cruelly gave his piano away.

"I always had your number on my phone, Mrs. Braganza. There was a time when we didn't have mobile phones, but the minute my dad got one, I searched his phone for your number. Luckily, he had saved it. And I wrote it down. Then, when I got a mobile phone of my own, I saved your number from that piece of paper I had kept in my wallet. But I never had the guts to call you. I'm sorry." Wadia lowered his head. First Mr. Fernandes, and now Mrs. Braganza. How conveniently we forget the people we once knew.

"Don't be," said Mrs. Braganza in the kindest voice. He recognised this tone well, too. It was the one she assumed on those rare instances when she would get emotional, like when the young Rustom had played a particularly difficult composition in spectacular fashion. "That's life. But you still have to tell me what brings you here. I know you've not come here checking up on how I'm doing. Pray tell me, what's on your mind, child?"

"Mrs. Braganza, did I ever play *Für Elise*?"

"Oh my, oh my," she said, and she looked through the window once again. When she turned to face Wadia, there was a remote look in her eyes.

"I was instructed to never teach you that piece. Ever. It was on that very condition that I was hired, quite literally. I found it the most absurd of requests, but I acquiesced because, well, I really needed to do something with my life."

"But – I could have found out about the piece from elsewhere. What would you have done if I had asked if we could play it in class?"

"I don't know. But does it matter, really? I mean, you played almost everything else to near perfection. You were even going to go to London with your dad, you know... at least that is what I had hoped..."

"London?" Uttered as though time had stopped.

"Yes, don't you remember? It was the *Great London Piano Competition*, held every year in London. World class pianists came there, to make their mark. There was a modest cash prize, too, but it was more about the recognition. It's always about the recognition, don't you think, for artists in general? I wouldn't have insisted that you enter the competition if you didn't have the money, and it was a lot of money, mind you, but you most certainly did, and I thought your father would jump at the thought of it. How wrong I was..."

Wadia was looking out the window now. So *that* had been it; his father couldn't bear the thought of his son performing in a competition because of the fate that had befallen his own father. Why couldn't he have seen the situation in a different light? That this time round, his son would make him proud?

As though Mrs. Braganza were reading his mind, she went on. "You poor child. I know what that must have done to you, especially when you were so very talented. I even came around one day and sat with your father for an hour, trying to reason with him to the best of my capabilities and when that failed, begging him to at least let me meet you once, but I was told that you were not in the right frame of mind to meet anyone. Ah... I should have known. How could you possibly be all right after what had happened?"

Wadia nodded. He had slipped into a deep depression after that incident and hadn't stepped out of his room for six long months. When he emerged, he had forgotten everything. Of course, nothing that deeply affects us is ever truly forgotten, and he had silently borne this pain inside him for ever so long; until now, when it was rising to the surface like a tsunami, threatening to drown him.

"You know, ma'am, it's a strange thing. I cry every time I hear the song Für Elise. Listen to it on the record player, that is. I haven't touched a piano in years. But that song does something to me that I cannot explain; nor do I know why it has the impact it does. While there are several other pieces of music that move me, evoke feelings of sadness even, those feelings are of the kind one might experience at the cinema. With this, the pain seems real. The strangest part is, I look forward to that experience of crying myself senseless every night. But I cannot for the life of me fathom why."

Mrs. Braganza was staring out the window again, her hand stroking her chin, lost deep in contemplation. That's when Wadia decided he had to tell her the entire story: about Toral Shah, a mysterious diary and, of course, more of that 'Für Elise.'

After listening patiently to the entire story, Mrs. Braganza seemed to have an air of animation about her as she spoke, "What if Petunia Shah were taking part in the same competition? You know, the one your grandfather went to London to participate in? I know this all sounds rather far-fetched, but..."

"No. I think you're right, Mrs. Braganza. I never thought about it earlier." Wadia seemed to be excited at the possibility of having come closer to uncovering the truth. "Let's see, my great grandfather took little Dhunji to London when he was only seventeen. That was around the time Petunia would have completed her course at music school. There was a good chance the competition would be held the summer right after she had finished her course, and that she would have taken part in it too. You might just be right, Mrs. Braganza; the universe might just have conspired to bring the two of them together, after all."

"Is there any way you can find out? What about the diary?"

"Alas, that entry when she came home and met my grandfather, well, that was the last."

"But – I wonder why. There would be plenty to write about, especially now that she was home. Why would a young girl write every single day for more than three months, only to wait for ten weeks without writing a single entry, and then finish off with only one?"

Wadia shook his head. "It beats me."

"I think you need to be calling that girl, Toral, and asking her who her great grandmother's best friend might have been. Of course she will be long gone now, like Petunia Shah herself, but she might have passed on the things she knew to other people. Go on then, get out of here. You have some work to do. It has been so good seeing you, my big boy."

Big boy Wadia was, indeed. She rose to her feet, as did he, and stretching her arms out to him, said, "This is something I have always wanted to do. Would you be kind enough to make an old woman happy?" But she needn't have said that. Wadia almost ran into her arms. He had always thought of her like his mother, especially since the latter had died when he was but a child. And he broke down and sobbed profusely, as though he might be nine again. Mrs. Braganza comforted him, patting his head as his tears fell relentlessly, until finally there were no more left to shed. Perhaps that was why he had come here, he thought subconsciously. To let go.

On the rickshaw ride home, Wadia thought of nothing. He just tried to clear his mind and focus on the hunger that was churning inside of him. Ramukaka had made one of his favourite dishes today, prawns pulao. It would only be a matter of time before he would reach home and all those prawns would find their way into his tummy, along with the yummy Basmati rice they were ensconced in. Not tiger prawns, mind you; you couldn't use those for pulav. As for the origins of this dish, Wadia was not all that clear. All he knew was that the recipe had been in his family for ages, and it had been passed down from generation to generation. Only his Gujarati cook, Hemali, refused to cook fish, as she couldn't stand the stench. It was a good thing Ramukaka knew a bit of cooking, too; on the days she had to go somewhere, Ramukaka would take over the kitchen.

At times it got to Rustom because Ramukaka fathered him as though he were a ten-year-old boy. Like his friend never really grew up after the death of his mother. Now, in the rickshaw on his way back home, he had to repeatedly assure his male servant that he was fine. It was on rare occasions that order was broken in the Wadia household, and on account of Wadia's age, it sparked pangs of fear in poor Ramukaka, who often thought his master might very well knock himself unconscious in the bathroom one day (and that was exactly why Ramukaka would check in on Rustom daily, while he was in his village, on vacation).

"I want to break free!" Wadia sang, mimicking good old Freddie Mercury (who was also Parsi by birth, mind you), and the rickshaw swerved wildly. The rickshaw driver looked back at him (not merely caught a glimpse of him in the mirror, but actually turned his head to look back) and Wadia gave him the broadest smile.

You got it right, son. I'm a mad bawa! And he looked out of the speeding autorickshaw and laughed hysterically.

Chapter Eight
By the Bay

Wadia had called Toral Shah the very evening after he had gone to Mrs. Braganza's place, and told her there was something of the utmost importance he needed to talk to her about; that if she could spare a few moments of her time, it would make an old man happy.

"You know what, Uncle? I'm actually coming to Bandra tomorrow, to stay with a friend. She's working, and won't be back until seven. What say we meet at around six, and take a walk along Carter Road? The exercise will do both of us good, too." Well, that had been easy. He had thought at first that Toral would call him to her restaurant again, or perhaps even to her house. He preferred to be in 'his' territory, though, just like his cat Fluffy had – until she escaped from his place along with his other beloved pet, Polly.

Also, it had been a long time since Wadia had had any sort of exercise. Perhaps this evening rendezvous might just kick-start his getting into a healthy routine. Dr. Parmar, a senile old man who had been their family doctor as far back as he could remember, had warned him that his time would come a lot sooner if he were not careful with his health. He hadn't visited the old Parmar in over ten years now, and this surely spoke volumes about his not needing a doctor. The last thing he wanted was to be incessantly popping pills.

After reading some *Moby Dick*, and right before he played Für Elise for the umpteenth time, he took some moments to reflect in silence upon what Dr. Parmar had said the last time he met him. He had been around sixty years old then. Now he was seventy. He had told him, 'You crazy bawa, have you spared a thought as to who is going to inherit your fancy house and all your money? At this age, it's high time you drafted a will." Says the wheezing klutz who looks like he needs to be handed a ventilator.

But now, he had his doubts. What if my time does come sooner, rather than later? What will happen to my money? Not that he had ever been obsessed with his money, but might it not be better if he gave it to some charitable cause? After all, he had no relatives, except for the odd Cattolic coming and telling him he was his uncle or perhaps even his nephew (one man had even said he was both – on separate occasions, that is). Right about then the strangest thought popped into his head. Why should he not adopt a child? Give a good life to someone, who would carry on the Wadia legacy like he had all these years?

Wadia sat up in his chair. All of a sudden he had a strong urge to do something with his life; a sense of purpose. He had been so focussed on his roots the last few days, he had not spared a thought towards how those very roots would be terminated, when he was gone. But who on earth would let him adopt a child? After all, he was seventy-years-old and not exactly in the prime of health. Also would it be fair to the child? To be bestowed a parent as though by magic, and then have that magic wrested away from you not long after? Because Wadia surely wasn't going to live to be a hundred, was he?

He got up and opened the case that held his vintage record player that was literally the most prized possession in his home. Nowadays, everywhere you went you saw kids who listened to music with those thingies plugged into their ears; devices that resembled cotton buds. What had the world come to? Once upon a time you could have an actual conversation with people. They were with you; not somewhere else.

As the haunting music filled the study and every pore of his being, Wadia thought of his father and the bond they had shared when he had been alive. There was a sense of safety he felt when he hugged his father tight as he slept, for a couple of years after the passing of his mother. A sense of being protected from all harm in the world. Even if he were in a plane that were going to crash, he would feel safe in the arms of his father. That was an image that always came to his mind, even though he didn't quite know why.

He visualized it again: him as a ten-year-old boy on a trip in mid-air, the pilot announcing that the plane was crashing and that he was sorry, but none of the passengers would make it alive. All the passengers on the flight going hysterical. His father hugging him tight. And him being happy, despite knowing that his life (as well as his father's) was going to end at any moment. Happy merely to have loved and been loved in return.

Couldn't he give that kind of unconditional happiness to someone else?

The next evening he sat on a bench on the promenade by the sea close to Otters Club, a suburban club on Carter Road that Wadia would frequent with his best friend Jimmy Mistry back in the day.

The food was not bad there, but the club on the whole wasn't anything like *The Willie* (which is what the Willingdon Club that he was a proud member of, was called). The Willie had been built in the British era and had that old world charm that always had you coming back for more. A place the likes of *Sea Lounge* in the iconic *Taj Mahal Palace Hotel* in Mumbai, where one could sip a cup of good old chai. Wadia drank chai from the saucer there too, irrespective of who was sitting around him. There might be newer, fancier hotels these days, but nothing could beat the imperial feel the Taj exuded.

"Hello, Uncle! Sorry – Rustom! I love your sneakers, by the way. Shall we begin our walk?" Ah! The sound of youthful exuberance! It seemed to lift his spirit.

Toral seemed all set to run a marathon. Wadia was just going to tell her how lovely it would be if they simply sat here and watched the sunset instead, but then he thought, how much do I get out anyways? It will do me good to take a walk. But what's with the cap with all that glitter on it? Ridiculous!

"My child, I will walk with you for sure, but it will be more of a stroll, mind you. I'm not in the best possible shape and I'm a good fifty years younger than you." He laughed, seemingly proud of his joke. She laughed too, but it was forced. "Don't worry, Uncle. The 'walking' bit is incidental. I've often found I can collect my thoughts better while in motion." And right then she did something that left Wadia flabbergasted. She proffered her outstretched hand to him.

"Please, I'm not an invalid," Wadia almost shrieked, clearly incensed. He got up at that very instant, surprising himself by the efficacy with which he did. What do people think I am? Just because I'm old, it doesn't mean I can't do things that younger people do. Why, I could even jog a mile if I tried. I just don't want to.

And stroll they did, by the lovely seafront.

"You know, my pets came here one night," he told her.

"How cool! I didn't know you had pets. You mean, you got your puppies here one night for a stroll?"

"What makes you think I would have puppies? No, they were a cat and a parrot. And they came here on their own. I might as well add in the fact that they are dead now."

"O–okay, she said," clearly not believing what she had just heard. Wadia didn't even bother following up with an explanation. What was the point? Nobody in their wildest dreams would ever believe that an indolent Persian cat and a parrot that couldn't fly, had made their way from a home in Bandra where they lived, to the rocky foreshore, and spent the night there. Why, they wouldn't even believe it if it were Mahatma Gandhi narrating it. Best to mention something relatable. And so, he went on to reveal all that he had discovered during the last couple of days, right from the stunning revelation he had found scrawled in Petunia Shah's impeccable handwriting in her diary, to his father telling his tutor all those years ago, that no matter what, she should not be teaching him to play Für Elise.

"Wow. What a story. But, no Für Elise? Really? Why, I absolutely adore that piece. No matter what happened with your grandfather, the matter should have ended then and there. You know what? I think we need to sit down for this."

And before she could change her mind, Wadia slumped onto a bench right next to them. She sat down on the other end, and they stared in the distance at the setting sun, and closer up, the fisherman's boats that were docked in a rather haphazard fashion; as though they might have been abandoned. This was a rocky beach, and Wadia would come here every single day in his early forties, when he thought there was something missing in his life. Velkar told him that what he was experiencing was nothing short of a mid-life crisis. Of course he had rubbished that thought.

He hadn't come here in a long while, and the sight of the boats seemed to have a calming influence on him. After what seemed to be the longest pause they had ever had in their conversations with each other (even though there had been merely two conversations thus far), Toral spoke, and what she said rocked the boat of Wadia's existence.

"You do know that Beethoven composed Für Elise for a woman, right? It literally means 'For Elise.' Of course, the identity of the woman was never ascertained, although there were speculations as to who it might have been. Also, Beethoven was turning deaf around the time he composed this piece."

"Really?" How had this little titbit of history eluded Wadia, especially when it was so closely connected with something so dear to him? The whole *Für Elise fracas* now had a sort of dark romance edge to it. Beethoven had been obsessed by a woman, it seems. How very fitting, then, that his grandfather be obsessed by the very woman who had been playing the magical piece, the moment he laid his eyes on her. And *Elise* – what a lovely name! Although Petunia was not far behind, of course.

Toral allowed Rustom to let that piece of information sink in, before speaking again. "I guess we'll never really know what happened in London. It's strange, but there was no piano in our house either; at least not since I was born. Also, I studied at the London School of Economics for four years before coming back to start this restaurant. My parents and grandparents are long gone, and I really wish there was some way I could help you... wait a minute. What on earth am I looking to relatives for, when the answer might very well lie elsewhere? Petunia had a best friend, I remember that well. And her daughter and her best friend's daughter were best friends too. My grandmother's best friend, that is. And you know what? She has a daughter too, but she's not my best friend. I think she lives in Vakola somewhere."

"The daughter?"

"The daughter *and* the mother. I remember it because I would often accompany my mother to their residence, to check in on them after my grandmother had passed. I must have been only around eight or nine years old, but I remember her well. I think I even have her number saved in my phone. Let me see." And she fished her cell phone from the right side pocket of her tracksuit bottoms that had been neatly zipped up so there was no chance of it falling out. Teenagers! Have to carry their bloody cell phones everywhere. Of course Wadia hadn't brought his cell phone along. That was a sure fire way of losing it. Besides, they had come out here for a walk, hadn't they?

"Bhathena masi? It's me, Toral."

Ah, just perfect! A mad bawi. A loud voice boomed from the other end of the line, almost hysterical, confirming he was indeed right.

"Yes, yes. Very long time. No, no, I'm not calling about Niloufer." Shaking her head. "No masi, There's a gentleman here who would very much like to meet you.... What? No, please. I haven't thought of him that way!" Covering the mouthpiece and looking at Wadia, laughing. "She's asking if you're cute."

Wadia was shaking his head in despair. He already didn't like this woman. The mere idea of being set up at this age should not be entertained. Why couldn't one live by oneself? After all, he had done a pretty good job of it for all these years.

"So, will you meet him? ...I know, tomorrow is Sunday – you want to schedule it for another day? ...definitely tomorrow because you will be cooking berry pulao?" Covering the phone and whispering to Wadia yet again. "Can I come? I just *love* berry pulao."

"I insist," Wadia bellowed back, the furthest thing from a whisper. Of course Toral had to come along with him; the lady would be all over him if she didn't.

"Thank you so much, masi. We will be there at one... Yes, I see. Of course, it will be a pleasure to meet Niloufer after ages."

The word *Niloufer* was not uttered with the same level of enthusiasm as the words *berry* and *pulao* used in conjunction with one another earlier on.

"Yay! I can't believe I'm going to be eating Bhathena masi's berry pulao. It's been so long. It's the best berry pulao in the..."

"*World* – after the berry pulao you will get in my house. The next time, my dear child, I would think you might like to broaden the gamut of your life's experiences before calling something the best."

Toral laughed.

All in all, Wadia was satisfied by what this evening had brought about. Tomorrow he would be meeting a lady who might just bring him closer to finding out the truth of his sordid past. Certainly Petunia Shah would have conveyed something to her best friend about the incident, and there was a slim chance that information would have been passed down to her daughter, and from her daughter, to her best friend.

"No matter what, no match-making tomorrow, child. I have been out of that for a long time."

"Really? I'm sure you once had someone who was the 'love of your life'."

"Ahh! I did, although I never had the courage to talk to her."

"You mean, you've never been in a relationship before? Wow!"

"Really? I would think that knowing this, you would probably think of me as a – you know, *loser!*"

"Awww. There's no way I could ever think of you as a loser, Rustom. You're so cute!" But Rustom was looking elsewhere. A short way off to the right, where an elderly man in shorts and running shoes was staring at him.

"Why Wadia, you sly fox!" It was Velkar. That too, at the precise time when Toral had called him 'cute.' He dismissed the Maharashtrian with an angry wave of his hand and turned to Toral.

"A classic example of a person who doesn't get the facts straight, before jumping to a conclusion."

"Aren't you going to introduce me to this beautiful young girl?" And Velkar proffered his hand to Toral, without waiting for Wadia to answer. Toral took his hand and shook it, while Wadia shook his head once again. These mechanical engineers are the real losers, he thought. All those years they spend in hostels has them scarred for life.

"I'm Toral Shah," said she, clearly amused.

"Enchanted," said Velkar, not letting go of her hand. Toral laughed, before slowly prying it loose. "And you are?"

"Anil Velkar. Mechanical Engineer."

That is what Wadia had expected. For Velkar to make an utter fool of himself.

"So, you guys are best friends?" She turned to Wadia, as though giving him the benefit of answering the question.

What do I say now? If I say yes, the bugger won't stop calling me. If I say no, I might offend him. And Wadia didn't like to offend people who were close to him (and even though they might not be the best of friends, they were close nonetheless).

"You could say that," he said rather sheepishly. It was a diplomatic answer. A 'yes,' but not quite.

Toral laughed. She could see where this was going, and she seemed to be gleaning a devilish sense of satisfaction from it.

"Velkar, this is the girl I was telling you about. The one who is helping me find my roots." That was the fact. Weren't engineers supposed to focus on the facts?

"Oh, right." Velkar seemed disappointed. "In that case, I must thank you, my dear girl, for bringing so much happiness to my best friend in the twilight years of his life."

"You're being too dramatic, Velkar. How come you're here for a walk today? Don't you usually go to that Patwardhan Park, for a walk with your wife?"

"She still does. I like it here," said Velkar, a bit defensively.

Undoubtedly he comes here to check out the babes. Wadia shook his head again. The engineer never ceased to amaze him.

"Well, I better be going then," said Velkar, and he gave his friend a wink before leaving. Wadia was terrified. Had Toral been privy to that crazy Maharashtrian's gesture?"

"Sweet chap, your friend," she said, staring out into the distance after him. Well, apparently not.

But seriously, what on earth was wrong with that chap? He made a mental note of reprimanding Velkar later that evening. No, Vidya would be around. And then Velkar would put down the phone and Vidya would sense that something was wrong, and the last thing he wanted to do was create unwanted friction between a mechanical engineer and his wife. Even though mechanical engineers knew all about friction. No, it was best to tell him to his face, that best friends don't do things like that to each other.

"I'm sorry," he said. "I think I better be going now. And you can run along to your friend's, too. What time do we have to meet Mrs...?"

"Mrs. Bhathena. You can call her Meher. I would often oscillate between calling her Meher aunty and Bhathena masi, but never Bhathena aunty or Meher masi." She said this rather animatedly, as though he might be interested in listening to such gibberish.

Wadia had decided. He would call the lady by her first name, Meher. He supposed her husband must have gone over to the other side.

"So should I pick you up in a rickshaw tomorrow from your friend's place? On second thoughts, why don't you come over to my place and have a cup of tea with me before we leave? I promise you the best Parsi chai in the world."

She was grinning now. He shouldn't have gone that far. Although Ramukaka did indeed whip up a delicious cup of Parsi chai every morning, it wouldn't be fair to say it was the best in the world. After all, he, Wadia, hadn't *broadened the gamut of his life's experiences* with regards to Parsi chai. On the other hand, he had tasted plenty a fine Berry Pulao during his lifetime at many a bawa friend's place, thus enabling him to say with an air of absolute certainty, that the berry pulao cooked in the Wadia kitchen was the best berry pulao in the world.

"You got me there," he said, reading Toral Shah's face. "All right, it might not be the best Parsi chai in the world but it's most certainly worth a shot. In my house we serve it with some lovely nankhatai biscuits, too."

"Uncle, you know what? I'm meeting my friend after a really long time. She just broke up with her lover of the last five years and is an absolute mess right now. She made me promise I wouldn't leave until noon tomorrow. So, if you don't mind, that chai needs to be a quick one. Otherwise we won't make it on time for Meher Masi's place. She's a stickler for time, you know. And please, no biscuits. I'm saving all my appetite for the berry pulao. As far as transportation goes, don't worry about the rickshaw. I have my driver with me, and he will take us to Vakola and even drop you home on the way back."

"Oh no, please. Let me take a rickshaw."

"Uncle, I insist. Really, I have the car. Besides, we will be going together. It's not a problem. Can I drop you home now? I'm going to Pali Hill. It's on the way to your place."

"No, child. Let this old man get some exercise, please. If it wasn't for you I wouldn't even have walked that one length of the promenade. Besides, my house is not all that far away from here."

Toral smiled, and nodded her head. She turned around to wave back at Rustom as she walked away. Velkar would have read into that gesture wrongly, too, he thought. He would have said it was like that famous Hindi movie, in which the girl turns around to look at her beau, played by Shah Rukh Khan.

Wadia walked home slowly, thinking about how the last couple of days had been ever so eventful. He didn't quite know where all this rummaging into the past was going to lead; although he did know one thing. It felt right.

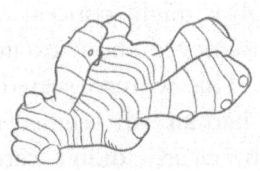

Chapter Nine
Meher Bhathena

"My little princess, you look lovely!" Toral's Meher masi hugged her fondly, while a woman who seemed to be in her early forties, stood demurely in the background. Undoubtedly that was Niloufer, the daughter Toral was not all that friendly with. Like her, Wadia too was a figure relegated to the background. Until Toral walked into the house, leaving him behind, that is.

"You must be Rustom," she said, and nobody said anything until a few moments later, when Meher Masi spoke yet again, her question directed straight at him. "Well, aren't you going to come in?"

"Right," said Wadia, and he sauntered in with a sheepish grin on his face.

The very first thing he noticed, as he entered the room, was just how much light streamed into it. It was the complete opposite of Mrs. Braganza's modest apartment, although the building had been just as decrepit from the outside. Wadia noticed a couple of maids walking briskly in the narrow corridor, from where a lovely aroma was wafting into the expansive living room. It wasn't the smell of berry pulao, but rather, fried Bombay ducks. He hadn't had those in ages. He bit his lip gently then, as though it might conceal his excitement. It was an absolute rule for him to never show excitement, even if he were dancing with joy inside. This woman seated in front of him on the bright orange sofa (that had already seemed to uplift his mood by its striking colour), though, clearly didn't care about concealing her rather obvious display of having fallen for him. God! What have I got myself into? He thought.

Toral and he were sitting in two large leather chairs, while Meher and her daughter sat on the orange sofa facing them. She had most courteously asked them where they would like to sit, and Wadia had instantly plonked in one of the leather chairs, because he couldn't stand the thought that this woman might just occupy the seat on the sofa right beside him. He would only ever sit on the sofa in his living room while watching television. And he would only tune into the BBC, to get a sense of what was happening in the world, and on rare occasions, the Discovery Channel. Ramukaka was the movie buff. His current crush was Salma Hayek.

"So, Rustom, what do you do?"

Really? The most clichéd question in the world. And for a man *his* age?

"Nothing." Grinning wide. Meher Masi looked as though she might have been the recipient of a tight slap. That word worked every single time.

"You mean retired, then?"

"No, it means I do nothing. I never did anything all my life, and I don't see myself doing anything in the foreseeable future." He had perhaps overdone it, but it was too late.

Meher masi shook her head. One of the maids Wadia had glimpsed a couple of moments ago peeked her head into the hallway, as though to ask if she should bring something out for the guests, but Meher dismissed her with a wave, rather angrily, as thought to say, *No Bombay ducks for this man.*

"Well, where do you live?"

"I live on Perry Cross Road—"

"Masi, he lives in that White House opposite the British Co-operative Bank.."

"Anjali, Bombay duck lao!"

Wadia ate the fried Bombay ducks with a great sense of relish. There was just something about biting into that delectable crispy covering and having the tender flesh of a Bombay duck melt in your mouth. The side tables had been drawn out for the starters (chips and nuts and a cheese platter apart from the piece de resistance that was the 'Bombay duck,' of course) and the plates and food laid elaborately by the help who looked like they might be nothing short of slaves themselves. I must expose this old hag, Wadia thought then, before sinking his teeth into those succulent Bombay ducks." On second thoughts, after a sumptuous meal like this, he wouldn't mind washing the dishes himself.

"Your ducks are very nice," he said, and everyone in the room burst out laughing, including himself. The ice had been broken, and the conversation rambled from Barack Obama to how Niloufer Bhathena almost had a great career in ballet, before she gave it up to study ornithology.

"You mean, you took a professional course in bird watching?" Wadia asked her, and Meher answered for her daughter, "No, she's leaving that to you," and they all laughed again, except for Rustom.

He noticed that the girl who sat across from him on the brightly coloured sofa hadn't said a word since he had entered her home. She seemed obsessed with Toral, what with the way she stared at her – as though she were going to take a hammer and smash her skull with it.

"So, Niloufer, you and Toral are friends?" And Niloufer didn't move a muscle before the reply came from her erstwhile tightly clenched lips.

"Best friends."

Spoken just like a serial killer; cold, detached. Toral, on the other hand, smiled forcefully and raised her Bacardi Breezer pint towards Niloufer, before looking at Wadia and mumbling something incoherent. Never mind what she had just uttered; he had got the message loud and clear. It was best not to bring up the subject of that 'friendship' again.

Lunch was served on the table. Wadia had just finished a large bottle of London Pilsner along with the several perfectly fried Bombay ducks he was still dreaming of. Nobody spoke for a while.

"So, Rustom, how is the berry pulao? Toral told me this morning that the one they make in your place is the best in the world?"

Wadia thought silently, If you're looking to score an invitation to my place, you can forget it, aunty.

"Oh, I think your Bombay ducks were the best in the world, Meher, and while this berry pulav is undoubtedly most delicious too, all I can say is that you must come and try the pulav we make at home."

"Is that an invitation?" That cocky woman!

The next moment there was the sharp sound of metal against china. Niloufer had literally smashed her fork onto her plate.

"My mummy's berry pulao is the best berry pulao in the world," she screeched, and that was that. The rest of the meal was spent in silence. It was only then that Wadia saw clear traces of pain in what had otherwise been Meher Bhathena's shiny happy countenance. About that scream, it was as though it were uttered by a forty-year-old with the mind of a girl not a day older than five. No wonder she thought Toral was her best friend. At that age you think that every kid who plays with you, is.

After lunch they were seated once again in their respective positions in the living room. Nobody said a word for the longest time. Niloufer seemed unfazed; as though she hadn't at all acted out of the ordinary a short while ago.

"Now Niloufer will have her afternoon nap."

"But Mama…"

"Don't mama me. I let you have lunch with grown-ups, no? Now go to your room."

"Yes, mama," Niloufer said, and after saying goodbye to Wadia and hugging Toral tight, she retreated rather sadly to her room. There was once again an interminable silence that permeated the air.

Finally Meher spoke, raising her hands in the air.

"Life!" she uttered, before quickly adding, "Not that I have any complaints, mind you. It's just that I wonder at times why this had to happen to me and not somebody else. Why couldn't my Nilu have a normal existence? It's not that I am inconvenienced in the slightest by the way she is; I will wake up in the middle of the night just because she saw a gang of bunnies out to get her. And even though that might sound funny to you, it's inexorably sad. I'm just worried about her, you know? I mean, what happens after I'm gone? Who will take care of my poor Nilu then?"

Wadia nodded, clearly empathetic. He didn't know if it were appropriate to bring up the subject of why he had really come here with her erstwhile best friend's daughter. But what Meher said next made his work a lot simpler.

"So, tell me what you want, Rustom."

Wadia cleared his throat. "This might take a minute."

"Oh, in that case, Anjali!"

Anjali appeared as though a character in a pop-up book would, when the page has been flipped.

"Ji, memsaab?"

"Teen cup chai lao, please." Toral gesticulated towards her tummy to indicate she was too full, but her Meher Masi waved her away, as though to say "You're in my house now and if I deem it appropriate that you have a cup of tea, then so be it."

"So, Rustom, begin."

And Rustom went on to narrate all that had transpired in the last couple of days, and the woman's look gradually went from one of initial disbelief, to utter amazement and finally, shock.

"Wow," was all she said after Wadia had finished narrating the tale and three piping hot cups of chai had been placed on the side tables that had already been cleaned while they were having their lunch. After their chai session these very tables would have to be cleaned again! So much work these poor maidservants do, thought poor Rustom. In that moment, it almost seemed as though he felt Anjali's pain. If feeling the pain of another didn't make you human, then what did? So what might he ask Meher Bhathena now?

"I was hoping you might know something about that piano competition. About what happened to Petunia in London all those years ago. Of course, her having entered the competition at all is based entirely on my presumption."

The old woman was silent for a long time. She was looking at her half-finished cup of tea for a few moments, before looking out the window. She drained the remnants of chai before saying, "Let's sit on the balcony, no?" And she got up without sparing a thought about what her guests might think of that idea.

Meher Bhathena hadn't spoken a single world for the five minutes they had been seated on her balcony. Overlooking it was a street that was distinguished by its beautiful canopy of trees and there was only the occasional sound of a horn, unlike the main road nearby that was heavily infested with traffic. This place had an idyllic feel about it. Toral gesticulated to Wadia to say something. After a great deal of deliberation, he spoke.

"I'm sorry, Meher, but if you feel uncomfortable talking about this—"

"Oh no, dear," she said with a smile before turning a bit sombre. It's not you I'm worried about, although you will have plenty to ponder over in the time to come. It's Toral.... I never thought this day would come, but it has."

"What is it, Meher Masi? Is it something about mama? What day has come?" Toral was clearly anxious, and so was Wadia. Although he would never show it, of course.

"Ah! What the hell. You deserve to know. She was your mum, after all."

Once again, deafening silence. It seemed like hours had passed before she spoke again.

"Something happened to your grandmother in London, that much I know. Your mother drove me mad trying to find out. All she said was that her mother never left the house when she came back from her trip to London that summer. It didn't help that her husband was a cruel, soulless man just like his father-in-law. All I know was that your great-grandfather moved into the Shah household and your great-grandmother's last name remained Shah. And she was a great mother, mind you; she raised Violet to be a lovely young woman, after all."

"Wait a minute. I'm a little lost here. Who's Violet?" Rustom said.

"Violet was Meher Masi's friend, my grandmother, that is." It was Toral, her voice having lost its erstwhile chirpy tone.

"Okay. I'm sorry. Please, go on."

Meher Bhathena, clearly irritated, went on.

"You see, there was some deep, dark secret your family had hidden, my dear." Meher Bhathena looked straight into Toral's eyes as she said this. "Every year, Petunia would travel to Udvada, which as you undoubtedly know is the holiest of all places for us Parsis. She would stay there for precisely a month, before she returned home. I think it was every January that she would visit the holy city, if I'm not mistaken. And then, when Violet was around thirty, the visits stopped. Completely. And Petunia never left her room again."

Wadia and Toral were rapt. The story was getting even more mysterious.

"When Violet was a bit older, she knew she had to do something to alleviate her mother's mysterious suffering. She couldn't bear to see her so severely distraught. There were nights when she would wake up to the woman's loud, hysterical cries while her father refused to get up from his bed and console her. She confronted your grandfather, Toral. He told her there were some things that they mustn't talk about at all costs, and this was one of them." Toral had a sense of resignation about her. As though she had already prepared herself for the worst."

Meher Bhathena was silent in the grips of nostalgia for a few moments. Then she went on.

"You know, the very first thing she did after that conversation with your grandfather, was call me. We decided we would discuss it at a sleepover at my place. At that time I didn't live in Vakola. I lived on Chimbai Road in Bandra, until I moved here after marriage. Of course, Homi, my brother, had already left for New Zealand. He said there was nothing left in this country. Well, I married a lovely man and we had a beautiful daughter together. I'm sorry I'm going off track here; it's just, I haven't thought of *Pesi* for so long. I miss him dearly, you know." And she burst into tears, and in a matter of moments, was reaching for her handkerchief. It was a very delicate moment and everyone was silent for a very long time. Before she found her composure.

"You see, your great-great grandfather was a terrible, terrible man. When he passed away, Petunia did not shed a tear, and I'm not all that surprised now, only since you brought up that reference to 'The Beast' in her diary. Then one day, the unimaginable happened." Pausing now and taking a deep breath, in anticipation of the blow she was about to deliver.

"One night, when her mother was in the bathroom, Violet discovered a photograph of a girl in your great-grandmother's bag. She couldn't stop looking at it, but had to place it back when she heard the sound of water coming from the bathroom sink. The photograph clearly showed a girl around thirteen years of age, and it was evident that she had Down's syndrome. On the back of the photograph was but one word: 'Elise'."

Meher took a break from speaking and Wadia buried his head in his hands. Dhunji Wadia... Petunia Shah... London... Für Elise... Elise – the pieces all fit together now, shining light on an inglorious past that people in their respective families had tried desperately to bury. Toral patted him gently on the back, but it seemed as though she might need some consoling too. A few days ago she had never met or even heard of this elderly Parsi gentleman. And now, can you imagine it, both their fates were inextricably linked together. And Meher Bhathena continued, because she had to finish the story.

"Whatever happened, both Violet and I felt, it was on account of *him*, or *The Beast*, if you prefer. We even decided to go to Udvada together and meet this girl. Of course, we had that nagging feeling that something terrible had happened to her, because why else would your great-grandmother stop visiting her? However, your grandmother needed that sense of closure and I was happy to go along with her. Besides, she was like family to me. But just the week before we were to go together, she passed away. Her death deeply affected me, child." She seemed to be lost, staring into space for a few moments.

"Now listen to me." Her tone had suddenly assumed a fierce baritone, and she was looking straight at Toral, who looked as though she had been knocked over by a bus. "Whatever you do, you are not to go to Udvada, do you understand me? There is no way your grand aunt is alive now, in any case." Looking at Rustom, "That applies to you too, all right? I have thought long and hard about it in the time that has passed since Violet's death, and I have come to the conclusion that perhaps some things really are better off undiscovered."

It was all in the open now. Petunia and Dhunji Wadia had a love child, and that child had been sent to Udvada to live a miserable existence all on account of her being born with Down's syndrome. Sadly, in all probability, the girl must have died a premature death. After all, a lot of children with Down's syndrome do not live very long. He looked at Toral and Meher and understood that they knew it too.

"I'm terribly sorry for your sadness, the both of you. I really wish there was something else to say. All I know is, life has a way of working itself out. Your great-great grandmother had Violet, who turned out to be the best friend a girl could ever have, and Violet had Rose."

"Wait a minute. I'm a little lost here. Who's Rose?" Rustom again.

"My mother," said Toral.

"Oh."

Meher masi continued. And then, Rose had you. And see what a beautiful young woman you have become."

Toral nodded in silence, her head down, trying in vain to suppress her tears.

What have I done? Wadia was deeply anguished. Not only have I caused myself a deep sadness, but I have hurt another soul, too. What has this poor girl done to deserve this? Why did she have to be unwittingly dragged into this mess?

"I think I need to go now," said Toral, and she got up, nearly losing her balance. Wadia gasped. "Are you okay, dear?"

Composing herself, eyes closed. "Yes, I'm fine. I just need some time to process all this information, that's all."

"Do you wish to lie down for a bit, dear? I have a guest bedroom. I'm so sorry I had to tell you, but there was no other way."

"You're right, Meher Masi. This was something I needed to know." Then, smiling at Wadia, "*We*, I mean. Something both of us needed to know."

64

Chapter Ten
De Souza and Sons

Later that night, in his study, Wadia contemplated the events of the day; how his world had been simultaneously resurrected and shattered. How he had craved to discover more about his roots and in the process, unlocked the deep, dark secret known well to both the Wadias and the Shahs that had preceded him and Toral. What a bundle of joy that little girl must have been, and to send her away to live with some godforsaken caretaker in a sleepy hamlet in Gujarat, away from the love and attention of her parents? Why, that was nothing short of abject cruelty!

What on earth had gone so terribly wrong in London? Dhunji Wadia had come home a broken man (or boy, for that matter) a mere six months after his visit to London. According to his father, he took over the family business but his heart was never in it. It was only after his passing, when his son Percival took over the reins, that the company began to flourish again. And then a thought struck him. Could the couple (Dhunji and Petunia, that is) have indulged in a dangerous liaison? Might a slave have fallen in love with a princess and gone on to defile her?

He needed to know more. What was that competition called? Ah, yes! The Great London Piano Competition. The society in question must have some website and if he could just find out if Petunia Shah and Dhunji Wadia had indeed played in the same competition together, then perhaps he would know more about what had transpired back then. Perhaps the answer lay somewhere in an archive in London. There was no Internet in those times, of course, and he only hoped the information had been preserved somewhere on paper, and had later been transferred to the digital world.

After what seemed like an hour, Wadia found an email address that belonged to The Great London Piano Society in south London. On their website there was even the mention of their upcoming competition. Wow. It most certainly seemed to be a prestigious competition, what with its having been around for more than a hundred years. It took only a few minutes of searching to find a contact email. After a bit of deliberation he shot off a mail to the director of the society, asking if they might have particulars of people who had taken part in the competition in 1897. Not that it was mentioned anywhere that the email address he was writing to, belonged to the director of the institute, but he was optimistic that he would get a reply signed by no less than the director himself. Or herself. After all, he was most meticulous in writing his letters and he expected a response every time he wrote a letter to someone, no matter how important they might be.

It certainly seemed like a tall order, but he felt that perhaps something might just come of it. After sending the email, and checking the 'Sent Messages' folder to verify that the message had indeed gone through (yes, he was a stickler for details, the mad bawa who otherwise forgot to carry his handkerchief to wipe the snot from his perpetually runny nose), he shut down the computer and for the first time in as far back as he could remember, walked out of the room without having listened to "Für Elise.'

"Sir, wake up! Sir!"

Wadia squinted his eyes to adjust to the light streaming in from his study windows, and looked around him. It was morning. It was obvious he had spent the entire night in his reclining chair. Something like this had never happened in his entire life. Was he falling apart? He wondered, as he reassured Ramukaka (who had been patiently waiting outside the door of his study like an obedient cat might) to the contrary. He went straight to his bathroom at the end of the long corridor next to the steps and showered, which was also something he had never done before (he did shower daily, but never at this time in the morning). A break in Wadia's routine was akin to him having a nervous breakdown; at least, that's what Ramukaka thought.

And Wadia thought of the exact same thing; that perhaps he might have gone well and truly mad. Come to think of it, he actually felt *terrific*. Even his cup of black coffee (chai would come later, close to noon) tasted better, and the boiled egg sandwiches Ramukaka had made for him, *absolutely divine*. When he left the house at nine in the morning, Ramukaka wondered if his master would ever come back.

Wadia hailed a taxi outside his house. It pulled up to the pavement.

"Meter pe jayega, baba?" How these taxiwallahs fleece you, thought Wadia. Once he had been charged two hundred rupees to merely go from Bandra to Worli. From that day onward, he made a decision: he would only ever sit in a taxi again if it went by the meter. That way, even if the fare was high, you didn't have the right to complain.

The taxi driver nodded, and reset the meter (that already showed a fare of two hundred rupees) so that it reached zero again. Something inside Wadia had snapped this morning. Even though he had suddenly been made privy to the kind of information that could break a person, something intense had been kindled in him. He felt himself rejuvenated; born again, perhaps.

The taxi pulled up right in front of the street where Wadia was heading. He looked quizzically at the driver, who turned back towards him.

"Iske aage nahin chalega, daddy." Gesturing to a signboard at the beginning of the street, before adding "No entry hain."

"Daddy? Kisko daddy bola?" Wadia was miffed.

"Uncle, don't get angry, please. I have a grandfather who is your age." Spoken in English. Probably another engineer who had failed to get a job.

He fumbled in his wallet for the three hundred and twenty three rupees he owed the taxi driver (all crooks, I will come back by train, he thought) and got out of the taxi, brushing his erstwhile neatly starched shirt that was now a collage of wrinkles. He got out and began walking down the street. He had no idea what the exact location of the shop was. All he knew was the name, *De Souza and Sons*. Was the love of music limited to only Parsis and Christians? He remembered his father telling him he had bought his piano from this shop, and he wondered what on earth a shop selling musical instruments might be doing in a place like this. Oh well, you know what they say about the lotus blooming in mud.

And then he saw it; right across the street, a sign in bold lettering read: *De Souza and Sons*. With some hideous looking guitars in the display beneath, the only musical instruments people played nowadays, it seemed. Why, in his time it was only the *violin* and the *piano*.

When he walked inside it seemed as though he had entered another world. The store had the most exquisite redwood interiors, and the air conditioning was set at the precisely right temperature. There were musical instruments in wonderful displays on all sides, from violins to more guitars (these were far better than the ones people might window shop at times), to the *sitar* and even *tablas*. All of them shining; each one of them beckoning to him, as though to say, choose 'me'! Like little puppies in a shelter. And in the centre was the jewel in the crown: a collection of ten pianos in two lines of five each; pianos you could see gleaming even from this distance. Right then a young woman in a suit came up to him, looking ever so eager.

"May I help you, sir?" And that smile was hard to resist, even though the idea of someone helping him in the slightest, made Wadia balk (it always had).

"You people should use a better word, when addressing customers," he said, and he didn't say this in a manner intended to hurt the woman who had just spoken, but rather to educate; or at least, so he thought. The woman seemed a trifle hurt.

"Can you tell me what that word is, please, sir?"

The audacity! He glanced around the store, as though in an attempt to find someone he could report this woman to, but there seemed to be no one around. Looking at her eyes that shone with innocence, though, he couldn't help but think that perhaps, just perhaps, she had said what she had, not as a taunt, but rather as a means of trying to understand what word could be a better substitute for the word *help*. He glanced at her name tag. It read 'Avantika.'

"Avantika, if you really must know, and you should, because it will help you in the future when dealing with discerning customers such as myself, you could say something to the tune of, 'Can I understand what you are looking for, sir?'"

It seemed as though she clearly didn't understand. The worst part was, she just kept smiling, as though *he* might be the one who was supposed to show *her* around the store.

"I'd like to see a piano," said Wadia, trying his best not to let his irritation show.

And the woman pointed to where the pianos were, with a grand flourish. Wadia sat down at the first one. He noticed the woman was standing right next to him, as though to ensure that he was not going to damage the piano.

"Can I play something?"

"Be my guest, sir!" Correct choice of words this time round. He looked at his fingers. They were trembling, and he knew the woman would have seen it too. Just do it, he thought. What's the worst that can happen? It's not as though she's expecting something to the tune of what Chopin might have played in his day.

And play he did. A piece he knew only too well, and it came rushing out of his fingers, eager, thirsty. It was *Prelude in E Minor, Op. 28, No. 4*, by Chopin. And as he played, it was as though everything in that crowded street of Girgaum came to a standstill, or at least that's how it seemed to the young Avantika Chauhan, who had been learning to play the violin for the last two years now and had never heard music as beautiful as this. It might very well have been Chopin at the piano. When he was done, Wadia's fingers lingered on the keys, as though he might be in a trance. He looked at her, crying. She was crying, too.

"Sir, that is the most beautiful music I have ever heard in my life."

It took Wadia a few moments to regain his composure, and to realize he had finished playing the piece. It had been a while, after all, since he had flirted with a piano. A long while, at that. And right then, out of seemingly nowhere, the sound of clapping filled the air. Softer at first, then louder, accompanied by fast approaching footsteps. Wadia turned to see a man about his age, with an upturned moustache, wearing a hat (a most ridiculous one, at that) walk towards him. He had not seen this man when he had come in. A few metres behind him, to the right, there were some steps, that probably led to an office. So the man had been listening to what he had been playing. What a cheeky scoundrel!

"Sir. In all my life I have never heard somebody play the piano like this in my store, and believe you me, I have seen plenty of people try their hand at these pianos, many of them professionals." He proffered his hand to Wadia, who took it reluctantly. 'Germs' was the word that came to his mind right before he took the stranger's hand. I should make it a point to not shake hands with strangers in the future, he thought. He had been swayed by the man's flattery, though, and that had made it impossible for him to refuse.

"Well, thank you. It's been a while since I played the piano. Close to fifty years, for that matter."

The proprietor and his employee both stared at Wadia in disbelief.

"Allow me to introduce myself. I'm Jason De Souza, and I'm the proprietor of this store. And you, good sir?"

"I'm Wadia. Rustom Wadia."

"And you're looking to buy a piano, sir?"

"Yes, but in all fairness I must say that the piano I played on in my youth was far better. Although this one will do perfectly, of course."

"If you don't mind me asking, what happened to your old piano, sir?"

"Alas. My father sold it. It was the best piano in the world. A *Steinway and Sons* so good it—"

"Wait a minute. Did you say Steinway and Sons?"

"Yes. Why?"

"And when did your father sell it?"

"Perhaps half a century ago. Why do you ask?"

"Come with me." There was an animated air about the man, and Wadia followed him. Might he know something about his grand old piano? Better still, might it *be here*? Wadia's heart quickened as he followed the gentleman, the son in De Souza and Sons, who led him into the back of the store through a door that was not visible until you came close to it. Wadia looked all around the secret room. There were all sorts of musical instruments neatly displayed, just like they were outside. A store within a store. The only difference was, the instruments here seemed vintage. Like they were items to be collected, not sold.

Mr. De Souza pointed to the large single window at the far end of the room, next to which a grand old piano stood. In a heartbeat, Wadia knew it was his.

"I can't believe it," said Wadia, tracing his fingers across the cover of the piano that still looked brand new.

"We touch this beauty up every now and then," Mr. De Souza told him. "All of these instruments here, for that matter. I like to think of them as the very best musical instruments in all of Mumbai. And yes – they aren't for sale."

"You mean I cannot buy this even if I pay you double its price? Or thrice?"

Mr. De Souza laughed, as though he were relishing this moment at poor Rustom's expense. "No, dear sir, I will not sell this piano to you even if you offer me *ten times* the price."

Wadia looked out the window dejectedly, after releasing his fingers from the piano he loved with all his heart. He had come so close to regaining what had been his one true love (in fact he was right next to it), and yet, he found himself so far away.

"You see, my dear sir," Mr. De Souza went on, this piano isn't mine to sell. My father told me the story of how a crazy bawa gentleman asked him if he could return the piano he had purchased from him. Of course my father balked at the idea, sheer businessman that he was. Until, of course, the gentleman told him that he didn't expect any money for it. All he wanted was for him to take it back.

He could do as he pleased with it. No matter how much my father tried, he couldn't for the life of him get your father to change his decision." Then he took a long pause before saying, "You see, my dear sir, the piano never really exchanged owners; it was just sitting here, waiting for you to come and take it back. That's what my father told me, you know. He said that when the time is right, the rightful owner of the piano will come back to claim it."

Tears streamed down Wadia's cheeks.

"You mean, I can really have this back? And you won't even take my money?"

"I will have it delivered to your residence this very evening."

Wadia was rubbing his eyes with his handkerchief.

"It looks like your father was a most wonderful gentleman. I take it he is no longer in this world?" It was just something Wadia sensed, and he hoped he was right.

"Yes." The man pointed to a picture that hung next to the window, that Wadia noticed only now. It was the portrait of a man that exuded class (that reminded him then of his own father's picture in his study), with a moustache even more terrific than the one his son adorned. In a strange sort of way, he was his benefactor. How had he ever known that the rightful owner of the piano would come back one day to claim it?

"Just so you know, all the other musical instruments here don't have a story. They were picked up by my father on his various travels worldwide. You see, my father was an avid collector of fine musical instruments. This room was an inner sanctum of sorts, for him. He would spend hours here, merely glancing at his treasures. And very soon there will be one less."

Wadia couldn't conceal his excitement on this occasion. He hugged the man with the upturned moustache tight, before returning to his senses.

"But – there's something I don't quite understand."

"What's that?"

"Your father could have easily sold this piece for a hefty profit. Why didn't he?"

And Mr. De Souza smiled broadly.

"Don't you know? Nothing priceless can ever be sold."

Chapter Eleven
Ramukaka

The evening went by in a blur. Wadia and Ramukaka were waiting outside the bungalow for the tempo to arrive from Girgaum. When Wadia had told Ramukaka what they were waiting for, on repeated prodding by his Man Friday, it had seemed for a moment as though the faithful manservant might be fighting away tears. That piano had been a member of the family, after all; at least to him it had. When the young Wadia would play (and Ramukaka, too, was considerably young at the time), the young Ramu would enter a distant place; one that was free from pain.

Even though he couldn't have asked for a better place in which to work, Ramukaka's personal life was in a shambles. His family was in the village, and it was a very long time ago, only a couple of years into his married life, that he had learned that his elder brother had slept with his wife. It wasn't as though he had forced himself on her, either; she had happily acquiesced, and when Ramukaka had confronted her about it she had asked him what on earth was she supposed to do, when her husband was gone eleven months of the year?

"You only ever make a special appearance at home," she said, when they had had a chance to discuss the incident at length. Ramukaka had rushed to the village, distraught of course, on hearing the news that had been relayed to him by a relative. The worst part was, his brother's indiscretion had been orchestrated in the very house he had grown up in, not forgetting to mention the fact that his brother lived there as well. How on earth was Ramukaka to ensure that nothing of the sort would ever happen again?

He thought back to the night when it had all begun. He had made love to his wife by the lake, back in the day when he had been wooing her, in the wee hours of the morning, under a grand old tree. That was the night the fifteen-year-old Ramukaka had become a man, and he had proposed to Sheela the very next day. She had said yes, and Ramukaka found himself married to his first love around a year later, when he was 16 and on his customary vacation. Since then he entered into a fairy tale world, only to discover shortly thereafter, that as in the books, there are demons in real life, too. Of course, the demon here had been none other than his very own brother, Shambhu.

It was around the time when he returned to Bombay from that unfruitful intervention, that *Wadia junior*, as Ramukaka fondly called him back then, was gifted that marvellous, scintillating musical instrument people called a 'piano.' It took him a few tries to finally say the name right, without sounding silly. What he found was, whenever Wadia junior played the piano alongside his teacher, it had a therapeutic effect on him. For that short time the little master played, the young Ramu forgot all his problems.

Only recently he had heard another song play on the radio, that took him back to the night he had spent under the tree, with his Sheela. It was the song that had played on the little transistor he had placed under the grand old tree under which they had conceived their son. As for Sheela, well, she had moved out of the family home long ago, to live with his brother. They had never divorced; never felt the need to. He was lucky to have been blessed with a wonderful son, Rohan, who was now a big man who headed a multinational company. He had got him to the City of Dreams some years after the 'incident' (with his brother), and Percy Sir had pulled all imaginable strings to get him into the best college in Rajasthan, where he had studied engineering before going on to get a job in a company. A few jobs and a few companies later, he was now Vice President of a respectable firm. He had entreated his father several times, to leave his menial job and come and live with him and his family in Calcutta, in a plush four-bedroom apartment. But Ramukaka had refused every single time.

Although Ramukaka visited Rohan for a month every year in the children's holidays, he told him that he could never imagine retiring from the life that had given him everything. Truth be told, he had been an orphan just like the late Dhunji Wadia, when he had arrived at the Wadia residence in search of work. Percy Wadia had taken him in at the tender age of fifteen and had even provided him a separate room in the servant's quarters that were located to one side of the expansive backyard. The household help had treated him like their own child, and he had instantly felt at home. Needless to say, the grand Percy Saheb had not let Ramukaka lift a finger until he was eighteen years old. That was what the Wadias were made of, he had told his son. And that was why he would never leave his work until the day he was not capable of working any more. Then he would go to the village with the money he had saved up, and spend the last few years of his life farming. That was the plan. At least for now.

Just then a tempo pulled up to the gates of The White House. Ramukaka ushered it inside the building compound, as Wadia looked on expectantly, like a little child waiting for a puppy his daddy has promised to get him. Because this was nothing less than *a thing of life*, thought Ramukaka. It was capable of moving people, after all. He directed the labourers to set the piano in the very same place it had been all those years ago, right next to the window outside which you could see the white brick wall of the Wadia bungalow, sans the bougainvillea flowers that had mysteriously stopped blossoming around a half century ago.. Perhaps the bougainvillea tree will spring back to existence with the music, he thought. Miracles did happen.

In a sense the piano had a deep symbolism for Ramukaka. It was as though it might be some kind of God. If he went around in his village saying this, he would probably be stoned; to think of God being an inanimate object, would be nothing short of sacrilege. But then, didn't people worship statues of Gods all the time? If you could think that God was in that statue of Jesus in church, why might he not reside in the piano?

Ever since the piano had found its rightful position in the house, Wadia had spent the longest time tracing his fingers across the fallboard; not opening it, merely looking out the window every now and then as though he might be expecting the bougainvillea tree to blossom all of a sudden once again. Ramukaka thought then, back in another time, Rustom had always found an excuse to play the piano, even if that meant skipping his homework or even his meals. And now, it seemed as though he just couldn't get himself to play it. Had he lost confidence in his ability to play the time machine?

He reflected on the menu for the coming night. It was chicken tikka masala with chapattis, along with some okra. That was Rustom's favourite vegetable. Probably the only vegetable he ever ate. Ramukaka had learned all his cooking from the late Elizabeth Wadia, whom he had been fortunate enough to meet in the last few years of her life (although neither he nor anyone else, for that matter, knew she was dying back then). She told him she had a cook in her ancestral home in Pune before she had been married, who had taught her cooking from scratch, when she had found herself being bored out of her mind. All this she had told Ramukaka in the little broken Hindi she could somehow muster.

It was a good thing she had trained him to make a few succulent dishes. She said it was important for him to know, for the times their regular cook would not come. Not that she ever forced him to cook, mind you. Perhaps she had known that she was dying, and that her beloved son and husband would not be able to cope with having simple food every single day. Of course one needed to have their basic *dal chawal*, but you needed variety too. Talking about variety, well, it was ever more important now, as Wadia had long since stopped going to the club he once frequented. Needless to say, Ramukaka was more than happy to oblige.

The moment had passed. He wasn't to be fortunate enough to hear his master play the piano that evening. Soon Wadia would retreat to his study. Ramukaka wiped the table as best he could. The maidservant left in the evening, and the only time Ramukaka ever did a bit of cleaning was at night, when he was the only servant around. Not that he needed to; Wadia had told him once, that there was no point in him dusting things when the maid had already done the job for the day. However, it was as though Ramukaka couldn't help himself. That was another thing Elizabeth memsahib had taught him; to keep things spotlessly clean. It was almost as though she had a problem; she couldn't see even a speck of dust on anything. While it might have troubled him at first, he was pretty habituated to it now; right to the point where he would clean things even in his son's house in Calcutta just because there was 'still some dust there' (whether that dust was actually 'seen' or 'imagined,' was another matter altogether). It took everything his son and daughter-in-law had in them, to try and get him to refrain from cleaning in their home.

"You're on holiday here, baba," his son would say. "Out here you're not a servant, you know. You are my father, and I don't want my father to work senselessly like he does in Mumbai." Not that he had anything against Wadia; in fact, he had a great deal of respect for him, knowing that his father wouldn't have been happy today, if it weren't for the kindness afforded him by Wadia's father. For that matter, if it hadn't been for Percy Wadia, he himself would probably be working at a tea stall. He had even made it a point to tell Rustom exactly that, when he had invited him and his family over for dinner when they had been visiting Mumbai.

"Don't keep thanking us, Rohan. Firstly, it was all my father. Secondly, you are where you are today because of *you*. We all need a little push in our lives, and I'm happy my father could do that for you.

But you must give yourself a pat on the back for a job well done." And tears had welled in Ramukaka's eyes when Wadia had said that.

And something magical happened just then, as Ramukaka was lost in those memories from long ago. Instead of retreating upstairs to his study, Wadia went to the piano, opened the fallboard and began to play. Ramukaka stood frozen, cleaning cloth in hand. His master was looking to a music sheet for reference, and the tune he played was one he had never heard the little master play before. Nevertheless, it moved him almost to tears. And it was in the very midst of his master's playing that it dawned on him, that what Wadia was playing was the same haunting melody he would hear sometimes when he went upstairs; music that wafted from the study where his master would retreat to for an hour or so every night. Of course there was no comparing that sound with what he heard now. The little master hadn't lost his touch, after all.

Chapter Twelve
Wadia's Animals

Wadia arose early the next day; far earlier than he was normally accustomed to. When he walked into the living room he had an unusual sprightliness in his gait. Ramukaka knew it was the piano that had arrived the previous day, that was solely responsible for the sudden change. His master even had a glow on his face after so long, and – wonder of wonders – Wadia was opening the curtains. Except for the solitary window next to the piano (that had never had a curtain over it), all the windows had been denied the pleasure of light for close to ten years, not counting the times when the maid had to clean the windows. Now, it was as though the house couldn't get enough of that beautifully stimulating light.

The thing is, after the death of his pets around ten years ago, Wadia had retreated into a shell. He had stopped going to the club that he would frequent almost daily, for ever so many years. The club had kept his mind stimulated as well as served as the go-to place for his favourite dish, eggs Kejriwal. He preferred the apocryphal version of the tale behind the dish named after a gentleman, Devi Prasad Kejriwal: that he was vegetarian at home and not allowed eggs, so to satisfy he egg cravings he would sneak to The Willie to get his fix. Now, he actually told the chef to prepare him some eggs that might pass off as something vegetarian (because everyone knew everyone in the club, and news of his 'sacrilegious' act of eating eggs would soon find its way to the members of his household). So, the chef doused some runny eggs with chillies, cheese and lots of chutney, and that's how the dish was born.

The Willie had indeed been a home away from home, for Wadia. He would play his golf and go for a drink or two with some friends. Or simply hang out there, doing nothing at all. Doing nothing in the club certainly beat doing nothing at home. Of course, this was the same club where his mother had died; the one that he had started frequenting only after her death. He told Ramukaka once that sometimes he felt he even saw his mother's face up there in the sky above the lawns, in the shape of a cloud, looking down at him, as though in an attempt to tell him she was happy. Ramukaka had merely nodded then as if in agreement with what his master had said. What else could he do? Although he believed in the afterlife, thinking of the late Lizzie Wadia manipulating clouds for her son's benefit was another matter altogether.

Wadia sat down at the dining table, not bothered about the fact that it wasn't 9 a.m. in the morning, which was when he usually sat down to have his breakfast. There was no separate dining room in the Wadia household; the story was, Jamshed Wadia had preferred a more expansive living room. Ramukaka appeared at his side shortly after, apologising profusely for not having breakfast ready. Wadia laughed and told him he needn't be sorry; that he was enjoying the fresh air that was streaming into the house after so long.

Something is definitely wrong with the world today, thought Ramukaka as he scurried back into the kitchen to prepare (first) that piping hot cup of coffee Wadia needed to wake up every morning. At least that's what he would tell his faithful servant, although coffee was not quite the thing that had woken his master this morning, Ramukaka suspected.

Wadia's request was for some scrambled eggs. Hemali, his cook, would come in by 9.00 a.m., which was the fixed time he had his breakfast. "Thank God I escaped eating that boring poha," he said and Ramukaka laughed, as only a short while later he placed the plate with eggs (scrambled in American fashion) and some buttered toast, on the table. Wadia was putting an apron around his neck that was in reality nothing short of the table napkin. Ramukaka asked his master then, if he would like some ketchup to go with his eggs and Wadia told him he would be tucking into his mummy's scrambled eggs, and needless to say, he wouldn't need any condiments with it. Ramukaka didn't feel bad when his master referred to the dishes Ramukaka made as his mummy's; after all, they were none other than the late Lizzie Wadia's recipes. All that mattered, as always, was that his master was happy.

The scrambled eggs were fantastic. Wadia asked for some more coffee, if Ramukaka might be so kind to oblige, and of course he was. In recent times his master had always picked at his breakfast. Today, he had even asked for a slice of extra toast to go with his scrambled eggs! Why, he would happily make him even a *third* cup of coffee, if his master asked him to. But that was not to be. After finishing his second cup of java, Wadia went to the bathroom and, emerging a few moments later, asked Ramukaka if he would like to come to the backyard with him. Ramukaka nodded, although he had absolutely no clue as to what was going on. And then he got it. Unless Wadia wanted to take a walk, there was only one other thing he could possibly want to do, and checking out the servants' quarters where he slept at night was clearly not it. When they finally got to the backyard, he realized he was, indeed, right.

Wadia stood in front of two large crosses, each of which had an epitaph inscribed underneath. The one on the left read: *Kitty Wadia. The most loving cat in the world with the most beautiful hair.* The other one read: *Polly Wadia. Best parrot in the world. Polly want a cracker?*

Perhaps not the best choice of words for both epitaphs, Wadia thought as he read them for the umpteenth time. On further reflection, he thought, 'who cares?' They were my pets and I loved them and that's all that matters. As if to well and truly hammer that point in, he had even added his last name to his pets' first names. After all, they were his children, just like human children. A name gave one a sense of belonging. He thought back to the final year of their lives, when they spent most of their time in meditation in the living room, next to the window outside which, once upon a time, you could see bougainvillea flowers. One morning Wadia had woken to find both their bodies stiff; he hadn't even had a chance to say goodbye to them. He had buried them in this garden himself, with his bare hands. And he had cried profusely the whole time.

"Pray tell me, my dear loved ones. What should I do?" Ramukaka glanced sideways at his master. Was he really talking to his dead pets? Ramukaka was a man of few words, but he understood every single word of the English language. He had studied till the tenth in a municipal school thanks to the benevolent Percival Wadia, but he had also got an informal education thanks to the private tutelage Lizzie Wadia provided him, ever so graciously. She would teach Ramu (she uttered his name with so much love, he could never forget that) English for an hour every evening, after she was done taking care of her son's needs. Even though she spent a lot of time taking care of her dear son Rustom, she ensured that Ramu never felt neglected. She was like the mother he never had. His birth mother had died in the village while she was delivering him.

Wadia was waiting for some kind of sign that might come out of nowhere, as though by magic. Last night had been a revelation. He had played Für Elise, and not shed a tear. In fact, he had felt an incredible thrill as he listened to the powerful composition, a thrill that indicated that something inside him had irrevocably changed. The sleep that had followed had been sound, and when he awoke he felt as though he had just walked out of his mother's womb.

And it was in the midst of these thoughts that Wadia saw the sign. Rather, *felt* it. A feeling of wetness on his right shoulder. Damn those bloody *pigeons*! Just as he turned to go back into the house and change, he had a revelation. It must be Polly reborn as a pigeon that had made her mark on him, he thought. He glanced upwards to look at the pigeon that might have bestowed upon him that much needed *good luck* (as it was widely believed in India, anyways), but there was no sight of any bird in the sky. In any case, the message was loud and clear: *Clean that shit*. Come to think of it, the message was as spot on as the pigeon's target. Elise Wadia had borne the brunt of a great injustice, and it was high time that she got her redemption. He knew what he had to do. Changing into a clean white kurta after a nice hot shower, he picked up his landline phone and dialled the number he had saved in his cell phone. He knew Toral might not pick up his call because she, too, was incredibly upset. But this was something that needed to be done.

"Who's that... Rustom, uncle? Sorry... Rustom. Yes, yes, I'm fine. Why are you calling from a landline? (Silence for a few moments). Really? Yes. Yes. No, it's okay. I just never thought..."

"I think we both need a sense of closure, don't we?"

And with that statement, the matter was pretty much settled. They would leave the following Monday for Udvada, as Toral was looking at a hectic weekend ahead (it was Thursday today). Even though he had absolutely no idea how they were going to find the place Elise had lived all her life. Of course his late father had never told him anything about it, let alone mentioned the fact that his half-sister was thrown away somewhere in Udvada like a prisoner.

How awfully cruel was the world. Dhunji Wadia had undoubtedly been dealt a bad card, but that in no way implied he should treat others harshly. And what had poor Elise done? She hadn't even asked to be brought into this world, and when she had, why, she had been thrust into an abyss all alone sans family – the one thing that would help her deal with the apparent ignominy of her condition (because that is how most of the world would have seen her, in any case, as a person with some sort of terrible deformity). No, he was going to do something right. He was going to honour her; he was going to go to Udvada and...

Clean that shit. Yes, that had undoubtedly been a sign from Polly, the Indian ringneck parrot that had spent so many years locked in a cage in his living room, by the window where the resplendent piano now found its rightful place. He knew she was looking out for him just like his mother. It was rather cruel that he had kept her enslaved in a cage for so many years, like so many people do, without sparing a thought for the poor birds they profess to love.

Love is as love does, indeed. And one day Polly had talked, and told him that what he had done with her and Fluffy had been awfully cruel. That's when he had given in and let Polly out of her cage. Did it matter that she couldn't fly and hence, was unable to escape from his house? No. Something had clicked that day. It was as though that fierce need to *possess* was gone. And one mysterious day, he had found both his pets dead; just like that. And they hadn't even been sick. The one thing that had absolutely defied his imagination had been this: how had they both passed away the exact same day? For all you know, they might even have passed away at the exact same time! It was a mystery to him unto this day. He had told Velkar about it not long after the incident had come to pass and the Maharashtrian had uttered but two words: *Joint suicide.*

The minutest shred of respect that Wadia had for Velkar's engineering prowess, was gone that day. Right then he thought about Fluffy. Might she too have a sign for him somewhere? In fact, Fluffy had been his very first pet. Over time, after the loss of his father, Wadia had found himself getting increasingly lonely, to the point where some sort of intervention was required, even though he knew in his heart that perhaps he suffered from an inextricable sadness that caused that gulf of need in him; a gulf that would somehow never cease to be, even if he found companionship. He had seen his friends, Jimmy Mistry and Anil Velkar, happily married to their wives for so many years, although he couldn't be certain if the happiness they displayed had anything to do with their wives. Now, while Wadia didn't have anything against women (he had fallen in love with a few, too), he couldn't imagine living with one. When he had got Fluffy, that erstwhile ideal of his – living the life of a bachelor, had been all the more reinforced in him.

He thought then of that trip his pets had taken all by themselves after having run away from home, and how shattered he had been that it was on account of a woman he had brought into his home, that the said event had come to pass. The next morning he had found her rummaging through his drawers, and that was it. She had only been after his money. He hadn't been as lucky as his friends Jimmy and Anil. He had kicked that woman out of his house the very next day after he had brought her home, and luckily, by the grace of God, been reunited with his pets only a few hours later, through a chance encounter in the market nearby. Perhaps all one needs is to find oneself in the presence of another living, breathing heart, to quell the sense of loneliness. That was one of the primary reasons he had set out to get Fluffy. After all, what difference did it make if the heart belonged to a cat or a human?

And he wished fervently then that he could have taken his pets with him to Udvada; how they would love the journey. After all, they had wanted to go *Outside*…

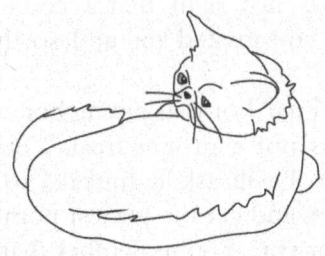

Chapter Thirteen
Maruti Suzuki Van

Wadia had invited Velkar to his home for lunch on Saturday afternoon. It was really an invite to an invite. Velkar had called him the previous night and asked him if he wanted to come over for lunch Saturday, as his wife was going out for lunch that day. They could order some takeaway (as Vidya was the only one who cooked in the Velkar household).

"She's going to a kitty party?" Wadia had asked his Maharashtrian friend, to the sound of a long silence. Mechanical engineers didn't speak mechanically, after all; they were always scheming, thinking of the most *in*appropriate thing to say.

"You don't understand, Wadia. Maharashtrian ladies do not go for kitty parties. They go for *cougar* parties," and he had laughed like he usually did – raucously, at his own jokes, until he realized the joke had in effect been on him.

"No, Velkar. It is not right that I come over to your house tomorrow. Last time you invited me and so this time I must invite you."

"Arre but you did na? For that piping hot cup of Parsi chai?"

"No boss, that is not a proper treat. You like fish, no? Please come over tomorrow. I will ask Ramukaka to go first thing in the morning to the market, and get the juiciest pomfret. He will make the best patrani macchi for you. You remember that time I had called you guys and the Mistrys over for dinner and you couldn't stop raving about the fish, the one you kept insisting was the best part of my humble Parsi meal? Well, that's exactly what you will get tomorrow! I will tell Hemali to go back home, and have Ramukaka cook instead."

"Arre? How can you ask Hemali to go back home like that?"

"What do you mean? If I want I can ask her to sit at home for the entire month, while she gets paid her salary in full. Velkar, you want to come or no?"

"You had me at patrani macchi."

The next day Velkar was seated on the comfortable sofa in Wadia's living room, as Wadia played Für Elise specially for him. Ramukaka had stopped halfway in his preparation of the exotic patrani macchi, just to listen to his master's haunting rendition of one of Beethoven's most powerful compositions. Velkar held a glass of lager in his hand, inclined to the point where the foamy liquid had reached the tip of the glass. It was only a few moments after Wadia had finished playing his musical masterpiece, though, that the beer spilt on the carpet. Ramukaka shook his head in frustration. One of the messiest of Wadia's friends, was this Velkar Saheb. But he overlooked it because he was also the nicest of Wadia's friends. At least in the way he treated him. Not everyone who came to this house treated him with the same level of respect; in fact, after Wadia, it was Velkar that treated him as an (almost) equal.

"I don't have words to express my admiration," a clearly stunned Velkar professed to his friend Wadia, who now sat across him in his grand leather chair. Wadia was beaming. Not only had he thoroughly enjoyed playing his favourite Für Elise, but he had also garnered his first critical appreciation for it. He had thought constantly about Mrs. Braganza after he had got the piano, and toyed with the idea of calling her over and having her listen to him play after all these years, but something had stopped him. He didn't quite know what it was, though. How thrilled she would be to hear him play the one piece she had been instructed not to teach him.

"Thank you, Velkar. I still feel I'm a bit rusty and that I could have performed much better."

"Much better? That's just about insane. Why, it seemed as though Ludwig Junior were playing the piano. But, tell me more about this piece. Is it your favourite?"

And then Wadia told him the whole story. Everything, right up to poor Elise Wadia being abandoned by both his great grandfather and The Beast. Velkar was shocked out of his mind, and it took him several moments to recover.

"I – don't know what to say. I'm really sorry, Rustom. Nobody can look you in the eye and know you are suffering from a personal tragedy of such proportions. Are you okay, my friend?"

Wadia smiled. "That's the thing, you see. I'm filled with a sense of overbearing happiness now, although it was sadness that hit me at first, mind you. All I want now is closure. And Toral needs it too, even though she might not admit it."

Velkar was shaking his head. "I still can't believe it. It was only the other day, that we were sitting in your study, trying to find that Gujarati lady named after a flower. Then we find her granddaughter, and what do you know? She's related to you!"

"Crazy indeed. The best part is, she's such a wonderful girl, that Toral. And we're leaving on Monday for Udvada. Getting closer to our roots, so to speak. The only problem is, I haven't figured out how we're going to get there. Do you have any contact numbers of some reliable car rental agencies, Velkar? There's a whole page of links on Google, but I'm not sure who I can trust. It's a long journey, after all, and I—"

"Take my car."

"What?"

"I said, take my car."

"I didn't even know you had a car, Velkar."

"Now you do." That cocky bugger.

"Oh, I simply couldn't! Besides, I would have to arrange for a driver."

"I have one."

"Really? But you would need him, right? To run Vidya's errands?"

"Not without a car I wouldn't. Besides, you won't be gone for more than a week, right?"

"Velkar, that's very kind of you, and I'm sure it will be three or four nights tops, but I really couldn't impose."

And right about then, Ramukaka began laying the table. It was *his* way of imposing on the two gentleman lost in conversation, telling them (albeit not in words) that lunch had better be partaken of with immediate effect. Not that Wadia ever minded, when he did that. After all, he was family.

The meal was spent mostly in silence, except for the loud smacking of Velkar's lips as he heartily relished the patrani macchi (steamed pomfret stuffed with chutney, a popular Parsi delicacy). It was undoubtedly the best fish he had eaten in his entire life. He would never admit to that, of course; his wife's kolambiche khadkhadle undoubtedly took the numero uno position, he told his wife silently, as though she could read his thoughts.

After lunch, they sat on the spacious balcony outside Wadia's study, to have a cup of green tea. Percival Wadia would come out here to smoke his cigars every now and then, because his wife Lizzie couldn't stand the smell of smoke in the house. At times he would nurse his glass of cognac, too. An image of the same flashed in Wadia's mind before he decided to pursue the conversation he had been having earlier with his friend.

"Is your van even in the right condition? Don't get me wrong, but I haven't seen a Maruti Suzuki van in years, Velkar."

"Are you accusing me of lying to you? That too, when I'm trying to be of some help here?" Velkar seemed a trifle hurt.

"Sorry, Velkar. Try and witness it from my point of view. The last thing I want is to let something happen to my friend's car. After all, we will be travelling on the highway."

"Don't be silly," said Velkar, dismissing his friend with a wave of his hand. "If something has to happen it will happen to you and the other people in the car. That car has already run its life."

"Run its *life*? You mean, you're giving me a dead car?"

"You want the car or not, Wadia?"

"Yes, please." Rather sheepishly. Although Wadia hated to admit it, he could be a real miser at times. In fact, all of his friends had been misers, and he found it hard to imagine that Velkar could have been so magnanimous as to lend him his car. Needless to say, the only real thing that had to be paid for was the petrol. Of course, petrol prices were crazy these days, but then he wouldn't be spending on a car (and a driver, too).

"You will have to pay for the petrol, though," Velkar added with a wry smile, as though he knew exactly what Wadia were thinking, and Wadia bellowed in laughter. "I knew there was a catch to it, you sly fox, you."

"It will be a great adventure for you, undoubtedly."

"*Adventure*? I'm going there on serious business, Velkar. For a matter of concern for my family as well as Toral's."

"Oh come on, Wadia! You people can easily make a picnic of it. Carry some chicken sandwiches and some piping hot coffee in a thermos, or your Parsi chai; whatever you prefer. Always look at the bright side of things."

"Will your driver be able to reach here at seven in the morning on Monday? I have told Toral to be here at seven a.m. sharp. We'd like to get an early start, you know, so we can reach our destination at a reasonable time."

"Of course. I will tell Yadav to reach here at seven. Sharp. And yes, please take nice pictures. It will be lovely to see the town of Udvada. Isn't that some sort of holy place for you Parsis?"

"Aah! The holiest, but look what's happening in the world around us, Velkar. It's not *places* that are holy or unholy, Velkar: it's *people*. That's the very reason I put off going to Udvada for the longest time. Because I don't believe in institutions of any kind, religious or otherwise."

Velkar guzzled what was the last of his green chai, and got up to leave. As though what Wadia had uttered from his heart moments ago, was of no real concern to him. "Well, I better be heading home. The missus will be back from her friend's home. And if you need anything else, do let me know. That's what best friends are for, right?"

And Wadia smiled sheepishly as he took Velkar's outstretched hand in his. The Maharashtrian was taking this *best friend* bit a tad too seriously. Oh well, let him have that delusion, if he must. He had probably been on formula as a baby.

Wadia waved to his friend as he exited the towering gates of the bungalow. He said he would be taking a rickshaw home, as Vidya had taken the car. Of course Vidya would have taken the car, Wadia thought. He always thought that people should be equals in a relationship, but Velkar's wife clearly dominated him way too much. How lucky he was, he thought. He didn't have to be answerable to anyone.

That night, after he retreated to his study, Wadia couldn't help but wonder if he was making the right decision. After all, Mrs. Bhathena had been most insistent when she had told them that no matter what, they shouldn't be going to Udvada. But no, he wasn't going to have some random Parsi lady dictate to him. On second thoughts, how dare she! This was *his* life, and he would do exactly as he pleased.

When Wadia went to bed that night, he couldn't sleep a wink. In the morning, right before he got out of bed, he went to the bathroom for the tenth time. He always got up to urinate in the night, but never more than thrice. Ten times was way too much. It was probably a world record. Did he have diabetes? Anxiety? He most certainly didn't feel anxious. No, it was rather a sense of emptiness that plagued him; an emptiness that stemmed from not knowing exactly what he was looking for.

And then Wadia thought of all those people who got up and went to work every day, thinking they could find meaning. And while finding meaning in your work might not be such a bad thing, what was truly important was finding meaning in your life as well; something that lent one a sense of fulfilment. There was more to life than work, after all.

The next morning Wadia packed his bag for his trip. He made sure to pack four pairs of underwear, in addition to the one he would be wearing on the day of travel. His mind flitted back to the time when he had set off on a cruise vacation with his best friend Jimmy Mistry. He had forgotten to pack any underwear on that trip. Luckily the cruise liner had laundry service, that allowed him to wear his single underwear on alternate days. Velkar clearly benefited in this instance; Vidya did all his packing for him, and he always had more than he needed. Once they had gone to Simla when they were in their fifties, their boy-gang (that is if you could even call a group of fifty plus men boys), the four of them including Jimmy Mistry and two Christian gentlemen, Joshua Dias and Aldred Demellow. Wadia had lost his sweater in the woods one evening when they had been out trekking. Velkar had given him another one to use the moment they arrived back at their hotel. Vidya always made it a point to pack more than one of each of the items he needed to be carrying, be it pairs of socks or handkerchiefs or shirts. Needless to say, he would never have borrowed Velkar's underwear.

When he was finally done packing (a large suitcase, at that – only because they might take three or four days instead of the intended one or two), Wadia told Ramukaka to take it to the living room next to the entrance, so he wouldn't have to lug it down from his room come Monday morning. He was all set to go. Come to think of it, the last vacation he had taken had been fifteen years ago (the one on the cruise liner with Jimmy Mistry). That cruise had turned out to be rather overrated. After all, you can't really go anywhere but within the interiors of the ship, except on those rare occasions when your ship is docked at the odd port. And Wadia had felt a gnawing claustrophobia eat into him only a few days into their overseas journey. After all, he lived in a large home, and to find himself cooped up in a room that was considerably smaller than rooms in hotels, was not very comfortable. Imagine how poor Petunia Shah might have felt, when she had travelled back from London all those years ago, on a journey that lasted around six months.

Perhaps Velkar was right. Udvada could be a holiday, too; it was just the way you saw things.

Part Two
For Elise

Chapter Fourteen
Road Trip

Wadia wasn't quintessentially a morning person, and this made it all the harder for him to move his bum out of bed. As if to make matters worse, the boiler in the bathroom attached to his room, was not functioning that morning (trouble always seemed to hit you right when you least wanted it to). I should have had a bath in the guest bathroom, he thought – it was at the end of the passage on the first floor, where the four spacious rooms in the bungalow were located, including the study. However, it didn't have access from inside the guest bedroom that it was adjacent to. Not that Wadia's guests would be inconvenienced in the slightest by some rather shoddy planning that had overlooked an entry to the bathroom from inside the guest bedroom itself. Truth be told, he had never had any overnight visitors. There had been plenty of visitors while Percival Wadia had been around, but Rustom somehow didn't like the idea of having people over to stay the night. After some time with people, he just wanted them to go.

He remembered the last time Velkar had come over, and had had a drink too many. Close to twenty years ago, that had been. Although the Maharashtrian didn't end up spending the night at his place, he certainly came close. Wadia had called Vidya and told her it was best her inebriated husband stay with him that night, reassuring her that things were fine now but since Velkar had brought his car, it was most inappropriate that he drive home. Vidya had slammed the phone down on him then, he remembered, and it seemed as though Velkar was in all probability going to end up sleeping in the guest room, until the bell in the living room rang a couple of times in quick succession and in came none other than Vidya Velkar herself. She caught our drunken buddy Velkar (who seemed to sober instantly at the sight of her) by the ear, and led him out of the house as though one might carry a kitten by the scruff of its neck.

That night, Wadia hadn't slept a wink. He thought that Vidya would blame him the next day for allowing (rather, coercing) her husband to drink way too much Scotch. Velkar had consumed three large pegs of the latest Japanese whisky Wadia had called him over to sample. Needless to say, the amount he had consumed had been far from a mere sample.

Vidya had called Wadia the next morning, as he suspected, but her reaction had been quite the contrary to what Wadia thought it would be. She told Wadia that he was the only person she could ever trust Velkar with and that no matter what had happened last night, things could have got a lot worse, like they did every single time he went to meet his engineering friends. There were times Velkar had been taken by stretcher in an ambulance, she said, although that did seem a bit of a stretch.

Wadia had felt a profound sense of relief after he had placed the receiver down. Someone actually thought he was a good influence. It was nice to be able to think of yourself in that way. Needless to say, after that day Velkar never graced The White House for dinner; for lunch, on several occasions, and perhaps even for that odd cup of Parsi chai, but never a meal post sunset. Of course it wasn't dinner Vidya was worried about; it was the happy hours that preceded it.

It was 6.55 a.m. when Toral Shah rang the bell, and Wadia ushered her in. She was five minutes early. That was good.

"My dear, I would love to give you a grand tour of the house but—"

However, it seemed as though she were not listening to him at all.

"It's beautiful," she said, looking all around the house. "Very Victorian."

"Thank you, dear. My mother was British, so I guess this house merely imbibed her sensibilities. We Parsis are anyways foreigners to non-Parsi Indians, so there's no chance this house could even remotely resemble an Indian home." But Toral seemed lost.

"What a beautiful piano! Was this the piano you had as a child?" She walked over to the magnificent *showpiece* (which was how Wadia saw it, at least). And then... "Can you play Für Elise for me, please?"

"Really? We must be leaving now." And then Wadia realized the car hadn't arrived yet. That bloody Maharashtrian! Toral sensed his discomfiture.

"Please don't be a stickler for time, Rustom. A few minutes won't make a difference. Besides, this is something I really need to hear!"

Wadia glanced at his phone. He would wait until seven-fifteen for Velkar's driver. Even though he shouldn't. After all, even though most people in Mumbai were inevitably late by fifteen minutes no matter where they went, that excuse certainly didn't hold at this time of morning, when there was not the least bit of traffic. He looked at Toral then, staring expectantly at him with all the earnestness of a child.

"Für Elise. Right. Okay, I guess it wouldn't hurt to play it. But, where are my manners? Ramukaka, please get the girl a cup of chai, will you?"

Ramukaka appeared out of nowhere, bowed courteously, and retreated to the kitchen.

"He is so cute," she said. "So *that's* the person who has been taking care of you for all these years?"

Wadia nodded, although he couldn't for the life of him fathom what might be cute about his manservant. Just then the doorbell rang. That darned driver. Dismissing Ramukaka (who had emerged from the kitchen once again at the sound of the bell), he went to get the door himself.

It was Velkar, wearing a driver's cap.

"Morning, shaabji. This is Anil Velkar, your driver, reporting for service. Besides English, I am fluent in Marathi and Hindi and—"

"What rubbish is this?" Wadia bellowed, and the milkman on the road outside lost his balance and nearly collided into a tree. He gave Wadia a dirty look before continuing his journey.

"Rubbish? You wanted a car and driver, didn't you? So, the driver is here, yours truly, of course, and so is my car (pointing to the dilapidated contraption that stood a few metres behind him). And then he gave Wadia a salute. There was a soft chuckle in the background.

"That was the idea. I wanted your *driver*. I don't want *you*."

"You break my heart, Wadia," and this time round there wasn't any chuckling, but the distinct sound of laughter. Was this guy for real? In any case, this wasn't the time to get into any sort of altercation.

"Anil, please, we don't have time for this. Besides, how will you even come? You can't possibly leave Vidya home alone, can you?"

"Oh, that's not a problem at all. You see, I have told her I am going to the *Iranshah Atash Behram*, to pray for the both of us. And this is something I do on several occasions, mind you. I walk into temples and pray to God for—"

"Don't you know, Velkar? You won't be allowed in the Fire Temple, at any costs. You're not a Parsi. Neither will Toral."

91

"Why I know, my dear Rustom. But I will be standing outside the temple while you say my prayer, so that, you know, my attendance is taken."

"*Attendance?* Are you ridiculing the Parsi faith? And why isn't your driver here?" Velkar was looking sheepish now, as though he had somehow been exposed.

"I'm sorry. I lied. I don't have a driver. It is none other than me who has been driving Vidya around all these years. She tells me I drive her crazy."

"With that ridiculous hat?" Wadia's tone had softened considerably now. "Oh, what the hell? You can come along, Anil. But just so we are clear, you will be splitting the cost of accommodation with us."

"But I brought khari biscuits…"

It was not one, but two piping hot cups of chai that Ramukaka prepared that morning, for both the fine young woman who briefly reminded him of the graceful Lizzie Wadia in her younger days, and the atrocious Velkar Saheb who he had seen plenty of times; he deliberated if he should give him some cookies along with the tea – on second thoughts, he might as well drop cookie crumbs as spill tea on his master's velvety carpet. When Wadia played Für Elise on the grand piano, time came to a complete standstill for him as well as his master's guests. When he finished, there was pin-drop silence. And then the sound of clapping. Ramukaka joined in the clapping too, but unheard by Wadia, in the corner of the kitchen, where he had heard Wadia play that haunting tune. Even though he had absolutely no love for music without words, something happened to him every single time Wadia played the piano.

"Rustom, you're a superstar! You know, you should make a *YouTube* video of this. I promise you it will go viral." Toral seemed clearly overwhelmed with emotion.

Wadia shrugged off the compliment, as though it didn't matter. "All I ever wanted to do was play the piano. I never really thought about having an audience."

The road trip had finally commenced. Ramukaka waved out to his master and his friends as the battered Maruti Suzuki van zipped out of Wadia's bungalow compound and onto quiet Perry Cross Road.

"Bandra buggers are so lazy. Not a single soul out in the morning. Do you know Vidya wakes up at 4.30 a.m. every single day to do her yoga?" He said this with a sense of pride; as though it were *he* waking up and doing yoga, not his wife.

Wadia, seated in the front alongside his driver friend, shook his head in dismay. Toral, though, seemed fascinated.

"Yoga? Really? Maybe I will take some tips from aunty."

"She doesn't like it when anyone calls her aunty," Velkar said before bursting into a rather hearty cackle.

Then he added, "Neither do I like being called Uncle."

"Okay then, what do I call you?"

"Call him Anil." Wadia said, exasperated.

"Call me Neel. It sounds cooler." And Velkar laughed and so did Toral. What does this bugger think he is, fourteen? There was no way on earth he was ever going to call him Neel, and he looked at Velkar then and the Maharashtrian nodded, as though his best friend had just said that out loud.

"Anil, please slow down. We're not in a hurry to get to Udvada. If you continue this way, we will—"

"We will all go to heaven, no? Now can anyone explain to me why that is not a good idea?"

One look at the uncomfortable faces, one beside him and the one he glimpsed in the rear-view mirror, and Velkar knew he had crossed a line.

"Okay, okay. I will slow down. But know this: Neel is the best driver in the world. Got it?"

Spoken like a four-year-old. Wadia sighed. "Got it."

"Got it!" Toral hollered from the backseat. And they were off on their journey, now at a far slower pace. If there were anything redeeming about Velkar driving them, it was this: he actually acquiesced to your demand of driving slow, even though he was, of course, an unpaid driver. Most drivers you paid money to, drove even faster if you told them to go slow. At least, that had been Wadia's experience over the years.

In barely a few minutes they were on the highway.

"Toral dear, do you see a bag on the floor behind Rustom's seat? Vidya aunty has packed some lovely cucumber sandwiches for all of us to eat. You must be hungry, no?"

The cucumber sandwiches were passed around. Velkar had parked his van on the side of the highway, so he could partake of the feast too. The least he could have done was pack some chicken sandwiches, thought Wadia. In any case, he had decided that at lunchtime he would have his favourite chicken dhansak at a restaurant in Udvada that had been around for many years. Jimmy Mistry's wife had told him that if he ever went to Udvada (the Mistrys had been there several times over the years), he must visit *Mimi's*. Back to the present moment. These cucumber sandwiches weren't the worst thing he had ever eaten.

"Please tell aunty these are the best cucumber sandwiches I have eaten in my life." It was Toral, and when Wadia looked back at her she was actually licking the butter from the sandwiches off her fingers. Like it might be a rare kind of butter. And Velkar looked pleased as punch, as he looked Wadia straight in the eye with a 'I told you I'm better than you' look, before looking back at Toral and saying, "Why, you can tell her yourself. When we get back, I'm hosting a dinner party in your honour. I told my wife there is this angel I met on Carter Road, and she told me she has to meet you."

Probably because she doesn't trust her devil of a husband, thought Wadia as he nimbly cleaned his fingers with a paper napkin.

"Oh really? That would be lovely. I'm sure Rustom would be there too?"

"Why, yes, of course Rustom will be there. Will you come, Rustom?" Clearly forced.

"I wouldn't miss it for the world," was the response that seemed part riposte, although (he hated to admit it) he wouldn't mind coming along to sample some more of that lip-smacking Pathare Prabhu fare, especially since it held the promise of meat on the menu.

"Well, that's settled then. Next Sunday at my place, guys. Now, are we ready to begin the journey again?"

Toral replied in the affirmative; Wadia didn't bother.

Chapter Fifteen
Udvada

The journey was not supposed to have taken more than three and a half hours, but after a couple of stops for tea on the way (on Maharaja Velkar's insistence) and a couple of visits to the bathroom at some service stations (Wadia made a note to never visit those bathrooms again), they finally reached the holiest place for the Parsis, Udvada.

Driving through the streets of the town, Wadia had a sudden feeling of déjà vu. It was as poignant a feeling as he ever had in his life. Strong, reminiscent of something he couldn't quite put a finger on. Just then a lady started speaking, out of the blue. Both Wadia and Velkar turned to discover that Toral had opened the Google Maps app on her phone, in search of Butterfly Villa, a place managed by a gentleman called Kaizad Patel, a courteous chap (well, at least he had been on the telephone when Wadia had called him to make a reservation), who was apparently the nephew of the man who owned it, one Behram Patel. Apparently, the now elderly Behram Patel had never had children, and he had gifted his place to his nephew, who lived in a one-bedroom apartment close by and rented this place out to guests. Travellers like them, in search of something. Weren't we all in search of something? Wadia let that thought slide for now.

Although it was Wadia who had made the reservation, it was Toral who had found the place to begin with. She had done her research well, zoning in on this place on account of the stellar reviews (apart from the pictures, of course, that were lovely as well), and the best part was, it even had hired help to cook all your meals if you so wished. Not that she could imagine anyone not having a meal here if they were to stay even a couple of days; this was Udvada, after all; not Manhattan with its several splendid restaurants. In only a matter of minutes (which was only logical, because how big could Udvada possibly be?) they pulled into the driveway of the large villa.

Kaizad Patel, a severely obese gentleman (the sight of whom gave Wadia some hope) wearing a T-shirt with braces clipped onto ridiculously tight trousers, rushed out to greet his guests, waddling like a duck. Velkar seemed drained. Poor fellow won't be up for going out to lunch. In that case he can stay here and I can go to the restaurant with Toral, thought Wadia. But first, let's get to our rooms and freshen up. He felt unusually sprightly; as if the long car journey had not tired him in the least.

It seemed like getting to their rooms would have to wait a little longer. For the next fifteen odd minutes, Mr. Patel led them around his property, naming all the plants (including some he had planted with his bare hands) with the kind of passion a botanist might exhibit. When they came round a full circle, he then started regaling them with stories of his uncle and how the property was passed on to him. Wadia was seething with anger. So much bloody money I'm paying for three nights, and this bugger is talking about his *plants* and now, his *roots*!

"My dear Mr. Patel (and Wadia said this is a tone that most clearly indicated that Mr. Patel was far from being dear to him), I'm sorry but we are all very tired now. Can we please go and lie down on our beds for a moment, if you don't mind? Looking to Toral and Velkar to back him up; not getting an iota of support from them.

"What's the hurry, Wadia? I know: he must be waiting to eat that chicken tikka masala he has been raving about ever since we started our journey. At that restaurant – *Mimi's* or something." Velkar said this teasingly, as though it was ludicrous to want to eat your favourite dish in a restaurant that had come highly recommended. Everyone laughed, except Wadia. Then Mr. Patel spoke, with a seriousness in his otherwise jovial tone, for the first time.

"My uncle's chicken tikka masala is the best in the world!" Suddenly Wadia had the shivers. It was as though Niloufer Bhathena (who had risen out of the blue in defence of her mother's berry pulao) had suddenly entered the body of this man, who was now championing his uncle's supposedly legendary chicken tikka masala. Wadia raised his hand in protest, but Mr. Patel dismissed it as though he might be swatting a fly.

"Nothing doing. My cook, Jamuna, will prepare vegetable dhansak for you all for lunch today. Of course you must be tired, and I insist you go in and freshen up. Lunch will be served at 1.30 p.m. sharp." That was an hour from now, but dictating the time? Who the bloody hell did this man think he was? Hostel dean?

The interiors of the house were clearly not out of *Architectural Digest*, but it was apparent the old Behram Petal had fine taste. A man called Satish led them upstairs and was even kind enough to place their luggage in their rooms, which was expected, of course, on account of the price they were paying for this overrated dump. Or was he going to have to pay for it all? Wadia plopped down on the comfortable four-poster bed in his room – rather, sank into it. It was apparent he was going to get a most blissful sleep tonight. Or perhaps even siesta, for that matter. He knew Velkar was accustomed to taking a nap in the afternoon. Toral had happily complied, saying she would check out the shops in the meantime. As for Wadia, well, what choice did he have? There was nothing to do here but sleep, when they were not eating or looking for Elise, that is.

"Wadia! Wake up." It took a few moments for Wadia to come to his senses and realize he had fallen asleep on the plush white bed, for well over an hour. Velkar had woken him up from his deep slumber. *Focus, Wadia, focus.* Only a few moments later, the three travellers found themselves seated at the dining table at the far end of the living room, close to the kitchen. Just like in The White House. Wadia couldn't help but notice there was another plate set at the 'head of the table.' He was seated alongside Velkar, and Toral sat directly across from him. He looked at Satish, the Man Friday with cheerful countenance, bringing what seemed to be the most unappetising salad he had ever laid his eyes on (as though his jovial face might be the saving grace for that unappetising-sounding 'vegetable' dhansak), and gestured towards the plate that had been neatly laid out at one end of the table, before looking back at him.

"Yeh kiske liye hai?"

Placing the salad bowl delicately in the centre of the table, Satish answered, "Mr. Patel ke liye."

It took a few moments for the realisation to sink in fully. Was the hostel dean coming over for an inspection? What kind of game was this?

"*I* invited him." It was Toral, who seemed to sense her elderly friend's discomfiture.

"You – what?"

"Relax, Rustom. You have come here in search of Elise, right? Well, who better to ask then, than someone who has been living in Udvada for the longest time?"

All of a sudden, Wadia calmed down. Perhaps Toral might be onto something here. His emotions could take a backseat. No matter what, Elise came first. And, as promised by his manservant, Mr. Patel was at the table before they knew it.

Lunch was a gastronomic delight. Even though that dhansak might have been vegetarian, it surprisingly did the trick. And that was no easy feat, especially given the fact that Wadia was a hardcore meat-eater. After they had finished, Toral asked their host in her ever-polite tone of voice, if he would like to have a cup of tea with them.

"Oh no, please. I have already imposed myself enough on you people."

"Not in the least bit. Really, there is something we need to talk to you about."

And just like that, a few moments later, they were sitting on the immaculately manicured lawn outside the main entrance to the house. Of course Mr. Patel must put a great deal of thought into keeping his lawn well mowed. After all, he's a botanist! A wry smile crept up the corners of Wadia's mouth.

"So, what is it you do exactly, Mr. Wadia?" That unoriginal question again. It was the proverbial go-to question for someone who didn't know what else to say; a question asked merely to make cheap conversation. Of course, there were several answers Wadia could proffer when asked this question, and in his earlier years he had indulged in responding to the question in several ways, saying things like 'I invest in the share market' (which was true, because he did dabble in stocks – well, at least his financial advisor did on his behalf), but now, he preferred to give the same answer he had been using for the last twenty odd years.

"Nothing," he said, and Mr. Patel stopped in the midst of stirring his chai. He looked to Toral and Velkar to see if he could get something out of them, and having got nothing he said 'Oh!' before proceeding to stir his chai again.

The question Mr. Patel had posed to Wadia five minutes ago, and the single 'Oh!' that had emanated from the former's lips shortly after the single word 'Nothing' was uttered by Wadia as a response to what he believed to be the lamest question of all time, had in effect comprised the only conversation between the trio thus far, in the five minutes or so they had spent in the garden, sipping from their respective cups of chai. It was Toral who finally broke the ice. She addressed their host as she spoke.

"We have come here looking for Mr. Wadia's aunt and my great aunt, she said, before continuing, "Her name was Elise. Would you happen to know anyone by that name?"

Mr. Patel seemed to be lost in a train of deep thought, before he finally looked back to Toral with an absolutely blank expression on his face. Then Toral looked to Wadia and he nodded. They had known that in all probability the girl would not be known to one and all by her real name, and then it would be time to ask the question they would be forced to ask.

"Mr. Patel, I'm sorry but I'm talking about a girl with Down's syndrome. Would you happen to know—"

And then something happened that sent shivers down Wadia's spine. The cup of chai Mr. Patel held in his hand was now shaking, its contents spilling into the saucer underneath. The trio that had driven all the way from Bombay stared, shell-shocked. It took him a few seconds to put it down, and then he was walking hastily away. Wadia ran after him.

"Mr. Patel, please. I will do anything. I will even pay you double rent for this place, if you can let me in on what you know, because it is clear that you know something. Mr. Patel—"

But Mr. Patel had already got into his vintage Ambassador and the car was moving. Toral came up behind Wadia and placed her hand on his shoulder, while Velkar simply stared aghast from a few metres away.

"Never mind, Rustom. We will get to the bottom of this. That is why we are here, after all."

Chapter Sixteen
Finding Elise

It was two in the afternoon on a sunny day in Udvada. Wadia was pacing around the living room, while Toral and Velkar watched in silence. They had made several missed calls to Mr. Patel. He hadn't even responded to the WhatsApp messages Toral had sent him, even though the blue tick marks were clear indication he had read them. At least he had the settings that enabled blue tick marks. She didn't trust people who had disabled them – they were the ones you needed to be most wary of.

"I'm telling you, let's go somewhere else to stay." Wadia was livid. "The very least the man can do is tell us what he knows." Toral felt the pain of not knowing, too, but was clearly not as badly affected as the Parsi gentleman she had come to know pretty well over the last few days. Satish had come in then, asking if everything was all right, and Wadia had shouted at him so fiercely he literally ran back into the kitchen.

"Tere boss ko bulao!" He had told him, and Toral had calmed him down, saying that in most cases, the owners of rentals didn't meet their tenants. They were certainly not obliged to, and if Wadia did something even remotely stupid they could all be thrown out at the drop of a hat. Besides, it was best if they just let Mr. Patel be, for now. Perhaps he would come around in a day or two, and tell them all he knew.

"I propose we go door to door asking about Elise." It was Velkar, who had not spoken a single word since they had walked back into Butterfly Villa, after the 'tea party gone terribly wrong.' Wadia was just about to dismiss the idea (what would a mechanical engineer know about the heart, in any case?), when Toral chimed in, "You know what? I think that's a really great idea. But not right now. Undoubtedly everyone in Udvada unfailingly gets their siesta. I propose we catch a few winks too, so we can be refreshed come evening time."

Truth be told, it wasn't all that bad an idea, thought the tired Parsi. Toral had told him and Velkar that she would wake them up at four in the evening, which was a couple of hours from now. Or was that late afternoon? Wadia had wondered on several occasions what the actual boundary might be, that separated afternoon from evening (and evening from night, for that matter). Oh well, a couple of hours' rest would do even him some good, though he was clearly unaccustomed to an afternoon nap. And while he had initially thought that he would get no sleep at all, he was pleasantly surprised to find, when he woke, that he had been terribly wrong. He felt rejuvenated, and after a quick cup of tea prepared by the efficient Jamuna Das (Wadia asked him his last name, as he always did with anyone he got to know a little bit better), they were off on their quest to find Elise.

They thought they would start with the old bungalows first, the ones with the lovely patios outside, which they had seen on their drive into town: elderly people sitting, sipping their late morning chai. As they drove into town in the opposite direction now, the entire place looked deserted. These bungalows were owned by people who had been living in Udvada for the longest time, and if they had to find something from a long time ago, what better place to start than right here?

In fact, these were the very people who would be most concerned with the happenings in Udvada. Just like in Bandra, Wadia was forever concerned about civic issues, like preventing littering on the streets and ensuring that the Punjabi superstar who had moved into the bungalow in the modest Christian community Wadia was rightfully a part of (and the film star most certainly wasn't), did not disturb the residents around him with his late night parties, even though it had no effect on him at all, as he lived a couple of lanes away. He had written a letter to Mr. Kapoor (the actor in question), stating most clearly (and perhaps a tad rudely) that if he did not desist from keeping those late night parties, he would personally escort the police to his doorstep and ensure he stopped the bloody party (yes, he had used the word 'bloody' in the letter, too).

The next thing you knew: the parties stopped, as though by magic. Now, the venue for Mr. Kapoor's partying had shifted to his actress girlfriend's plush penthouse on Carter Road; that is, if the tabloids were to be believed. Of course, there was no mention of any mad bawa's letter in the papers anywhere. As for the residents of Carter Road in close proximity of the aforesaid actress's home? Who really cared? Wadia had done this all for himself. He was utterly selfish and he was proud of it!

Velkar's rickety van stopped outside a cottage that had clearly seen better years. It was in close proximity to the beach, which they planned to visit later. Of course there were other things to see, too, like the Iranshah Fire Temple, where Wadia had vowed to go and offer his prayers, along with the prayers Toral and Velkar would be entrusting him with, of course. Velkar had been in a bit of a conundrum when Wadia had told them about this. He had told Wadia, 'Arre, baba, then you will know what I am praying for, no?' Wadia had told him that of course he would; what other way was there, to offer prayers on someone's behalf? 'In that case, said Velkar, I will tell you what to pray for right before you enter the gates of the temple.' Wadia had thought then, 'What a foolish man'!

The door to the cottage creaked open. An old lady stood watching them with a thick layer of suspicion. She wore spectacles that resembled the ones worn by the late Mahatma Gandhi, and she had a walking stick in her hand. Wadia was immediately reminded of Mr. Fernandes, who he had presumed dead for all these years. How many *very old people* there must exist in this world. Largely forgotten, living in homes whose outsides were crumbling like their insides...

"Excuse me, aunty." Toral had decided the opening would be hers, in whichever house they went. Wadia and Velkar had agreed instantly, even though at first the latter had wanted to be a hero, saying he would make his way into not only into the homes, but also the hearts of the people they met; that is, of course, until Toral intervened and told him it was a better idea if she spoke instead.

"Yes?" The voice was tinged with fear, contrary to the rather stern expression on the lady's face. It seemed as though she had had no visitors in years. She probably had children who had long forgotten her, thought Wadia wearily.

"If you would be kind enough to spare a few moments of your time, Aunty, it would really mean a lot to us."

"*Time?* Nobody wants my time." The voice was feeble, but the fear seemed to have gone. It was practically the same reaction he had got from Mr. Fernandes. And none of them spoke a word for the next several moments.

"Come in," she said finally, looking at the hapless faces of the people who had rung her bell, somehow feeling sorry for them. When they walked into the house behind her, they were met with an unbearable stench. It seemed as though there might be some rotting food lying around. In all probability the poor woman didn't even know about the smell, what with her diminishing faculties; or perhaps she simply didn't care. When the three of them sat on the sofa at one end of the living room, it creaked even more noisily than Velkar's car. Wadia wondered then if the springs might give way; on closer inspection of the fabric it seemed as though it might have once been a rather resplendent thing – an imported sofa, undoubtedly, from a time when this woman, much younger, might have waltzed in this very living room with her husband while a classic played on the record player. Her husband was surely long gone, although there didn't seem to be a picture of him anywhere in sight.

"Tell me what you want." Straight to the point. Wadia liked that. She was in no mood to chitchat; and why would she be? The curtains were open to a view of the street at the back of the house. The windows at the front of the house were shut. There was plenty of light that streamed in through the window at the back, though, and that perhaps spoke of her resilience. To life.

"I'm sorry, aunty, but we have come all the way from Bombay in search of someone who we believe lived in Udvada quite some time ago, and we were hoping you could help us." Toral did indeed have a way with words, thought Wadia. If either he or Velkar were to have spoken first, they would have probably been kicked out of the house by now.

"What was her name?"

"Elise."

"Never heard of her. And mind you, Udvada is a small community. Everyone knows everyone here."

This time Toral didn't look to Wadia before she asked the question that would invariably seal the matter.

"Aunty, she had Down's syndrome."

And again there was the kind of reaction that brought goosebumps not only to Wadia, but this time, Toral and Velkar too. The old lady started shaking her head, as though in the process she could shake something out of her mind; something terrible from the past, had just clawed its way in at the mere mention of 'Down's syndrome.' Only a few moments later, she assumed a bold expression and when she spoke, her tone was seething with anger.

"What do you want from me? Why have you come here? Get out of my house, this very instant!"

Velkar spoke next.

"My lady, will you please tell us what is going on here? We just asked this question to another gentleman not long ago and we were met with a similar reaction."

"Who *are* you people?" She bellowed. And Wadia said, "Do you have a few minutes to spare, aunty?" She glared at him then, as though to say, 'Who are you to call me aunty, you old fogey?' But it seemed to have done the trick.

A heavy silence had descended into the cottage after Wadia finished his story. The stench seemed almost gone now; perhaps on account of him being accustomed to it by now? Or perhaps because his mind had been diverted by the woman's adverse reaction not long ago. Finally, the old lady spoke, and there was that fear in her eyes again.

"She was the sweetest angel in the world. I knew her well, but her name was not Elise. At least, not to us. We called her Diva, because she was just like a diva, you know. A goddess in the true sense of the word; perhaps that was what we should have named her, 'Goddess.' She had a caretaker. A man called Shankar, who took care of her in a bungalow close to the beach, like mine is. In fact, it's not too far away from here." She seemed to be lost in a train of thought, before she went on.

"I always wondered why they let a small girl like that, stay with a male servant who could have done just about anything to her, but when I saw the bond they shared, time and again, I realized that she was indeed in the best of hands." Glancing at her guests now, who were hanging on to every word she uttered. "I'm so sorry. I really should have offered you a cup of tea. That's the very least I should be doing. I can still make you some, but it will take me a while. I'm not as agile as the ballerina I used to be in my youth and my servant has gone for the day."

"Please, aunty. Take no trouble. What you are telling us will fill our souls. Who cares, then, what the body needs?" Velkar the philosopher.

"Okay, if you insist. But I'm warning you. What I am about to tell you might not be for the faint-hearted." Looking at Wadia and Velkar, and then back at Wadia. "Especially you." Wadia shuddered, and this time his fear showed. Toral, who was seated between Wadia and Velkar, patted Wadia on the shoulder. She was nervous, too, but she knew her heart was in better physical condition than Rustom's.

The old woman went on, and she addressed Wadia as she spoke. "There were only a couple of months in the year, January and February that is, when little Diva had visitors. In the month of January there would be a woman who would come to stay with her, and in February, right after she had gone, a gentleman would arrive – a Parsi gentleman, much like you. Like almost every man in Udvada, for that matter. Of course, that was your grandfather. I know that now. The really strange thing was, they never left the house. Neither the Parsi gentleman nor the lady who visited before him. As though they might be ashamed to be seen walking down the streets of Udvada with their deformed daughter. Of course all of us in Udvada knew they were her parents; who were they trying to fool?" Again, she seemed to be lost in thought for a while.

"You know, I even went there once, with some fresh chicken cutlets I had made. It was on Valentine's day, I remember clearly. Not that I had a secret crush on your grandfather. Besides, I was happily married then. Anyways, that was the day I decided, 'enough is enough.' I simply had to find out why they kept that poor angel trapped in there, when she loved the outdoors ever so much. And you know what happened? Your grandfather answered the door, and he told me, 'Diva is not here. Please don't come back again. Ever.' Initially I thought to myself, what a rude man. Who does he think is, all aloof, upturned moustache and everything? But later, when I went home, I thought of the deep sadness in his eyes, and decided to never pursue the matter again. She paused, perhaps in an attempt to gather her thoughts.

But who was he fooling? I knew Diva was there; everyone who knew her, did. Mr. Behram Patel, the man whose place you're staying at, would have a great time playing with her. He must have been in his thirties then, and Diva must have been around five or six. She lapped up every bit of his attention." The old woman paused, and Wadia could see a tear trickle down her left eye. Then she dabbed it with the back of her hand and went on with her story, seemingly with a newfound resolve.

"It's not easy to live with Down's syndrome, especially if you're an abandoned child. Her parents seemed to have spared no expense on the bungalow she lived in. Would you believe it was the nicest bungalow in all of Udvada? That too, occupied by a single girl. Perhaps it was by divine grace that she had a diminished understanding of things. That probably spared her some of the anguish of being so cruelly abandoned. In any case, she grew up to be the most loving, special girl, until–" And she paused then, and the trembling resumed. This is the moment of truth, thought Wadia, as he braced himself for what was to follow.

"Until what, aunty?" It was Velkar, who was as eager to know the truth as the rest of them. It was right then and there that Mrs. Bhathena's warning rang loud in Wadia's ears. She had told them not to go to Udvada. Perhaps some things are best left unknown, he thought. But it was too late now.

"She was raped, the poor child." She let that bit of information sink in. Wadia covered his face in his hands. Velkar was shaking his head in disbelief, and Toral looked as though she might burst into tears. There was no point waiting any further, the old woman thought. It would take far more than a few moments for that kind of information to *really* sink in.

"One night Shankar went about screaming in the middle of the streets, as though in an attempt to wake up everyone in Udvada. It must have been around three or four in the morning. He was simply unable to speak, at least to those who came out onto their patios in the wee hours of the morning. By late morning, it seemed as though all of Udvada had gathered outside her palace. "And what a palace it was," she said wistfully, before the sadness returned in her eyes. "Truly befitting of the princess she was."

There was pin-drop silence for a while before she continued, "Everyone wanted to know what the matter was, but the next thing we knew, it had become a police case. The policemen came later that morning and took him away, that poor Shankar. It was a terrible sight, seeing him cry manically as he was being led away. In only a matter of moments, it seemed, your father was here. The very next day he took Diva away and she was never seen again. Nobody has lived in that house since."

The old woman became silent for a long time, staring out the window into nothingness. Wadia thought to himself, No. That can't be it! That cannot be the end of the story.

"Do you know where my father might have taken Diva?" He noticed he said *Diva*, not *Elise*. In any case, that's how the old woman remembered her.

"No, my son. I can understand your pain, but you must understand ours as well. Diva was Udvada's daughter; she was the loving child most of us had lost to the world. Look at me; my children migrated to London and except for phone calls once in a blue moon, they never come here. They will visit Mumbai to meet their friends, but they won't come and see their ageing mother in Udvada. And you know what they tell me when I ask them why they won't visit me? They say there is nothing here. What about me? Anyway, forget about them. Where were we? Ah, yes, Diva. She was gone too soon. And they blamed an innocent man for the crime, I tell you. I was there, you know, when that Shankar was being led away. And he looked me in the eyes and said, 'Please; maine yeh kiya nahin.' And you know what? I believed him."

Something else was slowly seeping inside Wadia now, besides the sadness that had engulfed him like a Venus Flytrap might a fly – undiluted anger.

"How old was Elise, when this happened?" Back to Elise now. That was how *he* knew her, after all. Trying his best to keep from falling apart.

"I can say with absolute certainty that she was twenty-two. We used to have a birthday celebration every year for her, you know? None of us knew the exact date of her birth, of course, but we did have a general idea of how old she was, given the fact that she came here as an infant. We had an office in this large building in the centre of town, where we held something akin to a town hall. We would meet once a month to discuss the local affairs in Udvada. We would have her birthday there, every single year. It was a random date we had settled on, April 4th, and I remember most distinctly that the last birthday of hers we celebrated, was her twenty-second. How she loved birthdays, that dear child. She loved stuffing her mouth with pineapple cake – that was her favourite – and she would make it a point to feed all of us with her hands, one by one, until there was nobody left to feed."

And then she couldn't take it any more. Tears started rolling down the old woman's face, as the memories came flooding back. What a terrible tragedy to have befallen this child, Toral thought. That too, a child who would have absolutely no way of knowing the evil rampant in the world. She had probably let someone into her home at night with all her innocence, before the unimaginable came to pass.

"Who do you think did it then?" It was Velkar, clearly incensed. No matter the several shortcomings of the Maharashtrian, Wadia knew he had the utmost respect for women and he wasn't going to let anyone get away with a crime as heinous as this. The sad part was, the person who had committed this horrific act would be long gone by now.

"That's the strangest thing. Nobody in Udvada back then ever really knew who could have been capable of a crime as horrific as this one, owing to the fact that everyone loved her. Thus it was that most of them relegated themselves towards thinking that it had indeed been Shankar who had been responsible for this monstrous act. And Shankar had a family, you know; it wasn't long before some of the other servants in town got together and forced his wife and young children out of their home. God knows what happened to them. I still remember his wife, Kanchan. She worked in a few houses here part-time, as a cleaner. I used to see her sometimes, walking along the road, humming a tune at times, always smiling. How that incident changed the lives of those poor people, it's so terrible."

"Did you ever see Elise again? Perhaps on the day she left?" Toral seemed far more composed now than she had been a few minutes earlier.

"No. The story is, she was taken away in the middle of the night. The house was locked and nobody has ever stepped foot in it again."

"Where is the house?" Wadia knew he wasn't going to leave Udvada without knowing where Elise had lived out a large chunk of her life.

"You aren't thinking of going there, I hope? I don't think anyone has gone there since the incident. The young children in town call it *Ghost House*." Then she looked outside the window and once again, with those dreamy eyes, she said, "We used to call it The White House."

The White House. Toral and Wadia looked at one another the moment the words had slipped out of the old woman's mouth. Perhaps my house will become a ghost house long after I'm gone, thought Wadia. And in the flash of an instant he knew what he had to do.

"Where is it?" he asked again, this time with a sense of urgency in his voice.

"It's called *Providence Villa*. You can use those fancy phones of yours to find out where it is," the old woman said, "but you should leave it alone. No good can come of your curiosity. The past is best left in the past."

"Who owns the place now?" It was Velkar. Good question. Wadia had not thought to ask that himself.

"A trust in Udvada. Your father sold it off to them, I believe."

Wadia rose from the sofa that creaked even louder than it had when he had sat in it. "Thank you for your time, ma'am. I know it has been difficult for you, as well, to have narrated this incident to us." And the old woman just placed the palms of her hands together as though to say 'namaskar.' In a way, it seemed she were relieved, too. This incident had clearly haunted her for a long time, until she had repressed it well in the deepest recesses of her memory. It seemed as though this had been a cathartic experience of sorts for her; letting the pain run freely through her. Until there was no pain left to feel.

Chapter Seventeen
Udvada's Secrets

Udvada beach reminded Wadia of *Bandstand*. Rather, of Bandstand *beach* in Mumbai, which was not all that far from the rocky seafront in Carter Road. It was something of a ritual for his father Percival, to take him there as a child, to the far end where the land ended (hence, the place being christened Land's End) to see the grand fort that was built by the Portuguese sometime in the sixteenth century. Apparently, it had been built so that passing ships could get access to some freshwater, which was to be found nearby. This beach in Udvada was very much like the beach in Bandra's Bandstand, in that it was mostly rocky. There was hardly any sand to be found, but it was sunset time and ever so panoramic. Who said a beach had to have sand on it to be called a beach?

They had had to pass through several by lanes in Udvada to get here, and there was an intersection in the road where Velkar had nearly knocked down an old man on a bicycle; a man carrying freshly baked buns that fell onto the road as he swerved to avoid Velkar's car. He had cursed at them, apparently in some form of Gujarati (it must surely have been the local dialect of the Parsis), before turning to continue his journey. It wasn't his fault that the man's hot cross buns were spoiled, thought Velkar. In any case, people had far greater problems to deal with. Like being born with Down's syndrome and discarded like a rag doll by one's parents, in an unknown city.

Wadia had chosen to extend his stroll long after the three of them had walked the beach together, letting their thoughts sink in. He was restless, not knowing what to do next. None of them had talked about the rape since they left the old lady's house; after all, how could one even think of discussing such a thing?

They had stopped outside Providence Villa at Wadia's insistence. "I can't bear having come all this way and not to at least see the place where she lived all her life," he'd said. Toral had eventually conceded. "Perhaps it will put our minds at rest," she had agreed. On first sight, Providence Villa had resembled a house in a horror movie. The façade was crumbling, and the paint had probably lost its lustre years ago. The two large windows in the living room and one on the first floor had their curtains closed. Another window on the first floor, to the right of where they were parked, had no curtains. Through it the only thing they could see was a blank white wall that faced the window, nothing else. Might that have been Elise's room?

It was Toral's idea to go to the beach for some fresh air and to clear their heads.

The sun had painted the sky a beautiful shade of red, but this particular hue seemed to depress Toral even more. It's funny how things can have a different effect on you at different times, she thought. Like when she had heard a song by *The Beatles* when she had been dating her boyfriend in London. It had seemed so beautiful then, but post her break-up with Paul (that had been his name), it hurt her immensely every single time she listened to it. She remembered the name of the song too; it was *Yesterday*. The song seemed to trigger an overwhelming sense of sadness inside her every time she listened to it. Like what happened to Wadia every time he listened to Für Elise, albeit not with the same intensity.

Talking about Wadia, where was he? Ah! There he was in the distance, staring at some seagulls, although in all probability he was just staring into space. It was certainly not easy on him. As for her, well, she might look strong on the outside, but inside she was putty; all she wanted to do was go home, lock herself up in her room, and cry.

She watched him for a while, and waved at him when he finally looked their way. He picked his way slowly back over the beach.

"Rustom, will you pray for Elise at the temple, from my side? That's all I want now. It's time I thought of someone other than myself; at least this once in my life."

The next morning, before heading out, they had a sumptuous breakfast of *akuri* (the Parsi version of scrambled eggs) with white bread (they had no multi-grain option, much to Toral's dismay) and a couple of cups each of piping hot coffee.

Their first stop was going to be the legendary 'first ever' Fire Temple, the place where the sacred fire of the Parsis had been burning for more than fifteen hundred years.

"You're so lucky, Rustom," Toral said from the passenger seat in the front, as Velkar was passing the railway station close to where they were heading. She had wanted to sit in the front today; had literally begged, as though she were a small child. Wadia had happily acquiesced; the further away from Velkar he was, the better.

"And why's that, my dear?"

"Well, you know, you get to enter this most amazing place, and we don't."

Wadia was silent for a couple of moments. "It's unfair, you know. I thought about it many times over. Hindus don't check if you're not Hindu, before they allow you into a temple. Why do we Parsis discriminate? The worst part is, they go on to say that this rule of theirs is not discriminatory."

Toral turned to look at Velkar, who hadn't been his usual chatty self this morning. "Is something the matter, Neel?"

"No – why on earth? Why should you think that? I'm okay, of course."

"Hey Velkar, you haven't told me your prayer yet. Toral told me hers. Both of us are going to be praying for Elise."

"Further, I have asked Rustom to pray that Bobby Chan will come and work at my restaurant." Toral certainly had no qualms about keeping her prayer a secret from Velkar.

"Bobby Chan? Who's that?"

"Just a star chef in a restaurant in Andheri, Neel. Do tell us, what do you want Wadia to pray for? On your behalf, that is."

Velkar seemed to be straining to see where they might be.

"Relax Neel. It's a left in 450 metres. I have it here on Maps." Smiling at Wadia. "You can tell us your prayer."

So that had been it, thought Wadia. The reason for Velkar's curious, almost total, silence ever since he had got up that morning.

"My prayer is that we get some closure in the Elise matter."

"And?" This Toral was very good at being persistent, thought Wadia.

"And what? Nothing." He seemed a bit sad now. Toral decided against pressing further.

"Vidya and me want to have a baby," Velkar blurted out then. Wadia was aghast. Toral was shocked, too, but tried not to show it.

"Velkar, your wife is sixty nine. She is in no condition to have a baby."

"Arre baba, adoption I mean." Clearly, Velkar didn't know how to express himself. 'Wanting to have a baby' was not the way to say you wished to adopt a child.

"But, don't you think it's a little late in the day? Clearly no adoption agency is going to consider giving you a child at your age. You know that, don't you?" It was Toral.

Velkar stopped the car. The next left they had to take was in 38 metres, and the Fire Temple would be there shortly thereafter.

"Will you be our child?" he asked her. Wadia nearly fainted. Toral seemed in a state of shock, and it took a few moments for her to regain her composure, as Velkar looked on like a helpless puppy.

"Really?" Toral seemed to be actually contemplating the idea. Wadia couldn't believe it.

"Yes. I mean it. I spoke to Vidya last night and she only confirmed what we both knew. We have always wanted a child but Vidya could never conceive, you know. And then you came along, and I told her all about you, not forgetting to mention you had lost both your parents some time ago. It won't even be a real adoption, in the legal sense, that is. Look, you don't have to stay with us. Don't even have to meet us if you don't want to. Just *be ours*, will you? Give our lives some meaning."

"Yes, I will." Said with the earnestness of a girl to a man who has just proposed to her. Tears were streaming down her cheeks. And then, a couple of moments later, she fell into Velkar's outstretched arms. And the both of them were crying profusely.

"What is happening here?" It was Wadia, who had leaned forward in his seat. But both of them seemed to not notice him at all.

"Wait a minute. I will call Mummy," Velkar said.

Mummy? Wadia was flabbergasted. "But no, this is—"

"It's all right, Rustom. I want this." And the look in Toral's eyes implied she was not being coerced into anything out of pity; she really did want to be a Maharashtrian. Wonder of wonders! Wadia shook his head. A couple of moments later she was chatting with Vidya on the phone, telling her how grateful she was to both her and Neel (she had to tell her who Neel was, of course) for even thinking of adopting her.

One of Velkar's prayers had already been answered, and that suddenly made his other prayer, namely getting a sense of closure for Elise, all the more important. Now, in a strange sort of way, he was related to Elise as well. Of course there was no real connection with Elise like the kind Toral and Wadia harboured, but it was there, nonetheless. Wadia had seen many crazy things in his life. Of late he had lost his faith in seeing the Loch Ness monster (he had travelled a few times to Scotland and visited the lake several times just so he could maybe catch a glimpse of the magnificent beast, and had even paid a ridiculous sum of money for some water from the actual lake), but after what had just happened, he thought he could undoubtedly get a ride in the Loch on Nessie's back sometime soon.

The drive finally resumed, and not long after, they reached the gates that opened to the Atash Behram, the most sacred Fire Temple in all the world. Wadia felt blessed to be here; even before he had gone into the gates and into the sacred temple to offer his prayers. As were newly christened daddy and daughter, who were looking at each other with moist eyes. And Velkar didn't even have to pray to get her to be his daughter, Wadia thought. Imagine, then, what prayer might do. And he stepped out of the van and gave daddy and daughter some alone time, as he made his way into the magnificent Atash Behram.

Even sitting out here, outside the gates of this magnificent structure, Toral and Velkar couldn't help but feel that the agiary had had something to do with their wishes being granted. Ever since her father had passed (not too long after her mother, that is), she had felt a sense of emptiness. She had tried desperately to fill the void, with the relationships she fell into post her becoming an 'orphan.' Although she had all the money in the world and even the house (according to Petunia Shah, the house had to be passed on to only a daughter of the home, unless there were none, of course – in that case it would go to a charity she had chosen), that didn't seem to comfort her much, although it would have certainly delighted plenty others in a world that was increasingly materialistic. She didn't know it, but subconsciously she craved someone by her side; not necessarily parents or a lover, but perhaps a best friend.

And even though Velkar and his wife would never be able to replace her real parents, the moment she had been asked by Velkar if she would be his daughter, she had felt a sense of exactly that thing she had been craving for, for so long – belonging. As for Velkar, he was literally on cloud nine. His wife had not been able to conceive all her life, and that was exactly why they had been especially close to the children of their siblings. However, the relationship one shared with nieces or nephews was not the same as the bond they might share with their own children. They had thought about adopting several times over the years, but something had always happened to somehow thwart that plan. All they ever wanted was a little one of their own; and now, that dream had been realized. Except, the girl was not so *little*.

After what seemed like well over an hour, Wadia emerged from the gates of the grand Fire Temple. He had a beatific glow on his face. Later on, as they made their way to Udvada Railway Station (that Toral wanted to check out and take pictures of because it was far too early for lunch and they might as well see it now that they were here), Wadia told them that it had been the act of kneeling down to the fire (that burned bright in the inner chamber that only the priests had access to), that somehow 'did it for him.' In that moment, it was as though everything inside him just vanished; the entire burden he was carrying. An idea came to him, too. Maybe this Fire Temple had indeed performed a miracle; a couple of miracles, really, he thought, as he glanced at Toral who seemed to have a sense of calm about her too. As for Velkar, well, he might detest the man at times, but he had always had a soft spot for him. And he was happy. Happy for his happiness.

In only a short while they reached Udvada station. Velkar parked his van in a spot nearby and they walked towards the building. He could see now why Toral had wanted to come here. The façade was resplendent if not imposing. As they were admiring the structure, Toral told them that it had only been a couple of years that the building, that was more than a hundred years old (closer to a hundred and fifty than a hundred, for that matter) had been restored. They had hired an architect from Valsad to do the job. What was her fascination with ages past? History had never been Velkar's favourite subject in school; it was always geography. He remembered that before his preliminary exam, he had failed in geography and his teacher had told him that if he didn't pay attention to his study of maps, he would fail his board exams too. That's when he had burnt the midnight oil studying maps, and in the end, topped his class in geography. Thinking over it now, he wondered why on earth studies had been so important. He still remembered from Geography class where Rwanda was on the map, but he had been clueless about where Udvada might be, although he had heard of it several times since childhood. A place more important to him that Rwanda would ever be, as it turned out to be. After all, he had become a father here.

Into the station they went and Wadia was delighted at how surprisingly charming the place was. From the outside, the building looked exactly like a Parsi home in that it had a carved exterior similar to the one in many Parsi houses (certainly most of the houses here in Udvada, at least). They sat on a bench by the railway track and waited for a train to pass through. Wadia hadn't heard the sound of a train in ages, let alone see one whiz past him at breakneck speed. They spent time there chatting, and Wadia let Velkar dominate the conversation. After all, he had become a father at the ripe age of seventy-one.

Wadia looked at the grand clock a few metres away from them, hoisted up in the air on a pole. The time read 12.00 p.m. The rumbling in his tummy had started. Although he ate his lunch at 1.00 p.m. every single day when he was in Mumbai, he didn't spare a thought to that sense of routine now. Of course, it didn't matter what time they ate; little seemed to matter, except for finding the truth. But that would have to wait until later. Now, it was time for lunch. And when it was time to eat, he didn't wait for anyone. He got up and said, "Are you starving? I most certainly am!"

It so turned out that Velkar and Toral were famished, too. None of them had eaten much the previous day, and they were most certainly making up for it now. Wadia was literally tearing into the chicken farcha at *Mimi's*, the establishment he had been meaning to go to ever since they had begun their journey to Udvada. Not that it was such a great place, though, as far as the ambience went; it seemed like someone had merely thrown some plastic tables and chairs together and christened the place a restaurant.

'Don't forget Mimi's,' Delna Mistry had told him over the telephone. Delna was Jimmy Mistry's wife; he had called the Mistrys the Sunday before they left for Udvada, and even though he didn't tell them the real reason for his upcoming trip, he thought it pertinent to bring up the subject matter as a matter of courtesy, because they had been on at him for the last several years to visit the place, and had failed every single time.

Going by this succulent chicken farcha, a Parsi-style fried chicken dish that he was relishing with a savage ferocity, the advice had most certainly been sage. Of course, there was a lot more to come. Chicken tikka masala with rotlis, patrani macchi and prawns berry pulao. All of this would be washed down with unlimited raspberry soda, which, it turned out, was marked 'complementary' on the menu (alongside an asterisk that indicated – only if you ordered something to eat). Wadia wondered how it could be complementary in that case, but let that thought rest. They didn't know how much they would actually end up eating, but it was well worth it to order dishes they loved. Like back at the Willingdon Club in Mumbai, Wadia would only order his eggs Kejriwal. What was the point of experimenting, when you didn't know what you were going to get? After all, didn't men go back every single day to the women they loved? (Wadia had thought about this several times over, even though he had nothing but the utmost respect for women, and held that they were infinitely superior to anything made in a kitchen).

Of course, the prawns berry pulao had been Toral's choice. Come to think of it, that had been the very thing they had feasted on in Mrs. Bhathena's house, the one dish Toral absolutely adored. Which meant that she was not all that experimental either. And she owned a restaurant that regularly garnered rave reviews, mind you.

If the last few days had taught Rustom anything, it had been this: when you sail into uncharted waters, you might just be heading someplace beautiful. Like he would never have imagined being out here in Udvada, enjoying all this yummy Parsi food. And yet, he was. He would never have thought he would play Für Elise on his piano, and feel happiness instead of sadness. Yet, he did.

There was one thing bothering him, though. The old Parsi woman who undoubtedly owned the café (she had taken their order, and bore an air unlike the waiters in this place), was sitting on a chair at a nearby table, glancing dreamily at him.

"I think she likes you." It was Velkar. Wadia almost spat a large piece of fried chicken out his mouth. He hastily picked up the half-chewed piece of chicken and resuming munching on it, then turned angrily towards his Maharashtrian friend of more than fifty years. Toral had even turned around to see who it was Velkar was talking about, and the wry smile on her face a couple of moments later, did nothing to better Wadia's mood.

"Are you people crazy? How can I enjoy the rest of my meal now, with this lady gawking at me? Doesn't she know she can lose a customer, if she behaves like this?" He said this quite loudly, as though he wanted her to hear it.

"Not if she wants to win your heart." The audacity of that Maharashtrian!

Then Wadia did something that took Toral and Velkar completely by surprise. He lifted his plate with the half-eaten chicken farcha, and went round the table to sit next to Toral. Now, he was facing an empty seat. Diagonally next to him sat Velkar. And the stalker could only see his back. Neither Toral nor Velkar said anything; they just chuckled, to Wadia's chagrin. They were getting a bloody thrill out of watching him suffer.

And just when he had licked his fingers clean after relishing the last piece of his beloved chicken farcha, the old woman plonked herself in the chair he had previously been sitting in; right in front of him.

"I hope you people don't mind if I join you," she said, with that same dreamy look in her eyes. *Mind?* She hadn't even given them a chance. What was it with these people in Udvada? First that Kaizad Patel comes and joins us for lunch (well okay, that had been an invitation from Toral but he should have declined in any case, any self-respecting man would have done that) and now, Granny.

"No, of course not. Please, it will be a pleasure." It was Velkar. All set to destroy his life. She's all yours, he thought silently. I will happily give her up for you; just let me eat my dhansak in peace.

But alas! Peace was not to be had; at least for the rest of the meal, that is. What had started off with a lovely chicken farcha was now undoubtedly doomed to be a meal replete with the cackling of an uninvited goose. She just seemed like one of those types, who would not let anyone else speak once she had started talking. Wadia hated people like that.

"You're so handsome, dikra!" she told Wadia in the middle of a one-sided conversation that included Ratan Tata and pelicans. The ill-mannered Velkar literally spat out the strawberry soda he had been rolling around in his mouth for the last couple of seconds, into his plate. Wadia was disgusted. But not as disgusted as he was with this woman. Could she be any more direct? A bit of clarification here, it wasn't that Wadia didn't find women attractive; clearly there were times when the sight of a lovely lass made him turn his head to look again. He had seen plenty of women like that in the Willie, and had even mildly flirted with them at times. However, the lady sitting in front of him was anything but pretty. And looks were important to him; at least, they would be important to him if he were looking to pursue a relationship other than friendship. But he wasn't. And Velkar knew it too. Why was he egging the lady on then? Sadist!

Wadia just nodded his head at that remark about himself being handsome (he couldn't deny that, could he?)

"I get it, he's one of those shy types," the old woman said, looking at Toral as though the young woman might just come to her aid. Luckily for Rustom, Toral sensed Wadia's discomfiture.

"Aunty, we have come here looking for someone very dear to us. In the process we found out something most upsetting and that is why we are not quite in the mood. I hope you understand."

"Well, *he* certainly seems in his element." The lady wagged her finger at Velkar, who had a layer of raspberry soda plastered all over his chin. He smiled sheepishly and raised his glass of Roger's soda to Wadia and then, Toral. Getting a dirty stare from Wadia and an even dirtier one from his daughter, he took a sip from it before putting it down on the table.

Then the old lady brushed the back of her head and her composure changed completely. That dreamy look in her eyes was gone, and it was replaced by a look of sympathy. "I'm sorry," she said. "I didn't introduce myself. I'm Mimi, and this is my place."

And that was when Wadia got it. So *this* was why the Mistrys were ever so eager to have him visit Mimi's. What they really wanted was for him to visit *Mimi*, without the 'apostrophe' and 's'. Mimi was undoubtedly a friend of theirs looking to 'settle down' (if you could even call it that, at this age) and their plans to fix Rustom up with a nice lady over the course of the last few years having failed (and there had been plenty of ladies they had introduced him to, mind you) they probably thought that Mimi was the best (and last) possible option. It was all Delna, thought Wadia. Jimmy would have never tried to set him up if it hadn't been for his wife, benign pussycat that he was.

After Velkar and Toral had introduced themselves (Wadia just stared angrily at Mimi, refusing to say a word), Mimi looked at the irate Parsi and said, "You must be Rustom. Delna called me from Vancouver a couple of nights ago, you know, asking me to take good care of you. So, can you let me? Take care of you?" She said this with a twinkle in her eye, and that was it.

"You could get the bill," he bellowed, and nobody laughed. What's worse, in the precise moments following his loud burst of laughter, the other tables suddenly went quiet, and that made the silence all the more deafening. Mimi, clearly unsettled, took a few moments to regain her composure.

"If you don't mind me asking, what is your problem?" The question was directed towards Wadia.

And Wadia just blurted it out. What had he got to lose anyways?

"I'm sure you know Diva. Rather, knew her. My father would visit her a few years, after my grandfather, of course, who I'm sure you remember. That was because she was his half-sister, from the liaison of my grandfather with Toral's great grandmother." Pointing to Toral. Even Bollywood could not have come up with a script as crazy as this, he thought.

Plates laden with scrumptious-looking food arrived then and the next thing you knew, Mimi was sobbing profusely. The waiters asked her if anything was wrong and that was when she somehow managed to compose herself. She took out her handkerchief and dabbed her tears, as well as the sweat on her chubby cheeks.

"I sincerely hope you enjoy your meal," she said. "Please don't forget to give us five stars on Zomato." Spoken almost like a robot, or perhaps even Siri. Then, she did the most unexpected thing. She got up and left. Just like that. Not just left the table, mind you. She walked up to the manager and exchanged a few words before leaving the restaurant in a rickshaw that looked like it had been sitting out there waiting specifically for her. Perhaps she owned it. Perhaps she even drove it herself.

She had behaved in the exact same fashion Kaizad Patel had, when they had told him about 'that girl with Down's syndrome,' Wadia thought. As they ate their food in silence, a meal they didn't fully enjoy on account of the event that had just occurred, he felt there was something larger that was purposely being kept from them. He hardened to the idea he had in the temple.

Chapter Eighteen
Not Just Your Regular Pit Stop

They were parked outside a building close to the Fire Temple. It was five thirty in the evening, approximately an hour and a half before sunset.

"Why the secrecy? What's going on, baba? Are you wanting to go to the temple again?"

The two-storey building they were parked out in front of, looked like it had been recently revamped, but what was distinct about it was its rather modest architecture – that made it unlike any other building, certainly unlike the elegant bungalows and even the railway station in the beautiful city of Udvada, for that matter.

"And what might this place be?" It was Velkar. Only Wadia knew; he had used Google Maps for the first time today, and he was mighty proud. He pointed then to a sign hoisted on the terrace of the building. Looking upwards, his comrades saw a sign in bold lettering: 'Udvada Police Station.'

"What's going on, baba? You have come to turn us in? What have we done? Please, Vidya, forgive me. I didn't mean for it to end this way." Velkar's eyes were closed while he said this.

"Relax Velkar!" Wadia bellowed. "Look, the reason I didn't say anything to you guys (*Guys*? Had Mr. Rustom Wadia really said *guys*?) was because I knew I would be met with resistance. Don't worry."

"Well then, why are we even here?" Velkar was certainly justified in being anxious; angry, even.

"They say the blame was placed on poor Shambhu, who probably rotted away in some prison in Gujarat, right? Well, what if the police might have been onto something else? Something that the general populace were completely unaware of?" Toral seemed to sense where this was headed.

"I get it. You want to see if the police might happen to have any records pertaining to the time."

"Exactly. Velkar, if you're not comfortable, you can wait in the car. This won't take too long."

"Why no, of course I will come. After all, I *have to*." And he looked at the quizzical expressions on the faces of his comrades before he continued. "You know, they will want to see who has served as lead detective on the case."

No matter what, Velkar could lift you when you were at your lowest.

They found themselves in a small room on the ground floor of the two-storey building that prided itself on being Udvada Police Station. Wadia wondered what might lie on the floor upstairs. Might it be a lock-up? The one they had almost found themselves in? Or perhaps find themselves in, if they were not careful enough? A chill ran down his spine.

The Maharashtrian-looking gentleman (his community being confirmed by the glossy gold nameplate that read *Chief Inspector Agashe*), seemed busy with paperwork of some sort. Who in government offices isn't busy with paperwork? thought Velkar, who looked at an open box with some candies in it. He wondered if he could take one without asking. Better not. If he did, he would probably be detained for stealing. The Maharashtrian officer had even caught glimpses of him staring at those toffees, but hadn't bothered to ask Velkar if he would like any.

Once the chief inspector was done with his paperwork, he leaned over his desk and spoke in the most impeccable English.

"So, how can I be of assistance to you fine people?"

It took a couple of moments for Wadia to get over the shock of seeing a man in a small town in India, speak in unblemished English.

"I– *we*, actually, are looking for any information you might have relating to a rape that happened here a long time ago; perhaps around fifty years to this date." There. It was done with.

The police inspector looked at each of their faces carefully. He knew they must be visitors. Most of the people in this town were too old to come here and launch a formal complaint; they did it over their phones, if the need ever arose.

"You do realise this police station was built three years ago, right?"

Wadia sighed. What hope did they have? Of course there wouldn't be records of any kind dating back to an almost prehistoric age, here. He almost got up to say thank you and leave, when the charming inspector spoke again.

"There *is* someone who might be able to help you."

"And who might that be, fine sir?" It was Velkar, and he spoke in a flawless Brit accent; as though he might score brownie points for matching his fake accent with the chief inspector's, and get something concrete out of him in the process. Toral stifled a laugh. If the situation hadn't been one of sheer solemnity, she was sure she would have burst out laughing.

"None other than my father, Mohan Agashe, retired Chief Inspector of Udvada. But you will have to come home with me for dinner, if you wish to meet him. Ever since his retirement, he goes absolutely nowhere except for a walk early in the morning. He glanced at his watch. I get off at six, precisely fifteen minutes from now. Would you all like to come to my place and have a conversation with baba? My wife has made the best crab curry and I'm sure you will thank me for it later, if nothing else."

"Sorry, but I must politely decline." It was Velkar.

"Excuse me?" The gentleman seemed offended.

"My wife, Vidya Velkar from Khar Road in Mumbai, makes the best Crabs Khadkhadla."

"Crabs what?"

Wadia was shaking his head. Really, Velkar? You do realise this is a police inspector you are talking to, right?

"Khadkhadla is the speciality curry of our Pathare Prabhu community." Uttered with a Brit accent once again. That seemed to irk Wadia. The last thing one wanted to hear was the word 'Khadkhadla' uttered with a Brit accent.

"Well, you can come and have the crab curry at my place and then decide if your wife's curry is better, or Savitri's. Oh, Savitri is my wife, of course. And you will get to meet retired police inspector Mohan Agashe. He will be delighted to discuss an old case with someone. It's been a while since he's been off the force, and he likes to be reminded of his former glory days."

All eyes were on Velkar now, as though going to that dinner was pending his approval. After a few moments of intolerable silence, he broke into a smile and said, "In that case, I will be happy to accept. Let the curry wars begin!"

And so it turned out that the quick stop Wadia had proposed, had not been so quick after all. They soon found themselves sitting in a modest one-bedroom apartment that belonged to Mohan Agashe. Even though the hall was nowhere as large as Wadia's living room, or Velkar's, it was cosy. It had the feeling of a *home*, as opposed to a *house*. Further, the warmth the senior Mohan Agashe exuded was the icing on the cake; especially so, when they had hit rock bottom in their search for Elise. Wadia had told Sunil (that was the name of the young Agashe, although he dare not call him that, *Inspector* Agashe would have to do) before they had come here, that they would have to make an early night of it. Now, he thought that perhaps it might not be all that bad if the night were still young.

Mohan Agashe did not touch a drop of alcohol, and neither did he serve it in his house. The very first question Savitri had asked them when they were settled on the pistachio-green sofa in the living room, while Mohan and Sunil sat on two of the dining chairs they had pulled out from under the table, so they could be seated in front of their guests, had been, 'So, what juice would you like to have?'

'I'll have the beetroot!' Velkar had said, and poor Savitri had to apologise profusely, telling Velkar that if he wanted she could go to the market and get some beetroot for his juice; it was still open, after all. Trust Velkar to embarrass such gracious hosts, Wadia thought, shaking his head. What's worse was, Velkar had said, 'I'll have *the* beetroot,' as though he might be reading off a menu that had several juices listed on it, out of which beetroot was one. In the end, they had all settled for orange. Velkar had made a mental note to himself, to always say 'orange' when anyone asked him what juice he would like to have. He was quite inept in social situations. Vidya told him he made a fool of himself wherever he went, but that was exactly one of the reasons he was so endearing to her, even though she would never admit it to him.

The evening proceeded smoothly. Mohan Agashe regaled his visitors with his sparkling wit, almost having his guests in stitches at times. Rustom wondered if the conversation would ever veer towards Elise; he was having a hard time bringing the subject up, especially since the senior Agashe seemed to be hogging the limelight, and rightfully so. It seemed as though he hadn't had a visitor in years.

A good half hour into their conversation, Savitri came in and asked them if she could lay the table, gently informing them it would take approximately fifteen minutes for the meal to be ready. Wadia took that as his cue, to make his move. If Sunil was finding it odd to bring up the subject, he would have to do it himself. There was no other way.

"I'm sorry to have to intervene for a moment, Sir, but we were at the police station earlier, looking for some information on a case from around fifty years to this day. We were wondering if you might know something about it."

"What case?" Mohan Agashe seemed serious, all of a sudden. There was pin-drop silence in the room, as Wadia mustered the courage to utter the words that were too painful to speak.

"The rape of a young woman. Who went by the name of Diva."

If the name had rung a bell in Mohan Agashe's mind, he didn't show it. He just stared straight at Wadia, and it seemed as though he might be staring right through him, into nothingness. Once again there was an interminable silence. Was this man going to react the same way as the others had? Perhaps they wouldn't be having Savitri's famous crab curry, after all. And then the senior Agashe finally spoke again.

"Who was she to you?"

And Wadia told him everything. Again there was a period of deafening silence, after which Savitri came in and said that the food was ready. Mohan Agashe's face registered confusion. It was as though he couldn't decide whether they should eat first and talk later, or talk first and eat later. One thing was clear, though; he did seem to want to say something. It was Toral who broke the silence.

"Agashe uncle, it's okay. We can eat first. You don't have to say anything later, too, if you don't wish. Savitri aunty has taken such pains to make the crabs, it won't be fair to allow the food to get cold."

Once again, Mohan Agashe's face registered a stony look. Then he said, "Rubbish!" The trio squirmed in their positions. He went on, "What *pains*? Have you thought of the pains *I* took in carefully handpicking each crab?" That stony look again, followed by raucous laughter. That reminded Velkar of the friendly banter he often indulged in with Vidya when guests were over, what with him saying that the credit for the fish should go to him, and Vidya countering him, saying that the proof of the pudding was in the preparation. Needless to say, Vidya was the winner. Every single time. Things weren't quite the same in this household. Savitribai smiled meekly and retreated into the kitchen. After all, she was married to a police inspector, not a mechanical engineer.

The retired police inspector was silent a few moments, before saying, there's not much I know, but I will tell you. But after dinner, please?" His three guests happily acquiesced; after all, what had they to lose?

The crab curry was simply outstanding, They all ate with their fingers, which was of course the only appropriate fashion in which one ate crab curry with safed chawal. Velkar was licking his fingers clean, when Sunil looked at him and said, "Well, who makes better curry? My wife or yours?" Savitri was looking at Velkar expectantly.

"Your wife," he said, happily defeated, while the Agashes cheered loudly. This is what happiness is, thought Wadia. Simple joys jointly partaken of by the members of a loving family. And it didn't matter if Sunil and Savitri didn't have any kids. They had his father (and Savitri clearly treated Mohan Agashe more like a father than a father-in-law), and when the senior Agashe were gone, they would still have each other. This is exactly what poor Elise had missed in her lifetime; the joy of a loving family. Although she did have a sort of extended family in Udvada.

Then Velkar said, "Please don't tell my wife." And that had everyone in stitches.

They were seated after dinner in the very same positions they had occupied before they had sat down to partake of that wonderful meal. Mohan Agashe lived in a housing association property and not a bungalow, and thus didn't have the luxury of seating his guests on a balcony. The mood had turned sombre again, and everyone was patiently waiting for the senior Agashe to say something; anything that might help them get ahead of where they already were in their search for Elise. Please, please let this man have something to say about Elise, that might shed some light on where she went after the terrible incident in Udvada that night many moons ago, Toral prayed. And then, Mr. Agashe cleared his throat, as though what he were going to say next would require every ounce of his strength.

"An innocent man went to jail that day," he said, speaking straight to Wadia. "I was not the officer in charge, but I went along with my senior officer to Providence Villa when that frenzied call came in the wee hours of the morning. I was young then, in my early thirties. Palekar Saheb was the Chief Inspector. I remember a gentleman in the house who sat at the table, looking utterly devastated. Shambhu lay in a corner of the living room, shivering in fear. The girl was nowhere to be seen, though. All I remember was Palekar Saheb telling me to put the handcuffs on Shambhu." He took a moment to compose himself. "How that man wept, incessantly begging us to please spare him, that he had nothing to do with the crime. In fact, he had wandered the streets at night after calling his master who lived in Bombay, screaming for someone to come and help him. If you see a man weeping like that, you know he isn't guilty. Nobody came to his help, though. Shame on all of us."

He stopped to take a large sip of water. Savitri was back in the kitchen, clearing up. Toral had told her to please let her help her, she was used to cleaning her own kitchen back home as she felt she did a better job than her maid, which of course stemmed from the severe case of OCD she had, but Savitri had firmly told her that she was her guest, and it was her duty to do the work all on her own. And back home they had servants getting them everything from a pen in a drawer to a glass of water, she thought. The things we take for granted. One only had to see how others managed, to know how easy they had it themselves. The old Agashe continued, once again looking Wadia straight in the eyes as he spoke.

"I almost had an altercation with Mr. Palekar then, and tried my best to hide what I was saying from the gentleman, who was slumped in a chair at the dining table, utterly depressed. I told him, shouldn't we look for evidence first? To which he replied, 'I told you to arrest him, Agashe. He is guilty. That is the end of the matter.' It seemed wrong, you know; almost as though he wanted to bury the matter, letting an innocent man take the blame for a crime he hadn't committed. You must know that in those days, there was no DNA testing, which only meant that it was harder for me to prove he wasn't guilty. In any case, I knew that even if I tried my very best to prove his innocence, even if I came up with some shocking evidence, for that matter, the chief had already decided that Shambhu was guilty, and that was that."

He let out a weary sigh, and Wadia felt bad to have dampened the evening for the old man, through the revival of these dark memories.

"That girl, she was the pride of Udvada," he went on. "I was never really close to her like a lot of the other residents of this city were, but she would bring a smile to my face whenever we met. I wonder what made your families reject her (he turned his attention towards Toral too as he said this). Why, if I had a girl like that she would be special to me in a way like no other. Not that you aren't special to me, Sunil, but–"

"I get what you mean, baba," Sunil said, taking his father's hand in his and gently squeezing it. He said to the others, "I'm sorry but I don't have any memory of her. She seems to have been a very special person, though."

"You were conceived the year after she left Udvada, Sunil," Agashe senior wistfully told his son. Then he looked at Wadia again, but this time there was a certain compassion in his eyes that Wadia hadn't seen earlier.

"What are you looking for, if you don't mind me asking?"

Velkar, who was seated in between his daughter and best friend, spoke instead. "Would you have any idea who the real perpetrator might have been? Were there any suspects at the time?"

"Hmm. That was the worst part. Even though I secretly tried to find out who might have been the actual rapist in the weeks following the crime, I couldn't come to any sort of definite conclusion as to what might have happened. I spent many an hour trying to solve it. There must have been a clue somewhere: something that house just wouldn't give up. But I had to follow orders, move onto the next case. So it was sealed up and time moved on."

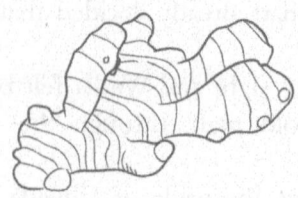

Chapter Nineteen
The White House

They partook of a nightcap reflecting on their day. All of a sudden Wadia seemed to perk up; as though he might have had a revelation of sorts. He put his hands up in the air, as though to say, 'Why didn't I think of this before?' He turned excitedly to his friends. "I've got it. We break into Elise's house in the middle of the night. Before the crack of dawn, we leave. That gives us plenty of time in between to, you know, find that missing clue that the house has kept secret all these years."

Toral and Velkar simply stared at Wadia as he egged them on with highly animated facial gestures, as though seeking their go ahead to what clearly seemed a most ingenious plan. Toral still bore a look of abject sadness. Velkar looked at Wadia as though the bawa might be completely out of his mind.

"Arre baba, I have watched all the *Mission Impossible* movies; enough to know that this plan of yours is impossible."

"Pray why, tell me?"

"It's as though you want to play *dark room*."

"What?" And then Wadia got it. Of course it would be dark in the wee hours of the morning, and they couldn't possibly use a torch (or three, for that matter), because that might just be the quickest route to Udvada police station. And just like that, his plan seemed to make no sense at all, until Toral spoke, with an air of absolute certainty in her voice.

"We go there in the dark, that much I can agree upon. But we go there a little before the crack of dawn; not too close to it, or we run the risk of being exposed, and certainly not in the wee hours of the morning. Then, we stay there all day, instead of night. That gives us plenty of time to conduct our search to the fullest. We tell Satish we are going for a picnic, and ask if he could be a darling and pack three meals for us. Just something snacky, you know. Something to 'make do.' Then, in the latter hours of morning the next day, we leave the bungalow and go back to our villa."

Velkar and Wadia were staring at Toral with a newfound sense of admiration.

She went on. "Of course, we must be careful. It will be simpler, really, if all the curtains have been drawn or if the windows have been shut. Then nobody will look into the house from the outside. But of course we mustn't make the mistake of closing the curtains if they are open. It will only serve to draw attention. So what I recommend is we do a bit of reconnaissance first, just to get an idea of how we might go about our mission." *Mission.* That had a nice ring to it. Certainly better than burglary, thought Wadia as a chill ran down his spine. They were getting into uncharted waters here, but it was simply too late to change their minds. They had to do something to find justice for poor Elise.

Toral raised her glass as though to secure a pact they were making, and even though it seemed rather silly, Wadia raised his glass too. Velkar's finally sealed the deal. After all, there was no point in the mission if even one of them backed out.

"Tomorrow, we're going to park outside the bungalow as though we're just waiting there for no particular reason. Got it?"

Wadia and Velkar nodded their heads in unison. After all, Memsaab had spoken, even though the 'waiting there for no particular reason' seemed a completely flawed notion.

The next day was uneventful for the larger part. The surveillance mission had been scheduled for the evening. After an extended afternoon siesta and some time spent at the beach, the trio found themselves outside the gates of The White House in Udvada. It certainly seemed an imposing structure, albeit a weathered one. The curtains being closed was fortunate. It meant that, at least for the most part, they would be safe once they were inside the house, unless they did something silly like open the curtains or put on the lights. In hindsight, of course, the electricity supply to the house would have been cut off ages ago. Toral laughed silently at the foolishness of it all; at their conviction in actually thinking they could pull this stunt off.

One look at Velkar and it seemed like he had pissed his pants. It certainly looked like a ghost house. Wadia, on the contrary, wasn't scared of spirits. He had always believed, over the years, that the spirit of his dead mother resided in the house with him, and she would never leave his side until he left for the gates of heaven. *If* he were going to heaven, of course. He wondered if he might sense Elise's presence here, like he did his mother's in his house in Bandra every single day. Especially when he listened to Für Elise at night. At times, if he wasn't mistaken, he actually saw the rocking chair rock a bit, when he was not sitting in it. That had been Lizzie Wadia's favourite chair. She would spend hours in the study sitting on it, reading books selected from Percy's vast library. Now, her son did.

He wondered how a lone girl in this sprawling house in Udvada might have felt being called *Elise* by her parents, when everyone else in town called her Diva. Might she feel special in a strange sort of way, despite knowing that neither of the people who called her that, would spend more than a month with her? He wondered which of the two names she preferred and what she even thought of her parents; if they had even told her she was theirs. After all, she had been discarded by them, hadn't she? Or might he be wrong? Might they have loved her dearly, yet found themselves helpless to do anything more for her on account of the wrath of their respective parents?

"It seems like a fortress," said Toral, shaking her head. There was a padlock on the front door almost as large as a jackfruit (well, perhaps that was an exaggeration, but it certainly seemed like that would be the worst possible way to try and get into the house). The place most certainly seemed a stark contrast to the palace it had once been (according to that old woman, at least), what with it seeming more a battered fortress. Just then, out of the corner of her eye, she noticed a by-lane where the wall of the house ended; more like a private road. The home adjoining Elise's bungalow seemed to share this road with Providence Villa. It was a bungalow that had a heritage feel to it, and was very well-maintained, unlike its neighbour. She pointed out the road to the others, and for a while none of them said anything.

"I'm going to go in that lane." It was Velkar, and before either Toral or Wadia could stop him, he had already got out of the car and was looking on either side of the road, trying to see when to cross over. Not that it made any difference. There were no cars on the road besides theirs. Neither Wadia nor Toral dared shout at him, because there were some passers-by approaching in the distance, and the last thing they wanted to do was draw their attention. In retrospect, they were simply two men and a lady in a van (make that a lady and a man in a van and a man outside it) parked on the side of a quiet lane in Udvada, outside a seemingly haunted house. Nothing fishy about it.

In a short while the people who had been approaching them had passed and turned the intersection a few metres down the road. None of them had turned to look behind at the trio, which was a good sign. Velkar was still standing there. Yep. Nothing to do with those people. He indeed must be seeing imaginary cars, thought Wadia. And then, all of a sudden, the Maharashtrian hurried across the street, and then walked alongside the bungalow wall as though he might be an FBI agent, crouching a bit and looking all around him. Toral couldn't help but laugh, although Wadia could not see the lighter side. That Maharashtrian might be the very reason they would find themselves in police lock-up.

And then Velkar disappeared. For a while, that is. He went past the point his friends could see and didn't come back. It had been five whole minutes since he had vanished. Wadia panicked. Might his friend have fainted?

He remembered the time Vidya had called him once, in absolute desperation. Anil had fainted, she told him, outside Churchgate station, in the summer heat. She was in Pune and someone had fished Anil's mobile phone out and dialled the last number he had called. Luckily that last call had been to her. She told Wadia that she was leaving instantly from Pune, but it would be a while before she got to Mumbai, of course, so could he please go to Churchgate station and rush his friend to the hospital? And Wadia had reassured Vidya that he would make sure he didn't leave his friend's side until he was completely all right, and had dashed off in his vintage car to Churchgate station, to get his friend some medical attention.

He remembered Velkar being absolutely dazed when he found him. Surprisingly there had been no logical explanation as to why he had fainted; perhaps low blood pressure, said the doctor, who had reassured Wadia and even a distraught Vidya over the telephone, that Anil Velkar's vitals were perfectly fine. That was the last day Velkar had ever taken a train in his life, although he had tried his very best to convince his wife that he had not even fainted in the railway station, let alone in the train. It was outside the station, didn't she get it? Apparently, not in the least bit. The very next month, Velkar's brand new Maruti Suzuki van had arrived, and after that day Velkar never harassed Vidya over letting him travel by train, ever again. He had fallen in love with that car; the very car that was a sorry excuse for one today.

Now, all of a sudden, he found himself worrying about Velkar. Why did he ever have to drag the poor chap into this? What would he tell Vidya if something were to happen to her husband? Panic bells ringing louder than ever.

Until he heard the sound of whistling, that is. A sound he knew only too well.

Velkar. If there was any time in his life he was happy to see the man, this was it.

The ride back to their rented villa had been a most sombre one. Velkar had not spoken a word since he had got into the car, despite continual prodding from Wadia and Toral. 'The walls have ears,' is all he would tell them. As if to make his point, he pointed to the interiors of the car. Wadia didn't push the matter further. All he knew, as Velkar whistled along endlessly as their car rattled through the streets of Udvada, was that a mechanical engineer had figured out a way to get the three of them into the fortress. And that was enough.

There was pin-drop silence at the dinner table. They had all decided to meet in Toral's room after their meal. This was the largest room in the house, located on the second floor. The best part was, the servants hardly ever wandered up there. The minute Wadia walked into the bedroom, he knew this was the room the legendary Behram Patel had slept in, before he had decided to retire and go back to Mumbai's Dadar Parsi Colony. It was spacious, and a cool breeze wafted through the open window, outside which you could see a large banyan tree. He was just going to tell Toral it was perhaps best she shut the window on account of the mosquitoes that undoubtedly lived in this town too, when Velkar, who had just ambled in, exclaimed "What a room!"

Not that the room seemed to interest Toral in the least bit. Talk about dysfunctional families; hers and Rustom's were probably the most dysfunctional families she had known in all her life.

A few minutes later Toral and Wadia found themselves standing over a large teakwood desk, on which Velkar was creating a diagram of some sort, on a piece of paper they had found in the living room. It took only a few moments for them to realize he was drawing the house they had undertaken surveillance of, only a little while ago; he drew the backyard, and what appeared to be a small gate. He then made an arrow at the side of the gate, and wrote 'Little Red Gate. Jump.'

Then he turned towards them, ecstatic, like a small child who has just created his first ever drawing.

"That's *it*?" Wadia bellowed. "A little red gate on the side, and we had to wait more than two whole hours to know that?" Toral burst into laughter. At least he made her laugh, thought Wadia. What's in it for me?

"Yes, that's it. What did you expect?"

"Why draw it then? Why not just *tell* us, Velkar?"

"Good point. You see, I am a mechanical engineer. We have been trained to express our thoughts through diagrams. Besides, you haven't heard the half of it."

"What's the other half?" It was Toral.

"I tried it out." Said with the cheekiness of a teenager telling his best friend he sampled some of his Dad's Japanese whisky without his father finding out about it.

"You what?" Wadia again, impatient this time round.

"I tried it out. I wanted to see if you and me could make it over the gate, so I jumped over it into the backyard of the bungalow and then I jumped over it again to get out."

Wadia put his hands over his head. The senseless dolt. "Which means you trespassed. Before we are all going to."

"Well, yes and no," Velkar said, still looking proud. "I mean, I didn't go into the house, if you know what I mean."

Wadia shook his head. "Still trespassing."

Then Toral spoke. "Okay, Neel, what next? How do we get in? Were the doors at the back of the house bolted? Any windows, that might have seemed accessible?"

"Oh," was all Velkar could muster.

"I propose we hold off the mission for a day," Toral said finally, and just when Wadia was about to say something in protest, Velkar spoke. "I think that's a terrific idea. We're clearly not prepared."

Toral nodded. "That, apart from the fact that we can't organise snacks at such short notice. We'll have to tell Satish first thing in the morning, so that he has enough time to pack us a picnic basket for the day after. Then, so as not to overburden him, I suggest we have lunch at that place you've been wanting to go to, Rustom. What was the name again?"

"Mimi's," Rustom said, rather demurely, clearly disappointed at having to hold off on the mission for a day, but knowing in the back of his mind that it was probably for the best. Nothing worthwhile should be rushed; it was an adage he had lived by for a long time. Furthermore, it gave them some extra time to do a bit more 'reconnaissance.' It was decided that the next evening, Toral would walk into the lane that ran between the two houses, and see if she could find a way they could enter the house apart from 'jumping over the little red gate,' which, she assured her daddy, was important nevertheless.

"Mango! Mango!" Velkar shouted then, and Toral and Wadia looked at him, stunned. Then he added, "That's what we say. If, you know, someone looking from the house opposite has caught us entering the building compound. We tell them we're looking for mangos. I saw some mango trees blossoming in the backyard."

The next day was pretty much uneventful. At least the first half was. In the afternoon they settled down for their siesta, but none of them could get any shut-eye.

In the evening, they headed to the beach again to watch the sun set, and straight after that, to Providence Villa, to see how they might make their way in the following day. Unlike Velkar, Toral simply walked across the road and towards the lane between the two cottages, as though she might be living in the house that bordered it, and going to the back yard to check on her plants. She looked at the house opposite Providence Villa. There were some clothes hanging on the first floor in the veranda that overlooked the neatly manicured garden. It was clear that someone lived there and that made it all the more essential to be absolutely careful.

When she came back, she animatedly told her friends that they had to be careful even in the early hours of the morning, as you never knew when the people in the next house woke up. She suggested they wake up at 4 a.m., get freshened up and have their tea before leaving at 4.45 at the latest. That way they could tentatively time their break-in at 5 a.m., which was neither too early nor too late.

"Did you see the little red gate?" Velkar said, excitedly.

"Yes. Furthermore, I walked right up to the back doors of the home. They are tightly bolted, with chains."

"I saw that movie, the Texas chainsaw killer. Perhaps we get one of those – chainsaws, you know?" Velkar, the film buff, but firstly, idiot.

"No, no. There is a window."

"A *window*!" Velkar and Wadia screeched in unison, as though a window might be something they had only ever heard about in the movies.

"Yes, but here's the thing. It's tightly shut, too."

The gasps of excitement that had escaped the elderly gentlemen's mouths a few moments ago, were now replaced with heavy sighs.

"But no, there's another thing." No gasps now, just two faces lit up in anticipation. What was she getting at? Can't she just say it already? Why do girls have to be so bloody dramatic all the time?

"Well, it seems as though a cricket ball has been thrown through the window sometime in the past, near or far there's no way to tell, and made a hole in it, but not shattered it completely. Luckily, the hole is close to the windowpane, which means that if someone were to put their hand in and move their fingers around, I think they could perhaps reach the latch and prise it open."

"But wouldn't that create suspicion if people see us? Won't they think we're breaking in?"

"Of course they would you imbecile!" Wadia's voice boomed, and Velkar went straight into a pothole. Toral looked at Wadia from the front seat, as though to imply that he might have been a bit harsh. Oh well, Anil was her Daddy now. It was best he mind the way he spoke to him in front of her. His tone of voice as well as his words.

"I'm sorry. That's a really good idea, Toral. But who might have thrown that ball? For some reason I can't imagine anyone playing cricket in that back yard, unless they might have been some urchins who trespassed on the property."

"I think it must have been the people who were trying to break in the last time round, that is, before the neighbours alerted the police, of course. Now, there's some good news and bad news."

"Tell me the bad news first," said Velkar. He thought of Vidya; she always asked for the good news first. They were opposites.

"Okay, Udvada police station is not too far away, which means that in perhaps five minutes tops, the police will be there, if they are alerted that something might be going down in Providence Villa. That doesn't give us a lot of time to get out of there, I know. But that's exactly why the earlier two attempts failed."

"And the good news?" It was Wadia, whose heart had sunk a little on realising there was a good chance they might get arrested today. That good news better be good.

"The good news is, half the job is done already. We know exactly how to break in. The ball is in our court, although technically it's in the other court." She chuckled as she said this, priding herself on her wit. Neither Wadia nor Velkar said something to the effect of 'That was a good one,' though, like people usually do when they hear witty remarks. Now was not the time, perhaps.

"Do you think we should leave a little earlier?" It was Velkar.

"No. That will seem a bit suspicious. Leaving the house anytime before 4.30 in the morning is bound to cause suspicion. In any case I have asked Satish to pack our breakfast, which we shall eat once we are inside Providence Villa. All he has to do, is make us those cups of strong coffee. All the more important for you, Daddy, because *you* will be driving."

Daddy. Velkar liked the sound of that word. Of course he wasn't the girl's biological father, but that didn't make him any less of a dad. No, Vidya and he would take good care of Toral, and be every bit like her true parents had been. Although, come to think of it, given their ages, it would probably be Toral taking care of him and Vidya. They had already decided that they would not inconvenience her in any way, nor would they ever move to her residence, if she even suggested it. After all, she had her own life, as did they. It was important they respect her boundaries. Talking about boundaries, there was this one boundary they had to cross tomorrow morning. Oh well, Velkar had crossed it before and there was no reason why Wadia couldn't. He would teach that fat Parsi how to jump.

Toral thanked Satish profusely for dinner, reminding him to start preparations for the next day's picnic hamper. Of course, it would be Jamuna Das who would prepare that hamper for them, but everything had to be overseen by Satish, who would pass on the necessary instructions. Kind of a Ramukaka of this place. Toral told Satish further, that they would be leaving first thing in the morning before sunrise and coming back late at night. Satish had looked at them with an air of suspicion, when he asked them where they were headed for that picnic and got no answer in return.

"We are going to Pardi," Toral had finally blurted out. Pardi was a small town less than half an hour's driving distance from their current location. In any case, as long as they didn't tell him they were going to be breaking into an old cottage in Udvada, Wadia thought, the hard-working manservant had no cause to complain. They left in a jiffy, lest he ask more questions, and went to Toral's room, to go over the scheme of things that had to be adhered to the next morning. The mood was rather sombre, punctuated by Velkar's dashing around the room every now and then as though he might be the great Sherlock Holmes, albeit without a clue to ponder on. Toral then decided to lighten the rest of the evening with several rounds of

Rummy. She always brought a pack of cards on every vacation she took, and even though she felt a sorrow as intense as Wadia's, she knew it would not do her any good to dwell on it. No matter what had happened to that poor woman, she thought, we will 'set things right.'

She knew now why those trips undertaken by her great grandmother Petunia Shah, had stopped all of a sudden. Without a doubt she had come to know of the horror that had befallen her child, and she couldn't take it. Petunia undoubtedly could never forgive herself for what she had done to her first born. Perhaps her only born. But – what control had she over the matter? Elise found herself in this place because of two people – The Beast and Jamshed Wadia. But, in spite of it all, little Elise Wadia (or Diva, as everyone in Udvada had known her by) had grown up to be a most happy child, loved by one and all whose lives she happened to grace. Well, until the incident, of course.

Wadia hadn't had a drink. Not tonight, after all they had found out about poor Elise. Perhaps tomorrow. They had to be focused the next day. It wasn't himself he was worried about; it was Velkar, of course. Velkar, who had to be taken home by his wife all those years ago, after he had become inebriated at his place. The very same Velkar, who had told his wife at least thrice in the fifteen-minute call he had taken in Toral's room between games of Rummy, standing by the open window, that he had not had a drink. Once the phone call had ended, he had looked sheepishly at the two of them before shaking his head and saying 'Women'! And then he had seen the look on Toral's face before realizing his mistake, and added "They're the best!"

Of course Toral got it too. She knew what marriage looked like, having witnessed it first-hand with her parents and with several members of her extended Gujarati family. Marriage was the last thing on her mind. At least for now. She wanted to do something with her life. She had big plans for 404 Juhu; she wanted it to be the best restaurant in the burbs. She couldn't compete with restaurants on the other side of town; they had the best chefs. So she focused on this side of town. If you think too big, you run the risk of losing it all, she thought. Like people who opened several branches of their restaurants when their one restaurant was doing well, and were later forced to close their flagship restaurant on account of loans that couldn't be paid.

You had to look at the small picture, she thought; so much so that it becomes the big picture. And so it was with the mission they had embarked on. At the end of it all, Toral went downstairs and told Satish they would be leaving the next morning at 4.45 a.m. sharp, just like they had decided.

And then, at eleven p.m, all the lights in Butterfly Villa went out.

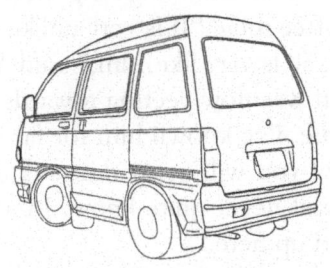

Chapter Twenty
Operation Für Elise

Wadia and Toral were already sipping their cups of steaming hot Nescafe (no foreign blends here; not that it mattered to Rustom, Nescafe would do just fine, thank you), and there was no sign of Velkar.

"I'm worried," Toral said, fidgeting nervously with the little silver spoon in her coffee mug. "It is very unlike him."

"Oh believe me, it is *very* like him," said Wadia, taking a large chug of his coffee that was now veering towards being called a cup of 'cold coffee.' "Trust me. I've known him for far longer than you have, although perhaps now you will get to know a different side of him; the likes of which I will never quite know. In any case, give it a few moments. He will land up here."

"But— what if he hasn't even woken up?"

"Just trust me," Wadia, said, and that was it. Even though Velkar was her daddy now, Toral trusted Rustom almost as she would her biological father. There was just something about that man, she had thought, after their first meeting in her café in Juhu. He commanded a respect that she reserved for only a few.

True to his word (Rustom's, of course, if Velkar had been a man of his word he would have been down earlier), Velkar waltzed down the stairs at precisely 4.32 a.m. A good seventeen minutes late. But— what was this? Wadia gaped at the sight of his old friend. He was dressed from top to bottom in black, right from the cap on his head to his brightly polished leather shoes. A black sweater to boot; one that seemed just perfect for this weather. Coupled with black jeans, it gave the effect of the Maharashtrian going to a discotheque, perhaps. Wadia even made it a point to tell him that.

"Party? Who, me? I'm going for a picnic." Of course, *picnic*. They must mention the word *picnic*. Wadia had almost forgotten. After all, Satish was a mere few metres away from him in the kitchen, and it seemed as though his radar was tuned into the optimum frequency, what with the suspicious glances he cast every now and then into the dining room; at Wadia specifically, as though he didn't trust him in the least bit. Wadia didn't like people like that. He was just a harmless bawa, after all.

As Velkar sipped his coffee nonchalantly, looking as though nothing might be the matter (after all, he thought to himself, did it really matter what clothes they chose to don for their mission?) they patiently waited until he had finished. Wadia was perpetually looking at his phone. He wore a battered, dead Rolex, the time on it forever set to 11:11. No social media for him on his phone, which was an old model of BlackBerry that Toral told him she had thought was extinct, and most certainly not on the computer in his study. After all, being self-professedly anti-social, how could he possibly be remotely connected to the word 'social'?

Wadia glanced at the sorry excuse for a picnic hamper: a three-compartment steel tiffin that had been carefully packaged with a golden ribbon tied into a bow, and placed in the centre of the table; from the looks of it, it would last them a couple of days, at the very least. There was not much else to do now, except to leave. That, being whenever Velkar finished his damn coffee and the two digestive biscuits that had been served along with it (Toral had instructed Satish to instruct Jamuna that they would not be needing an elaborate breakfast) and stopped humming like a jackass.

When they left the house that morning it seemed as though Velkar had been right to wear that sweater, after all. By the time they got to the car, which was parked in a specially reserved spot next to the front gates of Butterfly Villa, Wadia and Toral found themselves chilled to the bone. Not Velkar, though. Velkar, who looked at Rustom as though to say, 'Who's the idiot now?'

It was a very short drive to their destination, but to Toral it felt like the longest in the world. She couldn't get over the idea of what they were going to be doing in a short while from now. Breaking into a house like hardcore burglars. Of course, the intention was never to burgle, but nobody would understand that, would they? No, the more she thought about it, the more she knew she was doing the right thing. All of this must surely have been preordained. How on earth else would she have met her Daddy?

They decided to park the car a couple of lanes away from Providence Villa. The road they found themselves in was pretty deserted (given the time it was in the morning, it didn't quite seem that unusual), and they made the slow walk towards Providence Villa, careful not to step on something that might make a crackling sound; worse still, something they might slip over. Toral held the tiffin in her right hand. They had all worn sneakers, so they wouldn't seem overtly suspicious. The dim streetlights helped, too. Just enough light for them to get by; not quite enough to be in the spotlight. By the time they were only a few metres away from Providence Villa, it seemed as though their plan had gone without a glitch. And then something happened.

A couple of savage dogs were growling in the near distance, right outside the house they were supposed to break into. Surely their project wouldn't come to a premature end? Because it seemed as though these dogs were sizing them up for the kill to follow. Wadia had even heard of some pet owners being maliciously bitten by their pets; what chance did strangers have against strays? And then the most unexpected thing happened. Toral knelt down and placed the tiffin she held on the ground beside her, while Wadia looked on helplessly and Velkar shivered in his boots. She held her right hand out, as though to give the beasts something, making a sound with her mouth; a high-pitched sound that Wadia had usually seen people use to call cats. These animals seemed more like wolves.

And the growling grew only louder and it seemed as though all hell would break loose, until it stopped all of a sudden, just like that. The two feral dogs just walked away, as though it hadn't been as big a deal as the trio had purportedly made it out to be. Wadia and Velkar looked at each other with a sigh of relief. After all, they had just dodged a bullet. Wadia knew that Velkar had an intense fear of dogs; he had been discussing the matter last night, when they chatted in Toral's room.

"That won't work when you come to visit me, *Daddykins*," she had said. As if the word *Daddy* wasn't terrible enough, thought Wadia. And she continued, "I have a Great Dane at home, and guess what? You're his grandfather!" And Wadia thought then, "Oh dear Lord, spare me, please."

Luckily nobody had seen them so far, or at least so they thought. The real test, though, would be going unnoticed from the time they entered the back lane, to the time they got into the house. This time round, Velkar did none of that 'FBI walk' one saw in the movies (it might play out the same in real life, too, but with real commandos, of course, not mechanical engineers). Nevertheless, they weren't quite prepared for what hit them next. The light was on in the balcony of the home right opposite Providence Villa. Had someone heard the dogs? No, that couldn't be it, thought Toral. In that case the light would have come on in the front of the house.

"Perhaps they leave the balcony light on." It was Wadia. He personally knew some people who left at least one light on in their homes at night, so that thieves would know there was someone home, and be deterred from breaking in.

"Maybe," said Velkar. "But do we wish to take the chance? Perhaps someone has gone to use the washroom."

Toral and Wadia glared at Velkar, who seemed unfazed at first, until he finally got it.

"I have an idea." It was Toral. "I will walk to the end of the road, crouching, of course, and see if I can glimpse anyone on the balcony.

"No Toral, my dear. I can't risk something happening to you. What if they call the police?" How sweet, Wadia thought. Anil, the concerned dad.

"And say what? That I'm trespassing? This road doesn't belong to either of the two properties. Besides, in all probability there's nobody on that balcony. It will be a couple of hours at the very least before the paper gets delivered here. I know that, because last morning the paper was delivered at a quarter past seven to Butterfly Villa. Don't ask me what I was doing up so early. Well, all right, it was yoga."

Wadia shrugged. He couldn't really say if this was the right thing to do, but he wasn't against it either. This was to be their last night in Udvada, and it didn't seem plausible to extend the trip just because there was a light on in the balcony. Tomorrow might bring a fresh set of problems; one never knew.

Velkar nodded. "I think you're right. The dogs were a sign. They were like the gatekeepers of the place. They had a sense of what we were going to do, but allowed us in anyway on account of our pure intentions. I think Elise must have played with them when she was a child."

Again Toral and Wadia looked at Velkar after exchanging glances, but this time round they both had large smiles on their faces. The dolt was clearly well intentioned, thought Wadia. Perhaps that was the only reason he was his friend.

And in only a few moments, after they had placed their hands on top of each other's and lifted them away in a flourish, Toral was making her way stealthily, proceeding towards the end of the lane alongside the neighbour's moss covered wall. It was amazing how one's eyes adjusted to the dark. When they had taken their first few steps into this lane, it had seemed near pitch black, the lone streetlight outside the lane losing much of its effect in the narrow lane. Operation Für Elise was finally underway.

After what was only a couple of minutes but seemed like a lifetime, Toral had given them the go ahead. Wadia and Velkar walked slowly, careful not to step on something like a plastic bottle, or perhaps a squeaky toy discarded by a child who might be living in the house opposite. That house seemed to reflect an old-world charm, and whoever lived there had old-world money, Wadia surmised. There were some fancy cars parked in the front of the house; he had noticed them the previous evening, in the dim light of the building compound. He wondered who might live there. A family, perhaps? The very thing the girl in the neighbouring house had so desperately craved. Ah! The tragedy…

The three musketeers finally found themselves on the threshold of what had once been Elise's home, casting furtive glances back and forth from the little red gate to the balcony with the solitary light. From here they could see that it was an ordinary light bulb hanging from the ceiling, that was the source of illumination. Finally Velkar whispered, "I will go first." As though there might be a deadly ravine underneath, and he were jumping to the cliff opposite. And he just walked over the infamous little red gate (it was really that little, which made one wonder what its purpose might have been; for letting a dog out, perhaps? Toral thought that was the only logical reason one would keep a gate this small. Had Elise had a pet? There was so much about her she didn't know). And Velkar had told them he had 'jumped' over it, thought Wadia. The gall of that man.

Soon they were inside and had stealthily made their way to the backyard patio. Toral walked over to the window at the far end of the patio, and the two elderly gentlemen followed. They glanced back at the balcony in the house opposite all at once, noticing they were still visible in this position. Then to the window with the crack. That hole surely seemed like it had been made by a cricket ball crashing into glass. At least, that was one of the visuals that came to Wadia's mind. The other was of a man standing on this very porch and hurling a ball like a baseball pitcher would. Okay, probably the former. Then, Toral took a deep breath and released it before putting her hand in. She struggled a bit, trying desperately to get her fingers to the level of the window pane underneath. And for the next several moments the struggle went on. Wadia panicked. Velkar, frozen, was staring at the balcony of the house opposite.

"Got it!" Toral lifted the latch she had found carefully upwards, and then pushed the window open by applying gentle pressure on the glass from the inside. And in a few moments the other window was open, too. Just then the most terrifying thing happened. On the balcony opposite, a figure of what appeared to be a man appeared out of nowhere, stretching his arms like one might after they have arisen from the deepest slumber. He looked straight ahead in the distance, and if he had turned to look to his left he would have certainly seen them standing like criminals trying to pull off a bank heist. They didn't even have masks on. But the stranger just looked straight ahead, turning ever slightly towards his left to plonk into an armchair that rested on the floor of the balcony – a deviation slight enough for the three of them to let out a collective gasp.

For the longest time, none of them moved. All they did was glance at each other, eyes filled with fear. Then all of a sudden, Wadia walked over to the window, rested his right hand on the window sill, and struggled to push himself over. Next, Toral coerced a trembling Velkar to go in. When he looked in, he saw Wadia, his hand outstretched, to help him.

"It's now or never, Velkar," he said. And the next thing you knew, Velkar had made it to the other side too, almost falling over Wadia, much to the latter's chagrin. As far as Toral was concerned, well, it was a breeze. Handing over the tiffin to Wadia, she literally waltzed over the sill, true to the ballerina she had been in her youth.

And then the three of them were inside. Toral shut the window in slow motion and they finally found themselves inside Providence Villa, a house that had held a secret as dark as the darkness that now engulfed them. A darkness that would ebb, nonetheless, in a mere couple of hours.

And it was a darkness that took them a few moments to get accustomed to. Using a torch, as they had earlier decided, was out of the question. Nobody would even care if they had broken into an old, dilapidated bungalow in Carter Road or Bandstand back in Mumbai. People had so many other things to contend with. Life was fast paced in big cities. Certainly not in a small, sleepy hamlet like Udvada.

The room they found themselves in seemed to be a study. Wadia could discern a large bookshelf on the opposite side. They had decided to wait here and not move around until some light filtered into the house, for fear of smashing into something in the dark and waking up their neighbour. And their neighbour was awake now, so they'd better be quiet. There was a desk on the wall to the right of them, and a chair. Someone must have used this as an office, thought Wadia. Perhaps his grandfather Dhunji, on his month-long trips.

"I don't like that man," said Velkar. "Waking up at this time in the morning? There's something fishy about him, I tell you."

"What logic Anil! So, if a person gets up later, like say, well after the sun has risen, then that clears him of suspicion, does it?"

"I'm telling you nicely, Wadia, don't get on my nerves. I'm always a diplomat when I speak to you."

"You have the nerve to think I get on your nerves. And *diplomat*? It's *diplomatic*, you bloody idiot!"

"Idiot? Who are you calling idiot?"

"Stop it guys!"

It was Toral. As much as she loved this love-hate relationship the two old men shared, this fight needed to be nipped in the bud, for fear of it escalating and their neighbour leading the cops to the door of this home.

And just like that, the fight had come to an end. In the next couple of minutes, the three of them were fast asleep. Without setting an alarm on either of their cell phones, of course. Toral knew sunrise would wake her up. It always did.

"Shit!" At the sound of the word, or perhaps the booming sound with which it had been uttered, Wadia and Velkar had both been sharply jolted out of their reverie.

"It's 8 a.m, Toral said, as the two elderly gentlemen squinted, adjusting their eyes to the light streaming in through the hole in the solitary window they had come in from, that was now firmly shut again, of course. The place was a complete mess. There were large cardboard boxes stacked against the wall alongside the desk, that Wadia had missed while his eyes had adjusted to the dark. Toral told them that the best way to start their search, was by splitting up and going into different rooms. If one of them found something they felt the others should know about, they should simply come and tell them (not shout it out, for obvious reasons). She said she would go upstairs and conduct her search in the master bedroom. Wadia could take this room if he liked, and Velkar, the living room. And they would all meet in the living room in an hour for breakfast – at 9 a.m. sharp.

That worked for Wadia; he was accustomed to having breakfast in his home in Mumbai at the same time.

"What if there's no living room?" Velkar. Who else?

"I'll start with boxes," Wadia said, with the earnestness of a man who might be eagerly rummaging through the contents of a vintage cupboard in his home, searching for coins he had collected as a child. The only downside was, this room (and undoubtedly the same applied to the other rooms in this house, too) was filled with dust and his hacking cough had started in full earnest. There was nothing he could do about that now. The dust had surely triggered his allergy.

Even though cobwebs and lizards abounded (Toral had seen three or four already and had been completely freaked out), the place didn't seem quite as rundown as they had expected. Of course, the windows had been latched for years, and perhaps the only kind of ventilation in this house might have been the air wafting in from that little hole in the glass window.

Toral wished Rustom luck. She climbed the steps to the upstairs part of the home, waving out to Velkar who seemed to have already started his search. Of course, she would be starting her search in the master bedroom. That's where the detectives first looked, in those true crime shows.

And in the study she had exited a few moments ago, Wadia took the box that was placed right on top of the others, and set it out in front of him as he sat cross-legged on the floor. Right then he thought to look back at the sofa on which they had sat and even slept on (sitting upright, of course) for a while. It seemed as though it might have been purchased from an upmarket store in London back in the day, given its undoubtedly Victorian feel. A lot of money had been spent on this place. As though the person who had designed it had believed money could buy you happiness.

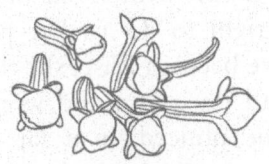

Chapter Twenty-one
Deep Shit

The first cardboard box was stacked with old clothes. Clothes of varying sizes that clearly belonged to a girl at different stages of her life: from small girl to adulthood. It was funny, thought Wadia. From the way the clothes had been placed in the box, it seemed as though the person who had placed them there had been running out of time; as though they wanted to simply stuff the things they needed as fast as they possibly could into them and get out of the house as quickly as possible.

The second box opened to reveal even more clothes. It seemed to Wadia, now that he thought about it some more, that perhaps Percy Wadia had expected to come back for Elise's things after taking her someplace safe post that terrible incident. Why had he not made it back to her with these clothes? Could something have gone wrong, further to that terrible incident?

In Elise's bedroom, Toral was surprised at how neatly the bed had been made. It seemed as though some terrible crime might have been committed within these very four walls, and someone might have tried to do a hush-hush job of it. Perhaps the intruder might have done it in the living room on a sofa, or even on the kitchen floor. After all, people who committed such horrendous acts were nothing short of monsters, and the people they did those terrible things to, mere objects used for their sadistic whims. In Mumbai, when she went for a walk sometimes on Juhu beach after dinner, she would look over her shoulder at the slightest sound, only because she was a girl, and as a girl you weren't really safe. No matter how much faith you had in the magnificent police force of your grand metropolis, there were always demons lurking around the corner that felt it was their birth right to do as they pleased with you, law be damned. She might have been an Elise, she thought then.

She looked around the room and wondered where she might begin. That's when she noticed, in a far corner, something large covered by what appeared to be a white bed sheet. Was it... Didn't it look like... Yes! When she uncovered it, she realised she was looking at the one thing in the Wadia family that had been the focus of so much attention so many years ago, and more recently, during the last few days. A piano. And she knew she had to let Wadia know right then. So, walking close to the wall like she had when she came in, well away from the window that faced the road where they had encountered those feral dogs in the wee hours of the morning, she went downstairs and made her way to the study.

"I don't believe it," said Wadia, as he stared at the magnificent piano.

"What?"

"It's the very same brand of piano, although not the exact same model."

Toral patted Wadia on the back. "I'm sure she must have been good at playing it, too. Wait a minute. What's that?"

A few pages had been scattered on the floor, by the window. Toral made it a point to crawl on the floor from her standing position by the piano, and with her outstretched hand grasped the papers and crawled back again to where Wadia was standing. She couldn't risk being seen even marginally, from an angle by the window. She looked at the papers. All sheet music that held absolutely no meaning to her. Handed them over to Wadia, who smiled upon seeing them.

"It's Für Elise," he said, and looked wistfully out the window that was only a few feet away from them. What were the odds? He sat down wearily on the piano chair, assuring Toral silently that, no, he wasn't going to do something as stupid as play Für Elise, even though it seemed highly improbable that the sound of his playing would reach the street outside. They had decided they wouldn't make any sound that was not required, and that was the end of the matter.

"What a lovely view!" Toral and Wadia looked up to see Velkar, standing by the window with a large smile on his face, trying his best to prise it open.

"Velkar, you bloody idiot!" Wadia almost screamed, trying his best to muffle his angry outburst. That fool had come in here and sauntered to the window when only moments ago his daughter had taken such great pains to ensure she wouldn't be seen through it. If she had been *Crouching Tiger*, was he *Visible Dragon*?

In a second Velkar realised the graveness of his folly, and instantly flung himself away from the window, losing his balance and falling onto the bed.

"Soft bed," he said, poking his finger into it. Spoken with the childish glee of people who throw themselves onto beds in their rooms in five star hotels. Toral managed to convince Rustom to not speak another word, by putting her finger to her lips and embodying a sense of utter calmness. Then she went over to the side of the bed, crouched low, and said, "Daddy, you do realize someone could have seen you, right?"

"Why of course. That's why I'm on the bed now." Wadia was pacing between the door to the room, and the piano. This guy is the very reason I'm going to be eating breakfast in prison tomorrow, he thought.

"I have a good idea, Daddy. Let's have breakfast." Then she looked at Wadia. "It's almost nine in any case, and I'm hungry as hell!" He nodded. He knew, of course, she wasn't hungry and this was merely a diversion tactic to ensure Anil Velkar got his act together again.

Breakfast had indeed been a good idea. The chicken sandwiches Satish had packed for them were pretty exemplary. They somehow reminded Wadia of those delectable sandwiches at a local eatery, *Candies*, in Bandra in Mumbai, that he would have several years ago, on many an occasion. Besides, the refreshingly (still cool) nimbu paani that had been packed in a couple of bottles for their drinking needs, along with two large bottles of Bisleri, served as the perfect complement to these yummy sandwiches.

"Oh shit!" It was Velkar. 'Now what?' thought Wadia. There was always something up with this character.

"I mean, *shit*!"

"*What* shit?" His daughter now. Wadia realized that the last couple of times, he had referred to her in his mind as Velkar's *daughter*. He had already become accustomed to the idea of the two of them being related. She had been a literal stranger to him not too long ago, and now she was the daughter of his (not best) friend. Talk about life being unpredictable. More like *unfathomable*!

"*Our* shit."

"Can we please eat?"

"Yes, but I have to go to the bathroom first." And Velkar just sat there, licking his lips like a lunatic.

"Well, go then!" Wadia bellowed furiously, little slivers of chicken and bread spewing out of his mouth as he said this. Really, he didn't have patience for Velkar's shenanigans. He pitied Toral. For what the future had in store for her.

"That's just it. I can't."

"Well, why not?" Toral now, in a tone that implied she had all the patience in the world.

"None of us can."

"What?" Wadia couldn't control his anger anymore.

"There's no water."

"What?" Velkar and Toral in unison. Wadia sighed. For perhaps the first (okay, not quite first) time in his life, Velkar was right. There was no water in the house. And how on earth might they have even thought this house might have a constant supply of water? Of course the water supply to Providence Villa must have been cut ages ago, like the electricity.

It had been decided, after careful deliberation, that each of them would use one of the three bathrooms in the house. There were four rooms in the sprawling bungalow (of which one of them was the study) apart from the hall and kitchen, and there should have been at least four bathrooms, Velkar had stated, but the others had paid him no attention. They were only three people, after all. Furthermore, after careful deliberation, it had been decided that none of them would do *potty*; only *susu* would be allowed within the walls of this house. Luckily for Wadia, he had already done his potty that morning, and on asking the others it was a relief to find out that they, too, had done their big jobs (the thought of even one bathroom having potty in it was disgusting, of course).

"But of course a man's got to pee when a man's got to pee," said Velkar, as he dawdled happily to the bathroom in the living room right next to the entrance to the study. In effect, he had secured rights to that bathroom without even asking the others if he could have it. There were two more bathrooms attached to a couple of the three rooms on the first floor, of course one of them Elise's bedroom. Toral offered it to Wadia and told her she would take the bathroom in the room next to Elise's, that had an attached bathroom as well. Wadia told her that no, *she* should take Elise's bathroom and *he* would take the other. And so, it was fixed.

When Velkar returned, Toral asked him if he had found something interesting in his search in the living room. Velkar told her he had found an old television set that didn't work. Well, that was that. Apart from some clothes, toys and trinkets, Wadia had not found anything of real interest in the study, either. He had just been in the process of putting the boxes back together, when Toral had come in excitedly, telling him she had found something in Elise's room that would really interest him. It had certainly been most interesting to have learned that their relative had a strong affinity for playing Für Elise, just like he had. Of course, it had never led to anything else. Music seemed to be both a boon and bane in his family.

"Leave the study for now," she told Wadia. There were two more rooms upstairs besides the one she had searched, and it seemed like the adjoining one was the one where Percy and Petunia would spend their time (separately, of course), when they came to Udvada. It had a large four-poster bed, and was all white, including the pretty artefacts on the shelves facing the bed. A room for people that assumed an air of elegance, it seemed.

Elise's room, on the other hand, was every little girl's dream. Although the shelves and wardrobes were empty, there was just something about those pink walls, carpet and comfortable looking bed with its beautiful pink upholstery and pink and white cushions. Like it were out of a fairy tale. Toral felt that she needed to check this room out completely, before they began with the others. She rifled through the large wardrobe, on the other side of the bed near the window. Of course she had to crawl to get there, just like she had done before. When she opened it, she seemed disappointed. It was completely cleared out. That would explain the boxes in the study, she thought.

But of course there must be something she could find that... She looked at the top of the vintage wardrobe, and a memory flashed to her mind. They had a wardrobe like this a long time ago. Once, when her father was doing his yearly spring-cleaning, he had decided to do away with the wardrobe, that was once her mother's pride and joy. Although Toral never knew her mother, her father would always tell her when she came to his room, that this wardrobe was her mama's wardrobe. Toral remembered crying when her father had told her it was time for the wardrobe to go, as he was looking to buy a new one. He told her that apart from her mother, nobody really liked that wardrobe. And Toral had looked at him and said, with all the innocence in the world, "But it was my *mummy's* wardrobe!"

She was there when the karigars came in; when one of them told her father the strangest thing. 'Secret compartment check kiya saab?' and both Toral and her father had looked at him as though they had absolutely no idea what he was referring to. Because they didn't, of course. Secret compartment? Where might that possibly be? Was it even possible, that there could be a secret compartment in something as ordinary as a wardrobe?

But the karigar had proceeded to go ahead, after a nod from her dad, and he had miraculously opened a secret compartment from out of nowhere. Looking at this wardrobe that looked eerily similar to the one in her own home, almost as though it had been made by the very same manufacturer (what a coincidence, to have a piano from Rustom's past and a wardrobe from hers, in the very same room), she proceeded to tap the upper right hand corner of the wardrobe (on top of the large mirror, through which she could see her reflection) twice. And wonder of wonders, it opened, like a door that has been left unlocked might open to a slightly ajar position.

There it was – the secret compartment. But her happiness was only short-lived. It seemed empty, just like the rest of the compartments in the wardrobe. She stared inside with a feeling of sadness for a couple of moments, and then proceeded to close it. That's when something shiny caught the corner of her eye. A glimpse of gold. She reached her hand inside, and there, amongst the thick layer of dust that had attacked the interior of the wardrobe with a vengeance, she found something. She felt its exterior. It seemed to be some kind of book. Grasping it firmly, she whisked it out of its hiding place. On closer inspection, it seemed to be a photo album. She opened it after dusting it thoroughly with a cloth she had found in the kitchen (one that she carried along to use in case the need arose) and found the picture of a smiling Elise; an Elise who must have been only six or seven years old, standing on Udvada beach (she recognised it at once, what with her having visited it only recently), her hair flying in the air, the most captivating smile illuminating her face.

She took a closer look at the picture. It was a black and white capture, one that had definitely been taken by a professional. These days, the only photos one ever took were from their cell phones. She turned the page to the next picture. It was of young Elise, aged about the same as the girl in the first picture, decked as though for a formal occasion, that pretty smile of hers once again the highlight. She was standing next to what seemed like a vintage car. Who had taken these photographs?

She flipped the pages and perused the pictures carefully, taking care not to miss a single one. All of them looked as though the photographer had a real interest in Elise; a *romantic* interest, perhaps? Well, it wouldn't have started when she was six or seven years old, would it? Unless the guy was a pervert. She shrugged the disturbing thought away. The photographs she was seeing now, were those of a fifteen-year-old girl. The strange thing was, there was nobody else in them. Toral shuddered. Had someone been taking advantage of this poor young girl?

She flipped through the rest of the photos, to see if there might be some sort of clue as to who the photographer might be, but there was none. In the final few photos, she sensed something was off, although she couldn't quite place her finger on what it was exactly. She shuttled back and forth between the pictures, and then it hit her. Elise was considerably older in the last ten photos or so – in her late twenties, perhaps. However, her smile was missing. It had not seemed all that strange to her at first, she realized, because she had plenty of old photographs of her own family, including those of her mother who she never knew, and the one thing she had gleaned from them was, people generally tended to smile less in pictures of yesteryear. It seemed odd in this world of smiling selfies, but that's just the way it was. The last few pictures, though, unnerved Toral completely. It was as though the erstwhile smiling girl seemed, all of a sudden, *terribly despondent*.

Chapter Twenty-two
Those Vacant Eyes

The three musketeers were sitting over an early lunch (might it be a brunch?), at the large antique dining table where they had had their breakfast only a few hours earlier. It was noon and this rather hurried lunch had been at Toral's behest. In that narrow window between breakfast and lunch, though, each of them had found themselves needing to go to the loo once for their minor jobs, in their respective bathrooms. It was pretty inconceivable to Toral, to have to use a bathroom outside of her home. She never used the bathroom when she were out; which is why she had to leave many an occasion early. Before using this bathroom that had not seen a visitor for years (and she couldn't quite tell whether the thought of that should serve to comfort or unsettle her), she had made sure she cleaned it as best as she possibly could, with a few wet wipes. God only knew what germs it might harbour.

"Oh dear, mutton kheema," Velkar said, after he had nimbly opened one of the circular metal boxes he had taken out of the large tiffin Satish had so painstakingly packed for them, and while at another time in his life he might have said this with the greatest sense of relish, he said it a bit warily, as though eating the sumptuous fare might just precipitate a premature shit. Not that he wasn't used to shitting at odd times; there were several times that wonderful Kolambiche Khadhadle had triggered the most wonderful shit at the most inappropriate time. However, in each of those instances he had a clean bathroom to do potty in; and of course, more importantly, clean, running water to clean his bum, too!

The possibility of having to rush to the bathroom all of a sudden was playing on Rustom's mind as well, as he glanced at the lovely *gajar ka halwa* the second dabba revealed. The key, well and truly, was eating in moderation. In any case, they would have to eat less. How else would they keep their eyes open after lunch?

"Time for a siesta, guys?" Oh well, one of them had already bitten the dust. Who else but the designated driver for their trip, Anil Velkar?

"Have you come here to sleep?" Wadia made it a point to show his irritation. Toral intervened just then; to save Daddy Dearest, of course.

"You can have your siesta, daddy, in one of the rooms upstairs. Not Elise's room, please." Before Wadia could cut in, she went on, "Before that, I have something to show you both. But first, let's finish lunch?"

The trio were sitting in the study on the very same sofa they had found themselves on, moments after their 'break-in.' Toral had the shiny gold album in her hand that she had miraculously discovered moments earlier. She thought back to the time her father had unearthed a similar compartment in his wife's wardrobe. That secret compartment had held an envelope, and she remembered her father opening it and looking at the contents within, as though he might be scared to more than glance at them. She remembered him wincing when he looked inside, as though he might be looking at something he should not be seeing. And then, he simply told the karigars to go ahead and take the wardrobe away, as though the contents of that envelope might have somehow firmly reinforced in his mind the decision to do away with it. Toral had been furious. Did he wish to erase every trace of her mother from the house? And what could that envelope have possibly contained? Might it have been a picture of Elise? What other secrets had her father been hiding?

"Toral? Are you okay?" It was Velkar. Of course she's not okay, knowing her dad wants to doze off in the afternoon when it would be more appropriate for the three of us to be continuing our search, thought Wadia.

"I'm – fine." She went on to explain all about the secret compartment in Elise's wardrobe, that Velkar told her he must see to believe (again the fool thinks of doing something completely irrelevant, Wadia thought). Then, taking the album from her bag and opening it slowly, she showed the two old men, who peered down on either side of her, exactly what she had discovered.

It was the second picture that caught Wadia's attention. Rather, the car in the picture against which Elise leaned. "That is one of the cars parked in the house next door," he said excitedly. And the three of them exchanged glances, as though it might be a confirmation of their worst fears. Might the neighbour next door have been the one who raped Elise? Who *was* the neighbour, after all? Might Velkar have been correct in his assumption that there was indeed something wrong with the man?

"I will strangle him," said Velkar, making rapid boxing gestures as though he might be a poor man's Muhammad Ali (at least that's how Wadia pictured it).

"Wait a minute." It was Toral. "Let's not get ahead of ourselves here. It might not even have been the gentleman's car. Rustom, are you sure?"

"One hundred percent."

"Okay. Let's all agree, then, that the car in the second picture was indeed the neighbour's car. That doesn't necessarily mean *he* was the photographer. Furthermore, the building the car is parked outside of in the picture, is clearly not the building next door. The location of this picture somehow resembles the road that leads to the beach from that lady's house (and at that moment she realized that none of them had bothered to even ask the old lady her name; she let the thought slide). As you can see, Elise is merely posing next to the car, which also means that they, and by *they* I mean the photographer and she, might have simply stumbled across the car in the middle of a walk, and decided to take an impromptu picture there. After all, she doesn't seem especially dressed for this one, which is an anomaly if you compare it to the others, in which she has made a conscientious effort to look her best."

"Wait a minute. I have an observation." It was the Maharashtrian Sherlock Holmes. They turned to him and he said, "Actually, no."

They continued looking at the photographs and by the end of the album, both Velkar and Rustom seemed consumed by the same emotion that had beset Toral earlier; a deep sadness.

"She looks so terribly sad in those last few pictures," said Wadia, confirming what Toral had felt. "And those eyes – so vacant."

"Look how happy she was in the first few pictures. Ah. That's what I wanted to say, but I didn't think to bring it up for lack of relevance." It was Velkar, flicking through the pictures as though to demonstrate his point. This was all Elise was reduced to now, Toral thought; a girl in a photo album.

"It *is* relevant," said Toral, grim-faced. There was something that haunted Elise in her last days and we need to get to the bottom of it. I think we might have to do some more asking around, and possibly extend the trip by a couple of days."

"I say we go next door and confront the man living there," said Velkar. "I tell you, I got a bad vibe from him."

"But he hasn't spoken a word to us, Velkar." Wadia was

exasperated. Someone better tell this Maharashtrian how futile his comments are; that's probably the only way he will shut up.

"Oh, but he will," said Velkar, staring up at the ceiling. And people think we Parsis are eccentric, thought Wadia.

"So, I guess this photo album is all we have come up with." It was Toral.

"I think it is," said Wadia.

"That means a 'yes' for that siesta, then?" Velkar, sounding wide awake. Once again Wadia swooped in to intervene, but he was deftly cut off by Toral.

"I think that's a really great idea. Daddy, Rustom, you can choose which of the two beds upstairs you would like to sleep in. Once again, not Elise's room as that is the only one that has the curtains open. I will take this couch here."

"And then what?" Wadia couldn't understand why they couldn't get a move on with things. For most of his life he had had no sense of purpose; now he suddenly seemed to have found one, and a siesta was the last thing he needed to get in the way of it.

"Then we get out of here." Sensing Wadia's discomfort, she went on. "Look, Udvada is a small, sleepy town. People here are used to taking a nap in the afternoon. What time is it? Wadia looked to his cell phone and Velkar, at the old Titan watch Vidya had given him on his fiftieth birthday. "One o'clock," they uttered in unison.

"Exactly. Now, most people in a sleepy hamlet like Udvada are accustomed to their afternoon sleep. That's exactly why they call places like these 'sleepy hamlets.' Even though Udvada is considerably larger than a hamlet, of course. But it has the same vibe, nonetheless. I figure if we sneak in a good couple hours of shuteye, we will be well rested for the evening, as well as find ourselves able to sneak away from this place in the afternoon itself. Why wait for night when there's nothing left to do here, anyway?"

"What about the man next door?" It was Velkar, and he said this with trepidation in his voice. He didn't want to go to jail along with his comrades. What would happen to Vidya if they got no bail?

"*Especially* the man next door," said Toral. "After all, he was up at 4.30 in the morning. If anyone will be sleeping in the afternoon, it will be him. Regardless of his age. Now, I think we should target leaving a little over a couple of hours from now. It will be 3 p.m. then. Nobody in this town is going to wake up from their afternoon naps before 4."

"And then, we go straight to Butterfly Villa? What do we tell Satish?" It was Wadia. He was right, thought Toral; although they were no mastermind criminals, they had to cover their tracks, just like any smart criminal would. They might just find themselves embroiled in an investigation, and it was better they be safe than sorry.

"We just tell him there was nothing exceptional in Pardi to do, so we had lunch and came back. Only if he asks, mind you. Not that it makes a difference, but you're right, if people get a whiff of this break-in and start asking questions, at least we have our tracks covered."

And just like that, it was agreed that they would enjoy their siesta for a good couple of hours. That little window of sleep would be good for them, Toral included. Unlike others that belonged to her generation, she needed her eight hours of beauty sleep.

It was 3 p.m. when Toral's mobile alarm went off. She had set it at an extremely low volume, so there would be no chance anyone outside would hear it (even though the thought of someone outside hearing an alarm on a mobile phone, seemed to be absolutely ludicrous). She hurried to wake the others up. Wadia had taken the couch in the study and Velkar, the one in the living room. She had slept in the room adjoining Elise's, thinking that her great-grandmother must have slept there once. Although all of them found themselves desperately wanting to go to the bathroom, they decided against it as it would only be a short while that they would be returning to Butterfly Villa. At the very last moment, they changed their minds (after Velkar told them that they might just have to use a dirty loo in Udvada police station), and decided to use their respective bathrooms one last time. And when they were done, they proceeded to the very window they had crawled out of; the window that now seemed all the more ominous, because they were proceeding to break out of it in broad daylight.

It was Toral who went first out, after staring long and hard at the balcony across, to ensure nobody could see what they were up to. When she was absolutely sure there was nobody watching them, she lent her hand to her Daddykins, who luckily managed to climb over the sill without stumbling, like he had when he had been making his illegal entry into the house. He was now assigned to keep a watch on any possible movements in the balcony of the neighbouring bungalow, while Toral extended her hand to Wadia so he could climb over. Just a few moments and they would all be out of this place. And in the end Wadia clambered out, too, and took a few moments to gather his breath.

Then, the three of them looked at one another, as though to say 'Let's do this,' and holding each other's hands, walked down the porch and into the garden that was covered with grass almost up to their knees. Then, almost nonchalantly, they all looked up to the balcony of the house opposite – and into the sinister eyes of Kaizad Patel.

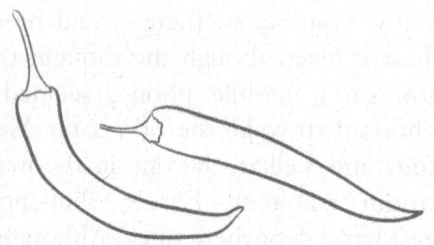

Chapter Twenty-three
The Clicker of the Clicks

The silence in the house next door was deafening. Nobody spoke a word for the longest time. The three fugitives sat on a plush leather sofa in the middle of a living room in what was obviously Kaizad Patel's home, staring at the man whose once gentle eyes now resembled black holes, sucking the life out of the three of them. Wadia had told Mr. Patel everything about their search for the young Elise Wadia, who had been a mystery to all of them until not very long ago. Kaizad Patel had listened in rapt attention, but either he didn't believe the story or he simply didn't care.

"You know I could very well report you to the police, right?" he said calmly, and the three of them nodded in unison. Why had he even called them here? It was clear he was hiding something. The terrible thought had struck Wadia, as they were walking to his house, that it might very well have been Kaizad Patel, who was responsible for the horrific rape that led to Elise being taken from this town to God-knows-where. Of course the thought had struck them earlier on in the day that the neighbour might well be responsible for the crime, but they had never thought that the perpetrator might be the very man whose house they had rented out. But of course they dared not accuse him of anything. After all, he had caught them red-handed, coming out of the house next door. Sure, they could deny it if confronted by the local police, because, after all, Kaizad Patel had only seen them in the backyard and not actually inside the house, but then their fingerprints were all over the place, and they would surely find themselves in the Udvada police station lock-up later, if not sooner. Please, let this be over, thought Wadia. If you want to report us, go ahead and do so.

Mr. Patel went on, "I think I gave you all a clear indication at our first meeting, to not pursue this matter. Am I right?" Again, the three heads nodded in unison. Then Velkar raised his hand, like a little schoolboy.

"Yes?" Spoken more like 'Principal' Patel.

Velkar put down his hand and raised it once again, this time with all fingers closed except one. Wadia glared at him. "Didn't you go for a leak just now?" He said this almost in a whisper.

"What to do baba? A little is remaining," he said in an even softer whisper, so that Toral couldn't hear it, but she did. She laughed then, and that seemed to immediately disconcert Kaizad Patel.

"Laugh all you like. I hope you know this isn't going to end well for you all."

Velkar ran to the bathroom. Not that the requisite permission had been granted, but then he hadn't been opposed when he had asked, either.

"What's that?" Mr. Patel suddenly said, catching the glint of the photo album in Toral's bag. Shit! She thought. How careless could she have been, forgetting to zip her bag when she knew very well that the photo album was in there. But then, the last thing she had expected was to have been caught.

"But – I thought you lived in a *modest* one-bedroom apartment." Wadia, coming to the rescue.

"Don't change the subject." Kaizad Patel seemed irritated, either on account of the 'subject change' or perhaps the 'modest one-bedroom,' bit.

Toral panicked. What should she do? Should she lie and say, perhaps, that it was her personal diary that was in her bag, and he had absolutely no right to lay his hands on it?

"This is something we found in the house," she said, gripping her bag tight.

"I see. Stealing now, are we?" Wadia was desperately looking for any palpable tension in Mr. Patel's face. All they needed was something that would give the man away; if they were in a pickle, well, he was clearly in a larger one. Then Toral spoke, in an unwavering tone.

"You can take us to prison, if you wish. I'm not handing anything over to you. If I give it to anyone at all, it will be to a policeman." Well played, young lady, thought Wadia.

All of a sudden Velkar emerged, looking completely spaced out; just like the hapless idiot he was. He was standing right in front of Wadia, preventing him from getting a good look at Mr. Patel. What was he doing? It was important to know if Mr. Patel had been intimidated by what Toral had just said to him, about handing the diary to the police.

"Daddy, please sit down." Well, *someone* understood.

It was apparent from the way Mr. Patel squirmed in his chair, after Velkar had taken his position on the couch once again, that he had been rendered uncomfortable by that last statement. It was clear he didn't want that photo album to get into the hands of the local police.

"Okay, then. I'm calling the police." Just a ploy to get them to hand over the photo album to him, thought Wadia; nothing more.

"No!" It was Velkar, who had missed what had transpired in the last few moments.

"Then hand over that photo album to me. *Now*."

"What makes you think it's a photo album?" It was Toral. Mr. Patel's apparent squeamishness, only served to confirm to her that he was indeed the very man who had cruelly raped Elise on an Udvada summer night, and then pinned it on the poor manservant who lived in the household, simply because it was far easier for people to believe that a servant had committed a crime so great.

"Saala! You rascal!" It was Velkar. 'What was he doing?' thought Wadia. And the Maharashtrian didn't say anything after that; merely remained mute, as though he had forgotten what he had intended to say next (or perhaps, and this was all the more probable, as though he had never intended to say anything more at all). What happened next shocked them. As though Velkar's random outburst were Mr. Patel's cue to let loose, he bellowed, "You have the nerve! Calling me a rascal in my own home. I need you to vacate Butterfly Villa with immediate effect. If you people don't leave Udvada in an hour from now, I'm calling the police."

Wadia looked at Velkar as though to say, 'See what you have done'? And the words Velkar uttered next to Mr. Patel, were probably the words he had kept to himself a few moments ago. The ones he had dared not let out for fear of what their captor might say.

"I know you are the photographer who has taken pictures of Elise, and I can prove it."

All of them looked at Velkar, stunned.

"You see, my dear Mr. Patel (he said this as though Mr. Patel were Watson and he, the esteemed Mr. Holmes), when I went to the bathroom, I couldn't help but observe a red light emanating from the room next to it. The door was ajar, and when I opened it, what did I see? A room filled with pictures. A darkroom."

Rustom and Toral stared at Velkar with a new-found sense of admiration. Wadia wondered if he should jump in and say something that would completely unnerve Mr. Patel and get him to admit to his horrendous crime. Then, all of a sudden, Mr. Patel's visage softened considerably. He seemed a bit weary as he said, "It's time you all knew. Come with me."

And Mr. Patel got up and led his three perplexed hostages, to the room Velkar had sauntered into, while he had gone for a pee. It was with a sense of reluctance that they followed him, hoping they weren't walking into a trap. When they walked into the windowless room (nevertheless, one that was illuminated, albeit dimly, by a single red light that hung from the ceiling), the first thought that hit Rustom was that this was a professional photographer's room. For a few moments Mr. Patel didn't say anything, as though silently inviting them to catch a glimpse of his wonderful art. And they did. The pictures were strikingly beautiful, but they were all of landscapes. A lot of them looked like they had been taken abroad, too; wonderful images of cliffs and grassy plains and beaches, but not a single image of a person, let alone Elise.

"Diva was the only person I photographed," he said with an air of nostalgia, as though reading the thoughts of the others present in the room with him. "She was very special to me. I was around twenty when she first came here, and like the rest of the town's inhabitants, I looked after her as though she were my daughter." He was staring at the only blank wall in the room as he said this, a wall against which rested a large desk that held some bulky equipment, presumably related to his photography. The wall at the rear, the one with the door through which they had entered this room, was plastered with scintillating photographs as well. Mr. Patel's face now exuded the same sadness Elise's had, in those final few photographs in the photo album. He went on.

"Elise grew to be very fond of me. She would come to my place all the time, when my father was around. Did you know he only moved back to the colony because of the incident?" All of a sudden Wadia felt this man wasn't quite who they had made him out to be. Mr. Patel continued.

"You see, Elise was fascinated with the photographs I took. They were mostly of natural locales, as you can see, but there were a few odd ones, like those of a fisherman somewhere or perhaps even a nun, that caught her fancy. She told me she wanted to create a picture album with photos of her taken by me. How she loved posing for those pictures... I was more than happy to click her, of course. Truth be told, I never saw the photo album myself, but she said it was safe and in a secret place."

A secret compartment was definitely as secret as secret could get, thought Toral. "Might I ask why she seemed extremely sad in the last few pictures you took of her?" Like Wadia, she, too, suddenly felt that this man had had nothing to do with the rape.

"I know what you all are thinking. That I might have had a romantic liaison with Diva. Or worse, still, did the unimaginable, that led to her leaving Udvada altogether. But no, I was the elder brother she never had. Whenever she was feeling low, she would come over. Whenever she was in a great mood too, she would come over. I was the person she could confide anything to…" Looking at Wadia now. "The reason I walked away from you that morning, was because I felt that you were like your grandfather."

"Like my grandfather? What do you mean?"

"Oh well, you know. Everyone in Udvada hated your grandfather."

"Why?" Was all Wadia could manage saying, even though he instinctively knew the answer.

"*Why*? Because your grandfather bought this house right next to mine – it belonged to a wealthy gentleman who lived in London at the time and whose children said they never wanted to go to that *shitty* town in India – and he just left poor Diva out here to fend for herself, all because of some issue in the family. *That's* why." He laughed before he went on, "Who did he think he was fooling? We all knew what the real issue was. And of course nothing could ever replace the love of a family, but we tried our best. We really did." Tears welled in his eyes.

A short while later they were sitting and having a cup of tea on Mr. Patel's veranda. He had assured the trio he would not be making a formal complaint to the police regarding their break-in. He had completely understood their reason for unlawfully entering the house next door.

"It would have been better if you had been the rapist," Velkar said out of nowhere in the middle of their conversation, and Mr. Patel nearly dropped his cup of tea.

"Excuse me?" Toral and Wadia were aghast, as well as the person at the receiving end of this utterly ludicrous statement.

"You know, then we would have a sense of closure. You would be the bad guy and we could go home." Wadia shook his head. Nut job.

"So you'd make *me* the rapist?" Velkar looked uncomfortable all of a sudden.

"I'm sorry. I don't think I should have said that. It doesn't come off as appropriate."

"Yes!" The other three chorused in unison.

And there was a long silence, that was finally broken by Wadia's sombre voice.

"Forgive me for asking this, Mr. Patel, but you didn't answer the question I asked earlier. Not that I suspect you in the least; it's just, why did you tell us you were living in a modest one bedroom apartment, when you are obviously leading a luxurious life in this bungalow?"

Mr. Patel smiled, and placed his cup of half-drunk tea into his saucer, before continuing, "It's good for business."

"I understand." It was Toral, who was undoubtedly an astute businesswoman. "Of course. It adds to the story; a good story makes for good business."

Mr. Patel raised his cup. Of course it had been a smart move, he reflected. There were people who would email him from places as distant as Canada and New Zealand, telling him they couldn't get over the fact that he lived such a frugal life, while allowing his guests to experience such lavishness. That story seemed to add to the allure of the property.

He's nothing but a bloody liar, thought Velkar. He looked at Wadia, who seemed to share the same sentiment. Oh well, what did he know about business anyway? He had worked in the same company for several years before finally retiring with a sense of pride. But he had never, never lied. As for his friend Wadia, he had never worked a single day in his life. What would he know, for that matter?

"So, what happened to Elise?" It was Wadia. He was desperately trying to hold onto something that would help them get further in their search.

"Ah! I wish I knew. All I know is, another gentleman arrived the morning of the rape, I think it must have been your father, there was a resemblance, and he drove the same car, and the very next day, Diva had lost its daughter to an unknown destination. I slid into a great depression after that. All this had happened in my own backyard; I could never forgive myself for that."

"It's not your fault," said Toral, in as comforting a voice as she could muster. "Surely, there must be some clue as to where he might have taken her?"

"Yes," said Wadia, almost imploringly. "Please, if you can remember anything from that time, we will be eternally grateful. There's nothing more we can do here, but hope that you might know something. After all, you knew her best."

Mr. Patel was silent for a few moments. "You're right. I did know her better than anyone else in Udvada did."

He paused, before continuing, "Most people won't even want to help you out because of your grandfather. But mostly, they want to have nothing to do with the incident because it brings back the most painful memories. That was the reason I behaved the way I did the morning we first met. You have to understand; the time following the incident was so traumatic I literally could not get out of bed for the couple of months that followed. I just buried the thought of Diva deep down inside, like the rest of Udvada did."

There was that sound of silence once again, punctuated by the sharp humming of some kind of bird, that seemed to remind them that no matter what, life must go on.

They were sitting on the beach on a large rock: the three musketeers who had successfully (despite being caught, of course) broken into a bungalow in the middle of town that morning. It was five in the evening; their last night in Udvada. The next day they would return to Mumbai and its monotony. They had tried desperately to find something that would help bring them a sense of closure, but without any luck.

"She was only twenty-five when it happened," said Wadia, rolling a pebble against the smooth skin of his right palm. "She had at least another thirty years to live, at the very least, if you take into account the average lifespan of a person afflicted with Down's…. How much more tragic can her story get?"

"At least we have these beautiful pictures of her," said Toral, holding the album she had discovered in the house, tightly against her chest. Imagine, her little feet on this very beach, pressing against the sand while her picture was being taken…" And she had tears in her eyes as she said this. This wasn't the end she had been expecting. Her phone rang just then, and she silenced it with one deft click. She hadn't taken several calls from her restaurant in the last few days. She had told them she wasn't to be disturbed at all, even if there was an emergency – her staff simply had to find a way of handling it themselves. After all, she had plenty of problems to deal with here herself.

"Perhaps it's for the best that we don't know about the remainder of Elise's life," Velkar said all of a sudden. "You know, maybe the actual ending was even worse than the ending as we know it."

"And knowing that is supposed to make us feel better?" It was Wadia, and even though he said this as though to insinuate that Velkar had said something highly insensitive, in the back of his mind he knew his Maharashtrian friend might just be right. Perhaps Elise's life had fallen apart completely after that. It might indeed be best to just think her life was happy in the years leading from the incident up to her passing away.

When they returned to Butterfly Villa, there was a police car pulled up outside. The three of them froze, as the wheels of the car, still in motion, came to a gradual stop.

"I think I need to pee," said Velkar.

"Maybe do it in the bushes while I see what Sunil wants," said Wadia. His heart was beating fast. Toral was in a state of shock. Might this be the moment they had all been dreading thus far?

They made their way like guilty little lambs to the junior Agashe. There was no expression on his face. As though to deflate the tension brimming within him, Velkar tried to see if there might be any nose hair protruding from the Maharashtrian policeman's nose. Nope. Not one.

"I have something that might interest you," said he. "My father did, actually – something he thought of after you'd left – but I would rather him rest at home, what with this bit of news already having made him a tad too excited. You see, years ago, his best friend called him out of the blue to tell him there was a rare vintage car he had seen parked in a by lane in Pardi."

The trio relaxed. They weren't in trouble, after all. That being said, there might just be something more to this new piece of information, thought Wadia.

"Rare vintage car?"

"Yes. You see, my baba and his friend were car fanatics, and mentions of the latest makes would always crop up in their conversations. My baba had mentioned to his friend the car make and model of the vehicle your grandfather used to drive, and voila! One day his friend sees the very same type on a deserted road in Pardi!"

"It could have been another car. Back then all cars were vintage." It was Velkar.

"According to baba, not that particular one. It was a limited edition."

Chapter Twenty-four
The House by the Lake

The 'good burglars' entered Butterfly Villa mentally and physically exhausted, and after they had bathed and dressed into their nightclothes, settled down in Toral's room.

They had also packed their suitcases, as they were due to check out before ten in the morning: Mr. Patel had told them he had new guests arriving the next day from New Zealand. Well, not straight from New Zealand to Udvada, of course. They were flying to Mumbai airport and from there they would take a cab to Udvada. They always made it a point to first visit their holy city, before they went back to Mumbai, where the rest of their extended family belonged. They were none other than Mimi's nephew and his family, but they never stayed with her, not wanting to inconvenience her. How sweet, Wadia had said then, rather absentmindedly, not meaning it at all. Nobody in their right mind would ever want to live with Mimi.

"I simply can't get over all that has transpired in the last couple of days," Toral uttered with an air of exhaustion, her head resting back on her pillow. "It all seems so unreal. In any case, what's the point of it all? It's not like we have reached anywhere in our search for Elise."

"Yes we have." It was Velkar. The others looked at him as though to imply, 'Why not?" After all, they had exhausted all other alternatives; perhaps Velkar had struck gold.

"Pardi is only a twenty minute drive from here," Velkar said. *Twenty-two* minutes to be precise, according to Google Maps. He was becoming quite an expert at this Google Maps thing. "I tell you what, once we check out of here we drive first thing to Pardi, go to the first house we see, and ask if they might know anything about a girl with Down's syndrome having lived there sometime ago. All in all, it will add not more than an hour to our trip. Come on, what say?"

Wadia, sitting on one of the large leather chairs opposite the bed (Velkar was propped up in bed alongside his daughter), said wearily, "You are right. After all, what have we to lose?" If he had lost all enthusiasm in the search, he would piggyback off Velkar's.

"And, we might after all find an ending to the story. Even if we found no clues to bring the real perpetrator to justice."

In the morning there was an intense conversation at the breakfast table about the legacy of Parsis and what could be done to ensure their numbers were upheld over time. Kaizad Patel had come over, and it hadn't been to inspect whether anything was missing from the minibar (after all, there wasn't a minibar in this joint). He had come here out of a genuine goodness in his heart, wanting to lift the spirits of his guests. Chatting with Wadia about the dying breed of Parsis did not quite seem the right way to go about doing it, thought Velkar, who felt a bit excluded from the conversation. He found himself growing increasingly proud of Toral, who seemed to know everything on the subject the two bawas were so vociferously discussing. After all, education wasn't merely limited to textbooks. Velkar should know; he read the comics section in the paper every single day.

They had decided they wouldn't tell Mr. Patel about their upcoming trip to Pardi; that is, if you could even call it a trip. More like a stopover on the way to Mumbai. This whole trip to Udvada seemed to be some sort of blur.

"I hope you will come here again. Despite all that has transpired." The question was directed by Mr. Patel to all three of them, when they had just got up from their positions at the dining table, to get a move on to Pardi (to Mumbai, as far as Mr. Patel was concerned). Their bags had already been loaded into the old Maruti Suzuki.

"It all happened a long time ago, Kaizad." Wadia noticed that he had called Mr. Patel by his first name for the first time. Then he went on,

"I will definitely come back, hopefully the three of us will."

"Yes," Toral and Velkar added meekly, sans enthusiasm. Kaizad Patel looked like a man who could use the company, even if it meant joining them for a mere cup of chai when they next visited.

"Thanks for your hospitality, dear Sir, and thank you for being so kind to my aunt." And saying that, Wadia proceeded to leave, the others trudging slowly behind him.

It was with a sense of pride that they finally left Butterfly Villa; pride at having tried their best to find out what had happened to poor Elise. And find out they had, but only up to a point, Wadia thought, as he observed the minutiae of the large palm trees that dotted the lane leading up to Butterfly Villa, for no particular reason. Perhaps Velkar had been right when he had said that it was best they don't find anything more, because that 'something more' might just turn out to be something they wished they had never known.

According to Google Maps, it would take them around 29 minutes to get to Pardi, on account of heavier than usual traffic. What traffic? Wadia had seen absolutely no sort of traffic on the roads in these here parts ever since they had arrived. Perhaps there had been a crash on the highway somewhere? No, in that case there would be the mention of an accident on the app. At least, that's what Toral had them believe. In any case, it ordinarily took around twenty-two minutes to reach Pardi. This was only seven minutes longer. Human beings measured time constantly and clung onto it as though it were in immense shortage. While you never really knew how much time you had, what mattered most was the 'quality' of time, not 'quantity.' A ninety-year-old man might have had a terrible life, while someone who died in their early twenties might have enjoyed their life to the fullest. Was it really a boon to live longer?

They took the Coastal Highway, which was pretty much the only road that would lead them to Pardi. It was a lovely road, but none of them were in the mood to marvel at the wonder of their surroundings. After all, this was no holiday. When they finally reached Pardi, Velkar parked the car on a deserted road, several metres from where it appeared to fork in different directions.

"Okay, so we're in Pardi. Now what?" He looked first at his daughter who was sitting in the front seat alongside him, and then back towards Wadia in the back.

"Let's just do as you said, Anil. Let's find the first house we can." From the tone of Wadia's voice, it seemed as though he had lost all semblance of hope.

"I suggest we go to the lake. And find the nearest house there." It was Toral. Of course she had done some stellar research on the place. She had to; that was her thing. And she was young, too; of course she would want to indulge in a bit of sightseeing.

"Yes, I think we can take some good snaps of the lake. Vidya will be happy to see them." Wadia was just about to intervene, when he thought otherwise. The poor Velkar had not only come along with him for support on this trip, but he had also been his chauffeur. Forget about the money he had saved thanks to Velkar's; it was certainly not easy driving such a long distance, at this age. If the mad Maharashtrian wanted to see the lake and take pictures of it too, then by all means, let him. This visit to Pardi might just be the 'cherry on top' of a largely forgettable trip.

"Let's go to the lake, then," said Wadia. In a way, he knew he was putting off that confrontation with whoever they were going to meet, because one part of him felt that he should just give this all up; that it was futile to be pursuing the ghost of Elise Wadia when they had already learned whatever it was they needed to know about her. His mind harked back to Mrs. Bhathena's words, instructing them to not go to Udvada. Maybe knowing more than was necessary was not so good, after all. Had she known? About what had happened to Elise that fateful night in Providence Villa? What else did she know?

Pardi Talav was only a few minutes from their current location. It's so funny, thought Wadia. You can find the location of a place at the mere click of a button now. In the good old days, there was a sense of mystery attached to locating a place. You had to ask around several times, and it was only then that you found your way. Losing your sense of where you were on the way to getting to where you had to, only deepened the mystery. Where had that sense of mystery gone now? It certainly didn't exist in today's digital world. What's worse was, when people finally got to those exotic locations, they would take pictures of natural habitats and in the end, diminish their experience of it. What was the point of standing in, say, a beautiful forest, phone in hand, trying to 'capture' it? Why was experiencing it in all its splendour, merely being there in the moment, not enough?

In only a short while they found themselves on the banks of Pardi Talav. It most certainly seemed to be worth the hype, and Wadia was surprised by the fact that he actually felt elevated. It wasn't every day that he found himself in a scenic location. Toral sat on the ground only a few metres away from the water. Wadia and Velkar exchanged glances with each other, and then they both sat down as well. They just stared at the placid lake for the longest time.

"Elise would have loved it here," said Toral, not speaking to anyone in particular. Perhaps she was speaking to herself. Wadia did that at times: speak to himself, even when he was surrounded by people. If the people weren't Parsis, they usually attributed his behaviour to the 'eccentricity of Parsis.' They were crazy too; they just didn't know it. How else could one survive in a crazy world?

Wadia found himself scrounging for some pebbles in the earth, and throwing them into the lake. Velkar was looking at him with a sense of agitation.

"Don't do that, Rustom. You will hurt the fishies."

See? *That* kind of crazy.

They spent nearly a half hour by the lake, before Toral glanced at her friends (because her father was her friend first), as though to indicate that they might wish to get back on the road. There was nothing to be found there. At least, that's what it had seemed until Velkar had pointed out something away to the right – a barely discernible cottage of sorts. Damn! That Maharashtrian has eagle vision, thought Wadia. After all, he had missed it and he was absolutely certain Toral had too, what with it being almost completely obscured by the trees dotting the lake.

And neither of them had to say anything. Toral started walking and the two gentleman followed her. It was a house, after all, and they had already decided that they would be going to the first house that they could find, in what would be their final search for Elise. As they approached their destination, they noticed the terrain was a bit too uneven for comfort. Toral had to lend her hand alternately to Velkar and to a rather irate Wadia (who kept telling her he was not an invalid and could manage perfectly well on his own, thank you very much). Finally, they came to some sort of clearing. From here they could see the whole house. It was a lovely cottage in the middle of nowhere, and Toral had the feeling that when she retired, she would want to live in a place like this. Oh well, that would be a long time from now.

The house had a lovely wooden patio and the overall sense of the place was that of a 'cabin in the woods,' although it was considerably larger than a mere cabin. It was a proper house, with a cabin feel to it. There were a couple of chairs on one side of what seemed to be the patio, and what appeared to be (Toral went over and glanced at it) – yes, today's newspaper on one of them. So there was certainly someone living here. Of course, they were probably trespassing on private property. However, there hadn't been a sign out here that said something to the effect of 'Trespassers will be prosecuted,' had there? At least not one they had seen. No matter what happens, I'm not getting arrested, Toral said to herself, as she went up to the front door and rang the bell, while Wadia and Velkar stood on the deck right behind her, trying their best to hide themselves, failing miserably.

An elderly lady opened the door. She had long, wiry hair and seemed to be a septuagenarian, at the very least. She looked at the trio as though she might be seeing fairies. As though it were pretty inconceivable that a human being would walk up to her house and ring the bell.

"Yes?" A smile appeared on her lips, with a faint trace of curiosity. She seemed to be wearing a nightgown, although Wadia couldn't quite be sure. How on earth would he know about what women wore, anyway? He hadn't shared his bedroom with one for all his life, except for one night long ago – but that was another story.

"I–we–" Wadia couldn't find the words. Then Toral cut in.

"I'm sorry, ma'am, but we have travelled from Bombay to Udvada on some serious business. Having finished, we thought we might stop by in this town on the slim chance that we might find some information pertaining to a relation of ours."

"And who might that be?" And what was left unsaid by the petite old woman was, 'And why have you come to *my* house looking for that particular somebody?'

"She was a young girl back then." It was Wadia now, his confidence seemingly bolstered all of a sudden. "She was not like the others."

The woman was silent for a few moments. Then she said, "Would you like to come in for a cup of tea?"

"Yes, thank you very much." It was Velkar. Wadia shook his head. They could have got the information they needed right on the porch where they stood, but then, their driver needed chai for the long journey back.

"But only if you let me help," said Toral. The old woman agreed in an instant, and they were soon inside the sparsely furnished, albeit elegant, house.

Wadia and Velkar settled into the comfortable sofa chairs in the middle of the living room, that had a large window that lent one a spectacular view of the lake. How wonderful it must be to live here, thought Wadia. All you had to do was hop, skip and jump, and you were in the lake. Of course, he didn't know if you could swim in it. It might just be infested with crocodiles like the Powai Lake in Mumbai was.

The women were in the kitchen, busy preparing tea. Wadia wondered if Toral had even told the old lady about Elise yet; however, from the excited chatter that came from the open kitchen nearby (which was cut off from the part of the living room where he and Velkar sat), it was safe to assume they hadn't gone there yet.

A few minutes later Toral came in with two porcelain cups of chai with steam emanating from them, and placed them on the large mahogany table in the centre of the four sprawling chairs. Only a couple of moments later the old woman appeared, holding the other two cups, one for Toral and the other, for herself. Wadia took a sip of the chai. It was surprisingly good; there must be something in it like the ginger and elaichi people back in Mumbai put in their tea. Some secret ingredient. It seemed almost impossible to put a finger on what it was, even though Wadia proclaimed himself a connoisseur of food who had surprised chefs in restaurants back in the day (when he frequented restaurants all over the world) by telling them he knew all the ingredients that went into the dishes he really liked, and then proceeding to tell them exactly what those ingredients were. He liked to guess the ingredients; never to ask what they might be.

"So, where were we?" It was the old woman, getting down to business. Oh well, she had been more than gracious so far; anyone else in her position would never have allowed three complete strangers into her home, especially when she lived in a place completely cut off from the world outside.

"Yes. Would you happen to know of a girl with Down's syndrome who lived in Pardi, sometime ago? Considerably long ago, I guess?" It was Wadia. The lady stopped stirring the tea in her cup. It was as though her hand had frozen in time, even though her eyes seemed to have suddenly come alive. She resumed stirring the tea a couple of moments later, and then gingerly placed her cup of tea on the mahogany table in front of them. Of course the lady knew about Elise, Rustom thought. But neither he nor his fellow travellers were even remotely prepared for what they would learn in the next few moments.

"Do you have a picture of her?" And Toral immediately fished in her bag and took out the photo album she had literally stolen from Elise's home. She handed it over to the old woman, fingers trembling. Neither she nor the others seemed interested in their tea. Not that it wasn't good tea; in fact, it was great chai. As the old lady flicked through the pages of the album, she cried dearly. Finally, when she set the photo album down, Toral got out of her chair, went up to her and hugged her tight.

"She was my sister," she said finally, regaining some semblance of composure. "I don't know who you people are, but she came here around fifty years ago. My mother found her with a gentleman by the lake. The man was clearly distraught. And *Princess*, which is what her name would be for the next twenty odd years or so until the day she died, well, she was glass-eyed when we found her. She was staring at the lake but not looking at it at all. There was this stuffed toy in her hand, a little teddy bear, that she simply would not leave. I must have been in my early twenties at the time, just down from London where

I was studying." She took out her handkerchief and blew her nose, before she continued. "After Princess came here, I never went back. But, don't get me wrong. It was the best decision I ever made in my life."

"I'm sorry, but did my father just leave her here?" Wadia didn't say this with any sense of shock, of course; after all, Dhunji Wadia had already abandoned his daughter several years earlier. And the old woman seemed even more saddened by the connection. Toral thought that perhaps now was not the right moment to explain to the woman, that *she* was related to Princess, too.

"Oh no. My mother and me just found him sitting at the water's edge, as he wept. We would take a walk by the lake every morning and one day, we were confronted by the sight of your father and Princess." And that was when Toral, unable to help herself, explained to the woman exactly how she was related to Princess herself.

"Oh my. That's quite a tale," the old lady said. There was a long pause before she spoke again. "I'm so sorry, where are my manners? I forgot to ask if you would like some cookies with your tea." Velkar started to speak then, and Toral was absolutely sure he would say that he would love to have cookies with his chai, and so she gave him the sternest look to shut him up at once.

"So, Princess lived here the rest of her life?" It was Wadia.

"Yes. Your father explained to us all that had happened, right from the time his father had abandoned her, to the night she was raped, breaking down several times while he spoke. He said he couldn't possibly take her home. And my mum kept her; just like that, to my jubilation. After all, my dad had died when I was only two years old, and it was only me and mum living in this house." Again, a pause as the woman took some time to gather her thoughts. This was clearly not easy for her, thought Wadia. Well, there was no stopping now. The old lady continued,

"You see, mum lived on the savings my father had left her. He was a highly respected businessman in Pardi and he came into a lot of money owing to an inheritance from his aunt who lived in Britain. She gave him an entire mansion, can you believe it? I'm not saying this to show off my wealth, mind you; I'm just enabling you to understand how we can afford this place without working, and how my mum could give your step sister all the things your father could have, had he taken her back to Bombay; to her rightful home. It was a while, though, before she was well and truly settled. First, we had to heal her.

Chapter Twenty-five
Healing

It seemed the story would take a while, thought Wadia, and he told the old woman to take all the time she needed. In a sense, they had already got a sense of closure, knowing that Elise had spent the last days of her life here, and that too, 'happily ever after,' as all stories should rightfully end. However, it was important to know the entire story, and he would listen to it patiently, even if that meant staying up till the wee hours of the morning. After they had all finished their chai, Toral told the old lady, whose name was Jasmine (she was also evidently Parsi, even though they hadn't asked her what her last name might be), that she would wash the cutlery in the kitchen and that was final. Unlike Mrs. Agashe, the graceful old woman happily acquiesced. Earlier on in the day, while the tea was being prepared, Toral had asked Jasmine how she managed to take care of such a big place (there was an upstairs, too) all by herself. And Jasmine had laughed and told her that no, she would go absolutely nuts if she had to maintain a place as large as this all on her own. She had a couple of maids that did the cooking and cleaning for her, and this was the one day in the week that they were on leave. Just like any other family in India, Toral thought. Ever so dependent on the help.

After Toral had washed the teacups, saucers and shiny silver spoons, and put them back neatly where they belonged (she had made a mental note of where they went when the old lady had taken them out), she settled back into the large, comfortable chair next to Jasmine's. The two men sat in front of the women.

"I just love what you've done with this place." Toral was always excited when she saw good homes; The White House had been one of them. And it wasn't only large houses, or houses on which tons of money had been splurged, that caught her attention. She loved houses that reflected minimalist sensibilities, like this one.

Jasmine broke into a laugh. "It's my father who should be credited with doing up this place." Gesturing with her hands to the space around her. "He wanted to bring a very British feel to the space. After all, his aunt had left him a lovely British house. He had this place constructed a few months after he sold that place. Neither he nor my mum were interested in moving to Britain. Earlier, we lived in a modest three-bedroom apartment in the centre of town. The wooden floors and exteriors of this place were all my father's idea. He wanted the house to blend with the forest, you know.

It most certainly did, thought Toral. They had almost missed it completely. If it hadn't been for her daddy's catlike vision, they wouldn't be here at all. "What happened to him, if you don't mind me asking?" The old woman shrugged it off. "It's perfectly all right, dear. It's been a while. What can I say? It was an accident. He had been returning from a trip overseas and on the highway, his car collided head on with a truck. I was very little at the time, but mum was completely devastated. After seeing Princess, though, she came to believe with all her heart that no matter what kind of pain you were going through, there was always someone hurting more than you. And you think these children don't understand a thing about the way the world works, what is *good* and what is *bad*, but they probably know better than us. Can you believe she didn't talk a whole year after she came to our home? We really thought we could get her to speak in a few days... days that turned into a year."

Her eyes brimmed with tears, and Wadia found himself fight back tears himself. This story had to have a happy ending. Hadn't the old woman said something about a 'happily ever after'? As if sensing his thoughts, Jasmine continued.

"You see, in the time following the incident, Princess was akin to an injured sparrow one might be nursing back to health; extremely fragile, untrusting. In the beginning, it seemed as though she might give up and never come out of her room. Forget getting out of her room; she was locked in the prison of her own mind." She looked wistfully out the window before continuing, "In the beginning she never talked. But once she started, she couldn't stop. She had an energy we just couldn't keep up with."

She took a long pause then, and said, "Would you like to see her bedroom?"

They took the stairs that led to the upstairs section of the house. Wadia thought back to what Jasmine had said about the house incorporating British sensibilities; while that might very well hold true, there was something very American about the house, too. Perhaps it was the choice of furniture – striking and modern. Elise's room was the first one to the right at the top of the stairs. Jasmine seemed to be fiddling with the handle to the door of that room, without luck. She shook her head then, as though she had forgotten that the door had been locked; then, she went further down towards what was undoubtedly the master bedroom, and came back holding a single key.

"I don't show this room to anyone who visits," she said, before putting the key into the lock and proceeding to turn it. "Of course, the cleaning lady opens and locks it every single day. But otherwise, we keep it shut." Wadia noticed she said 'we.' Might she be referring to her dead mother? Her father? Elise? Or perhaps the four of them together? Plenty of times people referred to the ones they loved and lost as though they might never have passed away. Just like he believed his mother still lived in his bungalow, watching over him and perhaps even Velkar when he visited (just to see if that naughty boy dropped any food on her precious carpet while he ate; which he did every single time, the sloppy Maharashtrian).

The room they entered was every little girl's dream. It was a literal 'White Wonderland,' with toys on shelves attached to the walls, that didn't seem to clutter the room in the least. The one thing that stood out for Wadia, though, was a white piano in a corner of the room by the solitary window. He looked at Jasmine and said, "Did she play the piano?" He realized it was a foolish question the moment he uttered it.

And Jasmine didn't say a word; she merely walked to the piano, and started playing it. Wadia was stunned when he saw this woman who had been a complete stranger to them only moments ago, play the one song that had haunted him all his life, Für Elise, to near perfection (Wadia always clung to the belief that nobody on earth could play any musical composition as perfectly as its creator). And when she was finished, she seemed completely refreshed, as though she might have just stepped out of the shower. The room was filled with light that wafted in from the single window that didn't have a curtain (much like the single window in Wadia's living room, where his old piano had found its rightful place after all these years). Jasmine noticed Toral staring out the window then, at the lake beyond. She decided to go on with the telling of her story.

"The very first day we moved Princess into this room that was erstwhile mine, she pointed towards this very window, as though she might be scared of it somehow. She was trembling, the poor girl, and it took us a while to figure out that she was actually terrified of the curtain that covered the window. So, we had it removed that very day. How she cried when the carpenter came into the room. We had to shift her to the guest bedroom downstairs, which had become my bedroom ever since Elise had moved in, until he had finished his work and left the house. Understandably, she had lost the ability to trust anyone. To be more precise, to trust *men*. In that case she would be pretty secure here. It was only me and my mum, after all, and the cleaning lady and cook, who were also women. Everything changed that one day in summer when she heard Für Elise play on the radio...

Her voice trailed off before it stopped, as it might as well have, to give Wadia some time to process what he had just heard.

"There was just something that piece of music did to her, in a way I cannot describe. It drained away her sadness; in only a few moments she came alive, like a little boy chasing a butterfly in his garden."

Wadia was stunned. Her parents had obviously named their daughter Elise after the one song they loved the most. Had they played it for her? Where had she even heard the song? As though reading his mind, Jasmine went on.

"It was the strangest thing. When I asked Princess where she had listened to this enchanting piece of music, after seeing her highly palpable excitement, of course, she said it had been when she was 'in the darkness.' At first I thought she might be referring to the house in Udvada where she had lived all her life, of course, but there was just something about the way she said those words – *in the darkness,* to be precise, that played on my mind for the longest time. And then, one day, when we had finally bought a piano for her and even hired a local tutor who travelled five days a week from Udvada to Pardi just to teach her music, I posed the very same question to her once again. Had someone played the wonderfully enchanting piece for her on a record player while she had been 'in the darkness,' as she had described it? Or had she heard it on the radio, perhaps? And then she told me, "It was dark and I was locked up. This music was the only thing I can remember. And you might think I'm crazy, but I can assure you that this girl was referring to the time she spent in her mother's womb."

The three visitors to the town of Pardi were at a loss for words. Princess' parents, the erstwhile Dhunji Wadia and Petunia Shah, had been almost manic where it came to playing this wonderful, haunting piece by Beethoven in their individual capacities. However, due to unforeseen circumstances shortly after they met, they simply couldn't introduce this child of theirs to a piece of music they desperately wanted to forget with all their hearts. Could it really be possible, that this bit of music the little girl had heard whilst in her mother's womb, might just have created an unforgettable impression on her young mind? Was it her only refuge while she was confined in that dark place? An escape that she would hark back to time and again, first in Udvada and then, several years later, in Pardi?

"How was she after that?" It was Toral. She wanted to know. They all did, and it seemed as though Jasmine had all the time. She had a beatific smile on her face now, as she looked out the large window through which the sun shone even more fiercely. And it wasn't only the sun that lit up her face; it was the glow from within.

"After that accidental introduction to Für Elise, it was as though the most beautiful chapter in her life began. We had the most wonderful time together, my mother, she, and I. We called ourselves 'The Three Musketeers,' and played board games and painted and did silly things like dance by the lake without music. Ah! The twenty years I spent with Princess were the best."

"How did she die?" It was Toral, asking the one question none of them wanted to, nevertheless one that was necessary to get that final sense of closure.

Jasmine looked out the window for a few moments, seemingly listless.

"She just passed away peacefully in her sleep. One morning, mum went into her room to wake her up. We never used an alarm clock, and whenever I or Princess wanted to wake up early for some reason or the other, it was mum who would rouse us. And you might think it pretty strange to want to wake up early in a house where you have nothing much to do except read books and look out across a vast expanse of lake, but there was so much we did. In any case, ten years later I lost my mum."

"Thanks for all you did for her," Toral said, and she started weeping profusely. Velkar got up from his chair, went up to her and placed his hand on her shoulder. It was difficult to see his daughter like that. Who would have thought he would find himself in a house by a lake in a town called Pardi that he had never heard of, with a girl who he didn't know a mere few days ago, but was now his daughter?

Jasmine went up to Toral next, took her in her arms and hugged her, as the silent sobbing became a piercing wail that rang shrilly through the air. Jasmine burst into tears too. As for Wadia, he remained seated where he was, by the edge of the bed, not moving an inch. He wanted to cry, but couldn't find the tears. When Toral had composed herself sufficiently, Jasmine proposed that they go and sit on the terrace outside her bedroom. Wadia insisted they leave, saying she had been more than hospitable and they had overstepped their time in this house, but Jasmine would have none of it.

"You all are like family to me now, she said. I would love to offer you lunch, but my maid is not in today and I'm eating yesterday's leftovers. Come, humour this old lady's wishes, will you?"

It had been hard to say no to such a nice old lady. Especially when she had told them everything they had been dying to hear. When she led the way through her tastefully done up bedroom to the large veranda where they now sat in the cutest chairs Toral had ever seen, Wadia whispered to the others that the conversation pertaining to Elise was now well and truly over, and neither of them should attempt to bring the subject up again. If there were anything pertinent left to say, Jasmine would make it a point to tell them. And so, they chatted about everything from Jasmine's love of gardening to the things there were to do in Pardi (apparently there were none, apart from spending time at the lake). At the end of what must have been an hour or so, Toral told Jasmine that they really needed to be taking their leave. After all, they had a long drive back to Mumbai. This time round, Jasmine acquiesced. And, after a long and tearful goodbye, they finally left the town of Pardi.

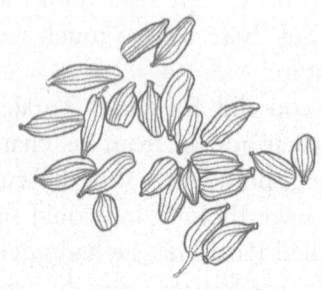

Chapter Twenty-six
Pain

The drive back to Bombay had been silent for the most part. *Mission Find Elise* had been a success; albeit with a minor hiccup. Of course that hiccup had in part been responsible for shedding light on yet more information pertaining to poor Elise. Not that what they had uncovered had any sort of comforting effect on them, though. On the contrary, it only served to stoke their angst. Poor Elise had to be taken away to an unknown place and forced to live yet another 'pariah' life. In hindsight, though, Toral felt that it was the best possible thing that could have happened to the young woman. Even though she had been cruelly snatched from the one place she felt she truly belonged, and whisked away to yet another. Because it was to a wonderful home that housed two wonderful souls, - and there she spent the remainder of her life. And yes, there was no doubt in her mind that Jasmine's mother had been an incredible woman, too; and their Elise had found her 'happy ending,' after all.

"I forgot to ask where she had been cremated." It was Wadia, although he didn't say this with any trace of eagerness. While it was widely known that in earlier times the bodies of dead Parsis were hung in wells for vultures to feast on, that practice had been abolished quite some time ago and there was a strong possibility that Elise's body had been cremated instead of being left to be devoured by a bird. No, of course she would have been buried in some crematorium in Pardi; why did they not think of even asking Jasmine where that might be, so that they might pay their last respects to her?

Over the course of their conversation, Jasmine had told them that when Percy Wadia had left Elise in their hands, her mother had thanked him for giving her a gift of such great magnitude, but instructed him firmly that no matter what, he was never to be seen in Pardi ever again. The last thing she wanted was for the girl to have mixed feelings about who was looking out for her, and if Percival Wadia were relinquishing his responsibility to take care of his half-sister, he must do so completely or not at all. In that case, what was his car doing, parked somewhere alongside a field in Pardi, a few years later? The very same car that had been passed down to him by his father, Dhunji (a car that also briefly belonged to Rustom Wadia before he had to sell it for scrap)? Now, Percy Wadia had told his son on numerous occasions that he was going to Pardi on business, but had that merely been a ruse? To ensure his son never found out about the dark secret he was hiding?

Might his father be driving all the way to Pardi every year, trying to get in touch with his sister, and being refused the grace of her presence every single time? Or might he merely be content standing by the lake near the house, catching a glimpse of her as she played in that clearing in the woods? And then crying in his car, knowing he would never get to meet his sister again? Was he even sorry for what he had done? Like his father, he had probably been *ashamed that she was born abnormal*. There was no other explanation.

They stopped at a dhaba along the way. Velkar needed his cup of chai, and to use the restroom. No wonder he kept going to the restroom, what with the copious amounts of chai he consumed, Wadia thought. Toral said she would use a restroom later, when they were closer to Mumbai. She didn't quite think the toilets on the highway would be clean. In fact, that was the very reason Wadia had ensured that he used the bathroom in Jasmine's place: so that he wouldn't have to use it for a while.

The chai was pretty substandard, although the Khari biscuits they had ordered to complement it, absolutely delectable. They took Wadia back to his childhood; when he would dip those wafer-like biscuits in his tea and relish the combination of 'chai-infused khari.' Needless to say, some of the biscuit matter would accumulate at the bottom of the teacup, and he would scrape it out with a spoon, happily relishing the soft mass that was undoubtedly the best part of the entire experience.

"So, it's back to the restaurant for you, now?" Wadia asked Toral in a matter-of-fact way. Perhaps all that was left, was to make mundane conversation. She was sitting opposite the two men, stirring her cup of chai lackadaisically.

"I guess. What else is there to do?"

"Don't say that, dear." It was Velkar. "This weekend, you're coming to stay with me and mummy, right?"

A tear trickled down Toral's cheek. Both Rustom and Velkar got up in their seats, concerned.

"Please sit, both of you. Like Elise, I too don't have my real parents around me any more. However, I have a family, who will look after me. Like Jasmine and her mother looked after Elise." And that solitary tear gave way to an avalanche of grief, and the young boy waiter passing by stopped in his tracks for a moment, before deciding better of it and making his way back to the kitchen. 'Was this what excessive happiness did to you?' Move you to tears? There must be a really fine line between happiness and sadness, Wadia felt. A thought struck him then. All those years, when he had seemingly 'cried' listening to Für Elise, might those in fact have been 'tears of happiness'?

It had been a tearful parting, that included Toral collapsing into Velkar's arms as he stood outside 404 Juhu, her sobbing once again, while he stood like a helpless lamb. At least, that's how Velkar appeared in Wadia's eyes. It was afternoon and the restaurant was open. A young man dressed in starched black shirt and black trousers (that seemed the exact shade of black as the shirt), undoubtedly the valet driver, stared at Toral as she wept. The manager from the other day (yes, that hopeless manager, stood at the entrance staring at his boss, seemingly unsure whether he should intervene and ask her if everything was all right, or if it weren't. Why did people have to do that? Say stupid things like 'Are you all right?' when it was clear they weren't.

Velkar stifled a sob as he drove home. None of this melodrama for me, thought Wadia. It wasn't as though he were insensitive; not in the least. He simply couldn't deal with public outbursts of emotion. Never wash your dirty linen in public, was an adage he had always stuck by.

Back home, he was hit with that feeling of emptiness once again. The feeling that had plagued him for the better part of the last ten years. Only these last few days had seemed to take it away. In his fervent search for closure, he had no idea it would be exactly that which would leave him feeling vacant. That's what people who do insane things like climbing Mount Everest must feel, he thought. Go back home and realise there is no mountain to climb any more.

Ramukaka had prepared a simple meal of dal-chawal. Wadia had called him beforehand and insisted he wanted nothing fancy, after politely declining Toral's invitation to have lunch at her restaurant. It was a good thing Anil had refused as well. From what he had observed, she could use some alone time. As for him, well, he needed space from Velkar.

Although their trip hadn't been that long, it had been both emotionally and physically draining for all three of them. Perhaps the fatigue had been triggered by their severe emotional exhaustion. Even though they had discovered that Elise had spent the last few years of her life happy, they couldn't ignore that one dark incident that had tainted her life's journey. Nonetheless, they couldn't really complain; she had been happy for the most part.

He thought then, had Elise known she was 'different from the others'? He had read somewhere that children with Down's syndrome, tended to know they had special needs; that the others were not like them on the inside, apart from 'not looking like them on the outside.' In spite of that, there had been nothing that could stop her. What an amazingly brave girl she had been.

That night Wadia slept like a baby. It was probably the tiredness, he thought when he woke up and saw the time had stretched well past nine in the morning, the precise time for his breakfast. This time he went down a little before ten. He glanced at his phone. It was 9:59. He waited until it was 10 a.m. sharp before sitting down at the head of the table (technically there was only one head as he had had the chair at the opposite end removed; there could be only one king, after all) and ringing a bell (the kind they had at the Willie to call the waiters). In a few minutes Ramukaka got his breakfast to the table. It was poached eggs with toast (butter on the side), one of his favourites, served with a piping hot cup of coffee.

Ramukaka knew the drill. Lunch would be at 2 p.m. sharp (instead of the regular one o'clock) There were very few instances when Wadia had made it late to breakfast, and even fewer times when he had been early for it. Needless to say, the silent instructions were followed: he would have his lunch exactly four hours from the time breakfast had commenced. Dinner, though, would be at 8 p.m. sharp. That bit was unchanged. When the late Percy Wadia had been around, dinner would be served at 6 p.m. every evening without fail, even on the days when he was travelling, and Rustom had stuck to this schedule until his father passed away and he discovered the marvel of creating one's own schedule. Needless to say, once he had carefully curated his own schedule, there was no tinkering with it. For instance, he would have a couple of drinks (happy hour would commence at 7 p.m. sharp, the second drink not before 7.30 p.m.), followed by dinner at 8 p.m. (sharp, of course). Such a stickler for time, was good old Wadia.

Post dinner, of course, it was time to indulge in some Cognac (Remy Martin only, no other brand would do), served in a precious glass his father would drink from. It was one glass only and it rarely went to a couple (if it did it was only on those occasions when he had had a single whisky before dinner – the subconscious rule was, never more than three drinks at dinnertime). Then, he would retreat to his study and spend a good hour there, before retiring to his room at 10. Lights in the Wadia household would be off at 10.30 p.m. sharp, and he would wake up at 8.30 a.m. every morning. He made sure to set an alarm, of course, as there was no way his schedule was going to be tinkered with. Yes, a good ten hours was what Rustom needed. He thought it one of the strangest things when people said they could get by with only a few hours of sleep. Especially older people (some people his age spent five hours tops in their beds). But then, he wasn't one of those people.

Of what use was it, he thought then, to be sitting at the head of a table when the rest of the chairs were empty? It was as though he were the king of an empire that had no subjects. Look at Velkar; he now had someone to carry forth his legacy. Well, not quite, because who on earth would want to carry forth the legacy of a mechanical engineer? Okay, at least his friend would have someone who would carry memories of him into the future. What about *him*? Who did *he* have?

After breakfast he went straight to the garden outside. This was a clear anomaly; the last time this had happened was when his master had gone to Gujarat, thought Ramukaka. He dared not ask him why he had gone there, of course; all he knew was, it had not been a holiday. People came back happy from holidays. He thought briefly to the time when Wadia Sir and he had been the best of friends (he never called him Wadia Sir back then, only Rustom, of course, like all best friends call each other – by their first names). And now, he served him. He certainly didn't regret it, though. Serving was in his blood. If he had to live another life, he would do it all over again. He wasn't a slave, after all, and what's more, his master most generously gave him whatever food he ate himself. Needless to say, Cognac was off limits (as was the Japanese single malt, of course). Not that he minded in the least. After all, Ramukaka had not touched a drop of alcohol in his life. Looking at his master now, he thought that perhaps in order to cope he might have to resort to becoming a full blown alcoholic: one moment it seemed as though he had lost his bearings, a short while later, he was on top of the world.

Wadia himself was lost in deep thought, looking at the tiny graves in the garden, that belonged to his darling pets. The very pets who had one day broken free and by the grace of God were found only a day later in Khar market. The most remarkable thing was, his late parrot, Polly, had made a point of telling him to his face that keeping her in the cage was tantamount to keeping a slave in one's household, even though she didn't do any work (obviously). There was simply no escaping the fact that he had clipped her wings and enslaved her, and that was a wicked, wicked thing to have done.

How the memories came flooding back. In the final years before they died, Polly had learned to fly again. She told Wadia (in a vocabulary as rich as anyone who is fluent in English possesses) that when she was on *The Outside*, which was 'outside this home,' she had discovered she couldn't fly. And for a while she had clung on to that belief, until she flapped her wings in all earnestness one day, long after they had come back home, and *voila!* she could fly once more. When Wadia saw her fly from one end of the living room to the other, he thought that she would be gone in a mere few moments. After all, in those days they kept the window (where the piano currently was) open almost all the time. But she hadn't gone anywhere. Would you believe it?

What would his darling pets have thought if he played Für Elise for them? That was what he wondered, as he walked towards the back door of the kitchen that led into the garden. Perhaps they would make fun of him, you never know. In any case, they were long gone now, and he was all alone. Even though he lived with a servant who was in the house for most of the day, and only retired to his quarters at night. But nobody who ever lived with a servant, even if that servant stayed well within the precincts of the house all day long, would say they 'had company.'

Wadia realized right then and there, that he didn't really have to sit all alone in his house; he needed to get a move on with his life. While playing Für Elise on the piano was nice, he couldn't possibly do it all day long, could he? Did he really have to read each and every section of the newspaper? He thought back to the last ten years of his life. They had gone by in a blur. What had he done, all those wasted years? He hadn't even gone to the club. The club! Why didn't he think about it before? He would regularly go to the club in the years before his pets had died; indeed, before he even had any pets at all. All of a sudden he was beset by a sense of excitement. The waiters at the

Willie would be so happy to see him. On second thoughts, perhaps some of them might not even be there any more.

But what would he even do there? The answer to that was pretty simple. He would sit in the library and read some magazines, until it was lunchtime, when he would be downstairs by the lawns where his mumma had died, wolfing down that lip-smacking eggs Kejriwal.

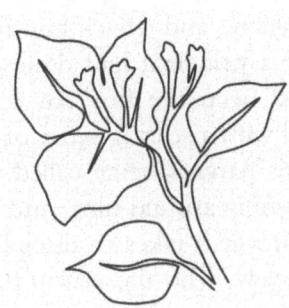

Chapter Twenty-seven
Wadia Goes to The Willie

The lady in the library on the first floor at The Willie hadn't recognised Rustom, or she was doing a pretty good job at hiding the fact that she was head over heels in love with him. Wadia was a little distraught by the changed behaviour of the woman, until she came closer and he saw it wasn't the same lady, after all. He was just about to ask her what had happened to the striking old woman he used to flirt with (he wouldn't ask her in those exact words, of course, he would simply ask her what had happened to the lady who had once worked there), but then thought better of it. This woman looked as stern as the principal of his alma mater that had stood by the sea in Mahim (it still did), and the last thing he wanted was for her to fish out a cane from somewhere, and whack him below the knees on the back of his legs, like his principal had done one day when he had played truant. That had been the first day in young Rustom's life, when he had been filled with a searing sense of shame.

He remembered his parents being called to school much earlier than that, when he was only around nine, and his mummy telling the principal, "You do whatever it takes to discipline him, Mr. Mackay." The very same Mr. Mackay, who dressed in the garb of a priest, but was the devil incarnate (you could see it in his dead eyes). And it seemed that Mr. Mackay had taken her words rather literally, and it would only be a couple of months after the day his parents had met Mr. Mackay, that he had been caned in front of all the boys during the school assembly. How ironic in a school that prided itself on instilling the strongest set of values in its children — that violence was never the answer! His mother had passed away only a month before; if she had been around, nothing of this sort would have ever been allowed to happen.

That day after he had been caned, he had gone home and played the piano with such a fervour that it seemed as though Mrs. Braganza might just fall off her chair. When he had finished, she had been speechless. The best part was, after playing the piano, all the anger he had felt towards his principal for having humiliated him in front of the entire school, had dissolved completely. In its place was a fluidity he had never quite experienced before. It was as though, by that vicious act of caning (and the humiliation that went with it, needless to say), he had somehow been set free. It had allowed him to enter a zone he had never previously inhabited; a zone he would keep returning to every single time he played the piano thereafter. One wherein the entire world was blocked out. It was that very day that his music reached another level altogether. Later on, when they had finished their class, Mrs. Braganza had asked him what had happened to him, that had made him play the piano with such intensity.

"Life," he told her.

Wadia was seated in a corner of the library, engrossed in the read of his choice, *Time* magazine. He always liked to be well informed, but he knew he could never be as highly informed as Toral. That girl knew everything about everything. He glanced at his watch. It was 12.45 p.m. How time had passed. It had been lovely to sit here and read, without being interrupted. Hardly anyone ever visited the library, come to think of it. How on earth could people let such great books and other reading material just 'sit,' when they could definitely find some time to come out here and enjoy a good read? It certainly beat going to the bar in the afternoon for a drink, which was what a lot of the old-timers in this club did. Those bozos would indulge in a drink or two in the evening too, in their respective homes. Perhaps they didn't tell their wives that they drank in the afternoon as well. Conversely, the set of bozos that made it to the bar in the evening, undoubtedly had a drink in the afternoon in their homes. Were the lives of some people really so sad they had to drink twice a day?

When Wadia finally went down and ordered his favourite eggs Kejriwal, he realized he was the only person sitting alone at a table. Occasionally he had caught a glimpse of people seated at other tables, people who seemed to look at him with eyes full of pity. They were probably thinking, 'Poor old man. His wife must have passed away a few years ago, now he's all alone.' Reminiscent of that person in the movie 'Up' that he had watched, and barely tolerated. He felt like getting up, walking to each one of those people, and saying, 'You bloody dolts! I have been alone all my life, and there is nothing I'd rather be than alone. So, enjoy your butter chicken or whatever it is you're having with that stuffed nan, and let me enjoy my eggs Kejriwal in peace.'

And those eggs were truly fantastic; just the way he remembered them. They must have the same cooks, he thought, although they would be pretty old by now, considering the number of years he had been coming here to have his favourite dish. Either that, or they had passed the recipe down to their juniors. The waiter was now indulging in some genial banter with him. He was asking him where his friend Jimmy Mistry was. Jimmy and Delna had been regulars at the Willie, and Wadia would often accompany them to the club, whenever he felt like playing a game of cards or perhaps having a drink in the bar. He had stopped driving a long time ago, and now balked at the idea of keeping a driver. What would the driver drive, in any case? He had sent his vintage car to the scrapyard a long time ago (a shame, considering the fact that it had been quite the rage in the day), and he wasn't going to buy a new car now. You got a driver for a car; not the other way round.

Thankfully, he reflected, his piano had not been scrapped. Not that he wouldn't have got another piano if he hadn't found his old one in that shop – after all, what were the chances of him finding it?. The fact was, he needed a piano and he would have most certainly purchased another. But it wouldn't have quite been the same, would it?

Yes, thought Wadia on the rather bumpy ride back from Haji Ali to Bandra in a rickety black and yellow taxi (okay, perhaps not quite as rickety as Velkar's van had been – the one that had surprisingly made it all the way from Bombay to Udvada and then further beyond to Pardi, before arriving back in one piece); yes, he might be attached to a lot of things, his piano clearly top of that list, but he never really held onto them, the way others held onto their possessions. He had seen his friends make a great fuss over a mere dent in their cars, blaming their drivers and threatening to take the money that would stem from their repair (a pittance to them, but a big deal for their drivers) from their salaries. As though they could take the money they saved with them to the afterlife.

In the evening, Rustom looked lovingly at the grand piano in the hall, the one that had played such a pivotal role in his childhood years, and he saw Ramukaka hovering around him, looking at him and the piano alternately, as though to imply what he couldn't quite say. Something had not been right with his master ever since he had returned from his trip to Gujarat. While there wasn't anything necessarily wrong with him (he had, after all, gone to the club after years, and that in itself proclaimed change of the good kind), it still seemed as though there was something missing. At least, missing in the version of his master from twenty years ago. The time he had spent with his parrot and his cat had been the best years of his master's life. Of course, there had been that brief burst of happiness a few days ago, after he had been reunited with his piano. And Wadia's brief flirtation with it had awakened something inside Ramu that he had not believed could have existed at all. As though it might have a life of its own.

As Wadia sipped his whisky, he stared at the piano that now would be relegated to being a mere showpiece, just like all the other artefacts in the house. There was all that lovely china, that his mother had elaborately selected on her solo trip to Paris, that was neatly showcased in the large glass cabinet behind the dining table. Then, there were those sculptures one might find at an art gallery; the ones you look at, trying to decipher what they might mean. Like a half-eaten hand or a ball that wasn't quite round. Not that he struggled to find meaning in what any of these pieces might convey (of course, one's perception of what a certain piece of art might seem to convey might be completely different from what the artist is meaning to imply). His parents had also been most fascinated by the several objets d'art they had collected on their travels over the years, to various exotic locales – artifacts that found their place all over the sprawling Wadia household in Bandra. The young Rustom had accompanied his parents on several trips, but a lot of those vacations had been when he was really small, and he couldn't remember the minute details of those trips, except for some random flashes of memory that burst to the surface every now and then. Certainly not pertaining to the moments when the artefacts or china were bought, though.

The one trip Wadia clearly remembered was the time they went to Mauritius, right before Lizzie Wadia passed away. He remembered sitting in the clear blue water amidst the corals with his mother, gazing blankly at the horizon, while his father lounged in the deck chair on the sand a few metres away, nursing his beer. That was the most powerful memory he had of his mother, and he felt his subconscious had emblazoned that memory in his mind even more firmly than it had the others, because it represented exactly how his mother made him feel – calm, while chaos abounded in the world around him.

As for his father, well, he did love him dearly, but he was always scared of him in a strange sort of way. He knew that if his mother had still been alive, his daddy would have never had the guts to give away the piano. Alas! His mother had not lived to see him play it. How proud she would have been. After all, she played the violin brilliantly; his mind harked back to the times when she would play it when guests were over. How she had everyone enthralled by the way she played, himself included. He knew that if there were ever a reason he loved music, it was because of the several times he had been entranced by his mummy playing the violin, either at dinner parties when guests came over, or for Rustom specially, when he was younger. All of a sudden his mind's eye went back to the sight of his father dabbing his mouth with his napkin at dinnertime, while Rustom and his mother were in the midst of having an animated conversation that was related to him taking a shot at playing a musical instrument, Percival Wadia not saying a word, not even wanting to. It was only all these years later, that he finally understood why his father was so averse to his love for, and pursuit of, music.

After dinner Wadia found himself in his study, reading a book he hadn't touched in years. It was *The Fountainhead*, by Ayn Rand. He marvelled at Ayn Rand's mind. Howard Roark was most certainly one of his most favourite characters in a work of fiction. And he didn't realise how much time had gone by, until he glanced at his cell phone and saw that it was nearly eleven. This was the first time he had entered his study after the grand old piano had returned home, and it seemed a bit strange to find himself here without playing Für Elise on the record player. But then, he didn't need to, any more.

It was rather strange that he would always end up reading a few pages before the point he had left off, and it was only after he had read several lines, that he would come to that realization. In any case, Ayn Rand ensured that her readers read the same lines over and over again, to garner a better understanding of what she was trying to say. And you could never have a sufficient understanding of what Ayn Rand was trying to say.

As he placed the book back, he gazed at his record player. And just like that, he caved in. Who had he been kidding? Of course he wanted to listen to Für Elise; the last time he had listened to it was before he had gone to Gujarat.

And so, he placed the record gingerly onto the record player, and let it spin. As the music played, he drifted off into a faraway place. He was in Udvada, and Diva was dancing at a ball with several Parsis, young and old alike, one by one. Dressed in a beautiful white silk dress, she looked absolutely radiant. If Wadia could have seen his face right then and there, as he sat in his large leather armchair, soaking in the music that permeated the very fabric of his soul, he would have observed it had an ethereal glow. Then, all of a sudden, he didn't know what hit him. Diva was lying in bed, bloody sheets over her, listless expression on her face. He burst into tears. That profusion of happiness only a few moments earlier, had been replaced by an overwhelming sadness. No! He couldn't get himself to think of her that way – but it was useless fighting it. He continued to descend down the spiral for the next several moments, until finally, he saw her as an angel by the lake in Pardi. Her face radiated a surreal sense of contentment; as though she had somehow discovered the secret of life. And Rustom held his hand out to her, and she took it, and he was instantly comforted. There was no joy now; neither was there any sadness. Instead, a feeling of serenity infused with calm detachment. He drifted away then, higher than his Cognac had ever taken him, remaining that way long after the music stopped playing, as though the vision had worked like an opiate on his mind.

Chapter Twenty-eight
La Familia

Wadia's hands trembled as he tried to take a family picture Toral had insisted he click, of her with her new mummy and daddy, in his living room by the piano. He had invited the Velkars (three of them now, of course), insisting he would like to be the first to honour the new family. He had repeatedly asked Velkar over the phone the Saturday before last, what he would like to eat for lunch. Velkar said he would eat 'anything that had moved once when it had been alive.' That request had been easy to oblige. Not a day went by in this house without non-vegetarian food of any kind being served at every meal, with the exception of breakfast (a masala dosa or cornflakes was a rarity, but one that somehow sneaked its way into the breakfast menu on occasion). He had made it a point to personally invite Vidya, too, and she had happily accepted.

"To be fair, I'm not particularly fond of Parsi food, Rustom. However, I can bring along a dish if you like. Would you like some crabs slow-cooked in the curry you loved when you came over for lunch the other day? I can see to it that Velkar personally goes to the market for those khekadas. With the exception of that time we had you over for lunch, he has been ordering fish online, lazy lout that he is."

As promising as that crab curry sounded, Wadia had told Vidya there was no chance on earth she was going to be doing any cooking. After all, she was his guest, and guests in the Wadia household came empty-handed and left with a full stomach. Moreover, Ramukaka would be honoured to cook the meal for them, and deeply insulted if any of his guests brought along any food.

"Pardon me for asking, but isn't Ramu a bit old? It will be easier on him if I just made a slow-cooked curry for the occasion." It was difficult arguing with women. They never seemed to give up. And 'slow-cooked'? Is that your newfound daughter's influence rubbing off on you?

But of course he had objected the second time round, too. He told Vidya that Ramukaka might be old, but he was still going strong, and if she really insisted on bringing something for Sunday lunch, it should be any dessert of her choice. Dessert sat on the border of meals; like they didn't really belong there. Even if the dessert Vidya brought turned out to be outstanding, nobody (Toral included) would really remember it when they talked about the fabulous lunch (of course it would be) they had had at Wadia's house; it was always the main course that truly mattered. That was why restaurants often outsourced their desserts; they didn't really matter enough for the in-house chefs to make them on their own. In the end, it had been decided that Ramukaka would cook a nice curry with chicken (that had moved once when it had been alive) and some okra (Vidya's favourite vegetable, although Wadia couldn't stand the bloody stuff, for the life of him). Little did Wadia know then, that he would soon have to strike a similar kind of conversation with Toral, who said that she would absolutely not accept his invitation, gracious as it were, if Rustom didn't allow her to bring a couple of starters (in the end, she brought four). Nevertheless, Ramukaka did have the honour of making the highly coveted 'main course.' There was good reason they called it 'main.'

Wadia showed the picture he had taken on his camera phone, of the three Velkars, to Toral for her approval. She had rejected the last three he had taken of them, including one Ramukaka had inadvertently bombed. Come on! It's just a bloody picture, Wadia had thought, as he had gone on to shoot the Velkars for what he had hoped would be the last time (luckily, it was). Then they all sat down, while the maidservant got out the starters. Not to the dining table; that was reserved for the mains.

"Can you please pass the fish fingers? They are really yummy." It was Velkar. Ordinarily, Wadia would think something to the tune of 'Why can't you get it yourself, bugger?' Now, he simply nodded gently, before reaching forward and passing the fish fingers that had been cooked in the kitchen of 404 Juhu, to Velkar Saheb.

At that moment Toral was in the kitchen, seeing if Ramukaka needed help with anything. If she had been in the living room, Velkar would have still asked Rustom for his help and not her, but she would most certainly have not let 'her Rustom' lift a finger. She had taken great pains to ensure that all the starters were taken out, and that each of them had a fork and spoon for the little plates they would be eating from. Furthermore, she had made cocktails for everyone (Velkar said he would never understand how she had got Vidya to have a drink – that too in the afternoon), and they were absolutely delicious (could you say that about a cocktail?), apart from being heady, of course. She came back into the living room from the kitchen, and asked everyone if they would like a repeat of her signature cocktail. They all replied in the negative, to which she said, "Okay. *I'm* having another," and then she proceeded to the bar and made her drink with the efficacy of Tom Cruise in the movie *Cocktail*. At least, that's what the movie buff Velkar thought. One look at Vidya and he knew she was drunk.

Toral had made them all bloody marys. Wadia often wondered how Christians could tolerate the fact that a drink had been gifted a name like that, and he thought about it again when Toral told them all that she made the *best bloody marys in town* (that didn't make it sound any less sacrilegious, of course). They had all agreed in an instant, for fear of dampening the enthusiasm with which she said it. He couldn't really speak for the others, but at least that was how he had felt. After all, he had absolutely no love for vodka. Or for Russia, for that matter. In the end, though, he had been mightily surprised. This superbly engineered bloody mary had made for a lovely Sunday afternoon drink. Earlier in the morning he had stocked his bar with two large bottles of London Pilsner beer for himself and Velkar, along with some bottles of Bacardi Breezer, that seemed to be the rage with women on a Sunday afternoon, according to his wine shop guy. His name was Mr. Patel (yes, another Mr. Patel), and he proudly claimed to have not touched a drop of alcohol in all his life (yes we get it, you do a pretty good job at resisting temptation).

An afternoon drink hit you pretty fast. Wadia knew that, which was exactly why he hadn't had a drink in the afternoon in ages. While the other glasses had been cleared by the lady who did all the sweeping and mopping in his house, Toral's second glass of bloody mary rested on the dining table, right next to her plate. After everyone had repeatedly assured him that the starters had been so filling they had no place for main course, Wadia used his trump card, saying that Ramukaka would feel hurt if they didn't partake of what he had so laboriously made for them – his famous chicken curry, of course! He had gone on to tell them further, as they were sampling his curry that they all found lip-smacking delicious (their being almost full notwithstanding), that he took an even greater sense of pride in making this curry than all the other dishes in this household, because it was his very own recipe, not merely one that had been passed down to him by Lizzie Memsaab.

The story of how this chicken curry had been conceived went like this. One day, Rustom was out for lunch. Before leaving, he instructed Ramukaka to prepare any chicken gravy he fancied for the evening dinner. When he had eaten what Ramukaka had made the following night, he had been absolutely blown away by just how delicious it was. He had expected Ramukaka to have prepared his mother's wonderful rendition of the classic Butter Chicken, but this was what he had got to savour instead – a dish he would lovingly call *Ramu's Special* from that night forward. Forget smacking one's lips, he actually *licked his fingers* clean. Even the lovely lobster thermidor he had relished at The Taj Mahal Palace with a friend earlier on in the day, hadn't come close to this wonderful creation. From that day onwards he made it a point to have Ramukaka's wonderful chicken curry at least once every month.

"Please, call Ramukaka out, will you?" Wadia loved the fact that Toral treated Ramukaka with the same level of respect that he did. On the other hand, Velkar and Vidya still referred to him as *Ramu*, like they had all these years, but Wadia didn't hold it against them. It wasn't as though they had any less respect for him. Well, perhaps a wee bit less, but that didn't matter. He called out to Ramukaka to come out then in his booming voice, a sound that led to Vidya dropping her spoon onto the floor. Velkar looked at her with a smirk, as though to insinuate that she was well and truly drunk. Vidya stared at him sternly, and he knew his wife had sobered up. Needless to say, so had he. Ramukaka appeared a few moments later, evidently distraught. Perhaps his chicken curry had not gone down all that well with one, or even worse, all of his master's guests. Maybe there was not enough salt in it – that in itself was enough to ruin an otherwise perfect dish. However, the look of sheer delight on all their faces set him completely at ease.

"Ramukaka, kya mast chicken banaya hai! Aapka Ramu Special mere restaurant ka speshal dish hona chahiye!" It was Toral. Vidya followed with a 'Farach changla chicken aahe." Ramukaka blushed right then and there, before running off to the kitchen after bowing first at Vidya, and then at Toral. Wadia noticed that Velkar hadn't said anything nice about Ramukaka's delectable dish . On second thought, he didn't have to; Vidya was his spokesperson in public.

"Is he Japanese?" Velkar asked no one in particular right about then, and the rest looked at him.

"You know, because of the way he bowed."

Lunch had indeed been a delightful affair. The plates had been cleared and Wadia asked them all if they would like to indulge in a bit of

Cognac. All of them politely declined. Vidya told him that it was best she stay away from his Cognac, otherwise they would have to rush her in a stretcher to the hospital because of an overdose of alcohol in her system. To this Wadia let out a large harrumph.

"Back in the day, the amount of alcohol we would consume, right, Velkar? In any case, I was just offering. My body isn't quite like it used to be either. I think I might just skip my evening drink, myself. Exactly how 'bloody' were those marys, Toral?" And Toral laughed before saying,

"Say, Rustom, let us hear you play Für Elise."

"Yes. It is like a slice of magic." It was Velkar.

"Magic? Barely. You give me way too much credit, Velkar."

"Oh no, no. Credit is where credit is due. I tell you, something happened to me when I heard you play the piano the last time I was here."

"Yes please, Rustom. I would love to hear it too." It was Vidya. Now how could he possibly say no, when all of them were eager to listen to him play?"

"Well okay, if you all insist," he said a bit sheepishly. He made his way to the piano slowly, as though he might be making his way on stage in front of thousands of people. And when he ran his fingers over the keys, a familiar feeling washed over him. Of being *in the zone*. The outside world dissolved. There were no spectators; he wasn't even in his house, as he let his fingers fly and played the tune that had haunted him all his life.

When he finished, there was pin-drop silence. His audience utterly captivated. Wadia caught a glimpse of his manservant, standing as though frozen, in the kitchen doorway. It took a couple of moments for Ramukaka to realize his master was staring at him, and pop out of his reverie. He slunk back guiltily, as though he might have consciously overheard a private conversation, and Wadia went back to his position in the large rocking chair, the proverbial 'head of the table' in this part of the living room. And 'head' he most certainly was, judging by the reverence with which the others gazed at him. It was none other than the head himself, who finally broke the silence.

"That was dedicated to Elise, the love of our lives." And then he sobbed. He cried like a baby and Velkar went up to him and took his best friend (to him, that is) in his arms, before Wadia found himself returning to the familiar feelings of calm and detachment he had experienced a couple of weeks ago. Vidya was squeezing Toral's left hand in hers. Needless to say, it wasn't easy for Toral, either. But it seemed as though she had got over it some time ago. She had let herself cry like a baby back in Pardi, something Wadia had not done. All the sadness that had been locked up inside of him seemed to have washed away now. All of a sudden he felt ashamed, for having allowed himself to cave in, in such dramatic fashion. Velkar seemed to sense this.

"You had to let it out sooner or later, Rustom. And I'm glad it was in our presence." That wasn't of much comfort to Wadia. He knew that internally, his friend would have enjoyed watching him wail like a baby.

"I think we had better get a move on." It was Vidya, and Wadia knew exactly why she had said it. She was used to having her siesta, like most old folks were. Toral said she would drop her parents off before heading back home. Wadia marvelled at the whole new life that had opened up for the Velkars, Toral included, of course. There would be several occasions when the three of them would be together and he wouldn't be around. And he had nobody at all. Being a bachelor had suited him for the longest time. Was he suddenly scared he was going to die soon, all alone?

After they had left, Wadia went back to his piano. Something had struck him as odd whilst he had been playing it. It seemed as though there had been dust on the lid, and perhaps even on the keys. Of course, that had nothing to do with Ramukaka's cleaning prowess; in fact, Ramukaka barely cleaned any more. The little dusting he did (on account of his OCD) was after the proper cleaning was already done. The cleaning baton had been passed on to Sushila, who was now in the kitchen, clearing up the mess left behind by the guests. Ordinarily Wadia would have never pointed out something of the sort to her. However, if there was one thing that always needed to be in the most pristine condition, it was his piano, his most coveted possession.

"Sushila!" he bellowed, in his booming voice. A couple of moments later Sushila appeared, Ramukaka closely following on her heels. Sushila did not seem to be perturbed in the least. Her master was a gentle giant, she knew that well. As for Ramukaka, well, he made it a point to be involved in anything related to household work. After all, the unofficial position he held in the Wadia household was that of 'manager.'

"Sushila, yeh piano pe dust hai re baba. Please, properly clean karo okay?" (Not even knowing if she understood the word 'dust.')

And Sushila merely turned to look at Ramukaka. What is this? Thought Wadia. Does she need permission from Ramukaka? Who is the master of the house, anyways? Ramukaka gestured to Sushila then, as though to tell her it was all right to say what she wanted to. And she said, "Saheb, aapka mehenga piano hai na? Agar usko kuch hua toh main jee nahi paungi." What rubbish – how would she not be able to live if anything happened to his piano? Besides, back in the day, they had another maid who had done the job perfectly well. And then a thought struck him. Why should he not clean his piano himself? It was, after all, the one thing in his household he truly loved with all his heart. To him it was just like that vintage car his dada would clean every single day with his bare hands. Not that he couldn't afford to employ a cleaner like all those Cattolics who lived nearby, did. He remembered his dada telling him one day, when he was in his teens, why he cleaned his car on his own, even in times when he was not in the best possible health, as he had been at that very moment (he had just recovered from a terrible bout of jaundice). He had told him that when you love something so much, you must take care of it yourself, in order to earn its respect. That had stuck with him.

And so he decided that tomorrow would be the day he would clean the piano. It was a Sunday, and it seemed like a fine day for cleaning. Perhaps he could make it a habit of cleaning his piano every Sunday? He could certainly make that work. After all, what did he do on a Sunday morning that was so important he couldn't spare a few minutes to take care of his priceless piano?

He instructed both Sushila and Ramukaka that henceforth, he would be undertaking the job of having the piano cleaned, once every week. Sushila seemed even more distraught, as though her master, fed up with her, was rubbing it in by telling her that he would be doing *her* job. It was only when he had narrated the story of how his father would clean his prized car every day, and not let anyone else touch it, that she finally understood, before folding her hands as a mark of respect and going back into the kitchen. Ramukaka gave his customary bow and followed her in silence. All he ever wanted was to see his master happy, and if he found that happiness in cleaning his piano, then so be it.

The next day, Wadia found himself thoroughly prepared. He had diligently researched how a piano had to be cleaned early the previous evening, thanks to *Google*, of course, and had sent Ramukaka off to the market to get the materials that would be required for cleaning his grand old piano. There were only two things he needed; a can of hydrogen peroxide spray, and plenty of cotton pads. After noting these down on a piece of paper lest he forget, Ramukaka had set off to the nearby market, in search of a store where he would get both. That was why Wadia loved Ramukaka; he did 'little' jobs for him, that amounted to 'a lot.'

A short while later Ramukaka returned from the market with a can of hydrogen peroxide that came with a spray mechanism, and a large packet of cotton pads. These would last Wadia a couple of months, if not more. He had already decided that after breakfast the next day, he would clean his piano for the very first time.

Relax, Wadia, it's just a piano, he told himself, as he began what he had decided would be a most clinical job. And so, elaborately he cleaned, right from the casing and the lid, to the keyboard and strings. Finally it was time for the pedals. He had noticed that while he had been cleaning the piano, the experience had seemed therapeutic. Like he was in a spa somewhere, completely removed from the world. Somewhat like when he played Für Elise, but not quite.

And then, something happened. While he was in the midst of cleaning the third pedal, he felt something underneath it. Some sort of paper, taped to its underside. He traced his fingers across the contours of both the tape as well as the paper underneath it. What could it possibly be? All of a sudden he retracted his hand and sat upright. He looked towards the kitchen. There was nobody there. Ramukaka had gone to the market, this time for veggies, and Sushila was probably cleaning the toilets at this very moment (she scrubbed them thoroughly every Sunday).

A few moments later he shook his head. Really, Wadia? Is it that secretive that you have to hide it from anyone? For all you know, it's just something that has been pasted beneath by the manufacturer; something they forgot to take off. And so he reached down again, and with a deft move, ripped off the tape along with whatever it held, and held it up to the sunlight that filtered through the window.

On closer inspection, it was a photograph. Of a large grey stone in the middle of what seemed to be a backyard. On closer scrutiny, Wadia saw the stone bore the name *Elise*. The backyard was one he recognised well. His very own.

Chapter Twenty-nine
Fragility

When he woke up, Wadia found himself surrounded by a few faces; some of which he knew, and others he didn't. There was Toral and Velkar and Vidya, a young doctor and nurse. He got up with a start. He was in a hospital!

"You'd all better explain what I'm doing here," he said then in his resounding voice, as though he could prove that he had absolutely no reason to be here. Right then the doctor, who clearly looked too young to be an actual doctor – must be something they called a *resident* – came up to him, took his hand in his and said, in the calmest voice he could possibly muster, "Relax, Rustom uncle. We don't want your blood pressure to go off the charts, now, do we?"

"What bloody blood pressure? I've never had a problem in all my life. And I'm not your uncle, mind you."

The thing was, Wadia hated hospitals. He had hated them ever since when only a kid, he had badly hurt his knee upon landing on a rock in a field while playing football. His mother had rushed him to the Emergency Ward of the nearest hospital (he couldn't be sure, but it seemed like it was this very hospital), and he had been terrified seeing people in white coats all around him, who were treating him as though he might have had a heart attack. After all, his mother was a philanthropist and this hospital, one of her charities. In the end he had returned home with a large bandage on his knee. All this after they had rushed into the emergency room as though the little Rustom might have needed a ventilator.

When it was clear to Wadia that he would not be getting a satisfactory response from anyone, he made as though to get up and leave. That's when the nurse placed her hand on his arm, and squeezed it gently, slightly pushing him back (What the hell?) as though to say he would be doing nothing of the sort. Of course there would be none other than a woman commissioned for this task. They knew men didn't fight ladies. If it had been that resident doctor who had placed his arm on his shoulder, why, he would have flung him against the wall on the other side of the room!

"You can't bloody keep me here like this." And it was at that exact moment that Wadia remembered exactly what had happened;

what he had discovered while cleaning his piano. He fumbled, trying to find the picture in his pyjama pockets (My God! Had they really brought him here in his jammies?) and found nothing. Nothing except the handkerchief he always kept in the right pocket of his pyjamas or trousers. Even shorts, for that matter, although he couldn't remember the last time he had worn shorts.

"Where is the picture?" he demanded. All of them were mute to the question.

Then the Velkars looked at each other and mumbled something incoherently. Of course they had found the picture. He sensed the drift of what they were about to say. It was easy. They would tell him he had had some sort of fall and had been rendered unconscious (that had to be it, right? Why on earth would he find himself here otherwise?) and that he had lost his short-term memory (which is why he recognised these dolts but did not remember what had happened yesterday, and instead concocted the memory of a picture of Elise's grave in his backyard), but he wasn't going to buy it. Before he could open his mouth to speak, though, the doctor intervened. And when doctors spoke, you listened. But no, this was a resident.

"The thing is, Mr. Rustom (it was sensible on his part that he didn't call him Uncle again, he had to give him that), you had a pretty bad fall. Your servant found you lying unconscious on the floor, right next to the piano – that seems to be the object you hit your head upon with brute force. Now, we have done some scans and are waiting for the results to come in. All we have to do is rule out any possible complications, like, say, internal bleeding."

Wadia felt a bit relieved. He had no doubt in his mind they would see nothing in those scans and that very soon he would find himself back in the comfort of his own home. The last thing he needed was to be told he would have to spend the night in a hospital bed. He glanced at the elderly Velkars, who were obviously guilty of hiding something. Then Toral spoke, her soothing voice comforting as usual.

"We're just concerned about you, Rustom. You see, Daddykins found the picture and he has instructed Ramukaka to keep it on your desk in the study. So, you needn't worry about it. It's safe and where it rightfully belongs. Undoubtedly, we need to have another conversation pertaining to this matter, but we shall reserve that for later. The important thing is getting you back home safe and sound." The last sentence uttered as though he were an invalid.

And then the doctor, who had seemed increasingly restless for the last several moments, cut in.

"The head nurse here (gesturing to the portly nurse who stood beside him), Mrs. Pinto, will call me as soon as the report is ready. I'm in the hospital all day, but only once Dr. Colaco gives the go-ahead, can you go home."

"Dr. Colaco? Who the hell is he? And why isn't he here?"

The resident, whose name was Arjun Shah (Wadia's vision was clearly not the reason he found himself in a hospital this Sunday afternoon) cleared his throat, and said shakily, "He has gone on a picnic to Matheran. But, don't worry. I will send him the scans via email as soon as I get them. Digital age, you know."

"And he sent *you* in his place?" The sheepish Arjun Shah seemed lost. He looked to the Velkars as though to garner some sort of assistance, but to no avail. They knew what he was now coming to realize: that you simply couldn't argue with the man in this bed.

"Well, you see, it's his son's birthday and—"

"Please spare me the drama, will you? Just get on with expediting those scans!" And this time it was not only the resident doctor who quivered, but the Velkars, too.

"Yes, Sir! See you soon, Sir!"

"No, I hope I *never* see you again!" Wadia's voice boomed louder than it ever had, as the nervous resident literally 'ran' out the doors of the emergency ward. The nurses in the ward, including the terrified one standing by his bed, seemed to be frozen in shock. Chattering noisily all this while like wild geese, they had been silenced in one deft move. Top job, Wadia!

After what seemed to be a rather long drawn-out silence, Velkar spoke, seemingly with a sense of conviction.

"Rustom, you have to understand. We thought you might have had a heart attack upon seeing that picture we found on the floor beside you; that it might have been the very reason you fell down, and were then rendered unconscious. The moment Ramukaka called me, I called the Holy Family Hospital ambulance. They were at your place in only a few minutes. It is in times like these that you realize it helps to have a hospital close by. In the meantime, I phoned Toral and told her what had happened. She told us to proceed immediately to the hospital, and that she would be there in no time. We were all here when they brought you in. You have to understand we – we were so very scared…"

His voice trailed off then. 'Just when I ask the resident doctor to spare me drama, this chap comes along and douses me in it.' At the back of his mind, though, Wadia was grateful to Velkar for having brought him here. He had heard several stories of people who had had nasty falls; old people like him, who had passed away not long afterwards. What if that fall had indeed precipitated some sort of internal bleeding? Staying at home, then, without any sort of medical intervention, would not help his cause, would it?

"Thank you," he said with the greatest difficulty. Not that he wasn't thankful; he just had difficulty expressing gratitude.

"You're welcome," said Velkar. Trust that idiot to be formal. The more appropriate thing to have said here would have been 'It's all right,' or perhaps 'You don't need to thank me' (the latter was far better suited). But, 'You're welcome?' Ridiculous!

Wadia excused the Velkars, who said they would grab a quick cup of coffee in the hospital cafeteria while they waited for the reports. Great! I'm lying here in a hospital bed and these guys are celebrating. He dismissed them with a wave of his hand, a wave that seemed more like he might be swatting a fly. And then he closed his eyes. It was really rather unbearable for him to have to listen to the incessant chatter of the nurses in the room, that had started all over again. He thought a couple of times whether it would be better if he screamed at all of them to shut up. In the end, he decided it was best he shut himself up; that way they would send him home, rather than take him in for brain surgery.

The reports finally came in, just after the Velkars had returned from their coffee break. What had it been? Harvest-your-own-coffee-beans coffee? The reports were all clear. Velkar explained to an excited Wadia that they were just going to proceed with the checkout formalities and then they would be out in a flash. Toral was paying the bill and he could pay her later.

"Of course I will pay her later. Why do you even have to bring that matter up, Anil?"

"I – because – well, you know. It just came out of my mouth. I'm sorry." Looking like a lamb that has walked into in a mutton shop.

And soon, they were heading home. Nobody said a word. It was 5 in the evening. Little had Rustom known, when he set out to clean his piano in the morning, that the day was going to unfold like this. As they pulled into the gates of his bungalow compound, he saw Ramukaka waiting nervously for him on the patio. His face lit up when he saw his master emerge from the car. He was *alive*. Wadia hoped he wouldn't do something ludicrous like place a garland around his neck. He turned to the others, who had got out of the car and were looking at him expectantly, as though they expected him to make some kind of speech. Well, if a speech was what they wanted, then a speech was what they would get.

"Thank you," he mumbled before turning around.

He didn't even look at Ramukaka's face; just acknowledged him with a silent nod as he walked into the house. Something terrible had happened; something Wadia would not share with anyone. He had just come face to face with the fragility of life. In all these years he had never thought of death; as though he might be the only person that ever lived, who would never die. But today, well, he knew he was lucky to be coming home. It had been a nasty fall, after all.

Later that night, he couldn't stop staring at the image he had discovered underneath the third pedal of his piano, in his study. Why had his dad plastered it there, well hidden from sight? How could he have not told his son that a dear, dear family member had been buried in their very backyard? Elise's tombstone was bang in the centre of that very place, towards the back. Eerily close to Fluffy and Polly's graves, which were just to its right. He shuddered to think he had almost made the decision to bury his beloved pets, in the one place they would find Elise's coffin. Now that he thought about it, a memory came to his mind. Ramukaka had insisted that they dig the graves to the right side of the place Wadia had just beforehand deemed appropriate. And then another thought struck him. Could Ramukaka have been a part of that 'secret burial' too? What on earth had happened to the tombstone? Had it been removed because it was best a girl with Down's be forgotten? He remembered his dad never coming to play with him in the backyard, although he would frequently play with him in the garden in front. Now he knew why.

Looking more closely at the photo, he noticed there was no date on it. And then it came to him out of the blue; a memory that served to show exactly how all of this was linked to his past. He remembered his dada telling him a long time ago, when he was a mere fifteen years or so (he remembered the exact age he had been because it had been around a year since his mother had passed, which was when he had been fourteen years old), to go and stay with his aunt in Surat because he had something urgent to do and he couldn't leave him alone at home. He remembered throwing a fit back then, and the strangest thing happening right after. His father breaking down, collapsing in a heap on the floor.

That was when the young Rustom had told his dada to please not cry, he would do anything he asked of him. It was set. Miranda aunty had been informed already. She would come to Bombay once in a while to check on her house, and incidentally, this was one of those very times. Furthermore, she was leaving for Surat that very morning, and she was the first one Percy thought of, when it came to keeping Rustom safe while he was away. Miranda had told her brother, Percy, that she could keep Rustom for as long as he wanted her to. 'Had she known too?' Wadia thought, as he placed the picture back on his desk. For a long time he did nothing but stare into space.

All this time they had spent searching for Elise, she had been right here in his home (because the backyard in one's home is part of one's home, of course), waiting to be discovered by him. And now, at long last, he had found her.

Chapter Thirty
A Tribute to Elise Wadia

A couple of weeks later, the Velkars were back in The White House. This time round, though, they weren't here on account of a brunch hosted by the piano man; they had assembled to honour the memory of Elise, and even though the exact year of her birth was unknown, Wadia had created what he believed to be a tombstone that truly did justice to the young lass who had filled the lives of so many people around her with sunshine. They all gazed at the large white stone (white was surely a far better colour to represent her purity than the drab grey that had been selected by his father, thought Wadia) that had been erected only a few moments ago, by a karigar whom Wadia had tipped most generously (far too generously by his standards, but then this was an occasion that merited an act of extreme generosity). On the tombstone were but two words: *Für Elise*. He had made sure the karigar did not dig too deep down, for fear of striking the casket in which Elise's body lay. It had been a most emotional moment for all of them, Vidya included. She had a handkerchief in her right hand pretty much all the time.

After paying their individual respects to Elise, they were all seated on the front lawns, for that piping hot cup of Ramukaka's 'speshal chai.' Initially Rustom had suggested they sit on the spacious balcony outside his study, but Toral had told him it would be difficult to carry all those cups of tea back and forth from the kitchen, and finally, with a great deal of reluctance, Wadia had agreed. He couldn't remember the last time he had sat on this lawn to have a cup of chai, although he did remember running across it when he was a child. As he sat here now, he wondered why he didn't do this more often. Have chai sitting here that is, not run around. The round table with its accompanying four chairs had been here forever, even though it merely served as a showpiece. He remembered his mama and dada sitting here to have their cups of chai, in an age gone by. Luckily, the table and chairs were cleaned every single day. After all, Lizzie Wadia's diktat of keeping the house spotlessly clean had been passed down to Ramukaka, who in turn duly instructed the house help.

"I'm so happy Elise finally got what she wanted," Toral said, breaking the heavy silence that had descended on them. "I'm sure she is looking up from the heavens and smiling as we speak."

"She is here," said Wadia, and all of them turned to look at him. He looked straight into his cup of cardamom chai, while he spoke. "I always thought the presence I felt all these years in my study was that of my mum. However, something happened last night that led me to believe otherwise."

"Could you elaborate please, Rustom?" It was Velkar, flashing his empty cup of chai straight in front of his friend's eyes, as though to indicate that it would be just splendid if he could have a refill. Ignoring Velkar's desperate plea for a second cup of chai, Wadia continued, "You see, last night when I was sitting in the study, the strangest thing happened. I couldn't get myself to read and I was staring at the picture of that tombstone for the longest time. A good hour must have passed, I think, before I realized my eyes were closing. I got up at once and just before I could leave the room, I thought of playing Für Elise."

"And then?" Velkar seemed to have lost all interest in that second cup.

"Then I did the only thing that came naturally to me. I played Für Elise on the record player. And the next thing you knew, I went through this whole gamut of emotions, ranging from extreme sadness to sheer jubilation. The strangest thing was, not long after, I knew it wasn't only 'me' who had gone through those emotions." And then, his face suddenly turned grave as he looked at the Velkars and said, "Do you think that all this while she could have been living inside of me?"

But Wadia's listeners said nothing, transfixed as they found themselves.

"You see, I came to realize that I was a conduit for her emotions. Through the music, she lived her life all over again; from the towering highs to the utter lows."

"I don't understand – are you saying she is inside you even now? Why, hello Elise!" It was Velkar, who was in reality terrified of ghosts. If anyone knew that, it was Vidya; after all, the Maharashtrian slept with a dim light on. The very fact that he were trying to befriend a ghost, would be to ensure it wouldn't attack him.

"I think I need some time to myself," Wadia suddenly said, as though to wrap things up. It wasn't like his words had come at an inappropriate moment, either; they had completed the ceremony, and finished their cups of chai. Not that his guests had overextended their stay, mind you; his home was an open house, after all.

Velkar warily took Wadia's outstretched hand in his. Wadia was almost tempted to say, "What is Elise going to do? Eat you?"

Then Toral said, "Don't think all that much about it, Rustom. We've had a pretty hectic last month or so. I think the best thing you can do, is take it easy. Maybe we can all plan a trip somewhere." Spoken as though she didn't believe him at all.

"That sounds lovely," Vidya opined. "Maybe we can go to Matheran. I've always wanted to see the monkeys there. Oops! I forgot, I already have one at home." That most simple of jokes got Toral and Wadia laughing, but not Velkar. And it wasn't because the joke was on him, Wadia knew that well. He still couldn't get over the fact that there might be a ghost present in the room with them. Worse still, inside the body of his best friend.

After his guests had left, Wadia took a few moments to gather his thoughts. Being alone had a whole different meaning now, he reflected, as he nursed his glass of whisky. He hadn't had an afternoon drink in ages, apart from that rather brilliant bloody mary Toral had prepared for him only a few days ago. He had opened that special bottle of Japanese whisky he had reserved for special occasions. Now was as good a time as any. He had played Für Elise non-stop for an hour or so, not tiring of it at all. Ramukaka had been his audience of one; he had defied his demure nature and ventured out of the kitchen to sit in the living room, cross-legged on the floor, of course, while his master played. The afternoon drinking some days ago had not disconcerted Ramukaka because his master had had company. As for today, well, he would let it slide too. After all, it was a very delicate time. Unbeknownst to his master (even though Wadia had had an air of suspicion about it lately), he had seen the body of that child brought to the house in the middle of the night, one day when the little Rustom was spending time in Surat. Of course he knew she had been buried later that morning. After all, he had helped bury her.

That night, in his study, Wadia scrutinized himself closely in the tall mirror that reflected the grand bookshelf, looking for some sign of Elise; as though her presence in his body might have somehow made him resemble her in some manner. But no, he looked one hundred percent 'Rustom.' Then he went to his bookshelf (that covered an entire section of the wall from top to bottom), looking for a book to read. He chose *The Little Prince*, because he was in the mood to start reading something he could finish off in one sitting. He absolutely adored Antoine de Saint Exupery's classic fable. It had, after all, been his favourite book when he had been a child. There are some books that leave a great impression on your mind when you are young, and this was one of them. Besides, there was another reason he had chosen this book in particular.

He knew Elise would love it, too.

It had taken him longer than expected to read the fable he thought he would devour in no time, partly because he wanted to savour it slowly, and also because his eyes were closing. Perhaps he should put off playing Für Elise for today? He waited a few moments by the record player, as though contemplating whether he should put an end to this ritual of listening to Für Elise every night, once and for all. But then he thought to himself, it has been a ritual for so long; why should I stop now? And so, he let it play.

When Wadia went to bed that night, he had the most beautiful feeling envelop him. He had played Für Elise in his study on the record player right before he retired to bed, and he had felt nothing. He hadn't even enjoyed listening to it, come to think of it; and, he wasn't that sleepy any more. Then a powerful thought hit him, straight out of the blue.

Elise had gone.

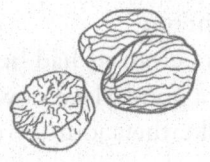

Chapter Thirty-one
Hidden Genius

The next morning Wadia woke up with a spring in his step. It wasn't as if he had become lighter, what with the weight of Elise not bearing on him any more. Unlike matter, souls didn't weigh a thing.

After polishing off his breakfast, which was a combination of his favourite scrambled eggs with toast, along with some sausages he had got from that fancy supermarket the other day, he made a mental note to buy more of the latter the next time round. Why travel all the way to Germany to eat *Bratwurst*, when you can have it in the confines of your home? Why, he could even organise an Oktoberfest in Bandra if he wished. And he could do it in November!

Ramukaka had shot off a dirty glance to Wadia, when he had placed the plate of pork sausages on the table. He had had to fry them, and even though it wasn't considered sacrilege in his religion to eat this type of meat, he wasn't quite happy with the idea of anyone eating pork, because he considered the pig a filthy animal; one that rolled in the mud all day long. He had even told Wadia this once when they were children, and the young Rustom had told him in turn that he himself was a sort of pig; one that rolled in his bed. And little Ramu had laughed loudly, but only because he did not want to displease Rustom, who was the only child who ever played with him. Little had he known then, things would change with time, and one day he would find himself serving the lad who had once climbed trees with him, in search of ripe perus.

Wadia licked his fingers clean. It had been a truly satisfying meal. He was happy Elise was in a good place now. He believed there was a time when spirits must make their journey over into the next world, and Elise had surely made that transition. In a sense it seemed almost cruel; to find happiness when someone you had grown to love (even though that love was only a few days old), left you forever.

Wadia had called the others for what he had proclaimed to be an 'emergency meeting.' They had all asked him what the matter was, but Wadia told them he couldn't disclose what he had to say over the phone. And so, only a day after they had all met to pay their last respects to Elise Wadia in The White House, the Velkars found themselves back there for tea the following evening. This time round it was Parsi chai and not speshal chai. Wadia was seated at the piano when they came in, like a musician who might be waiting for his audience to trickle in and fill the auditorium. Except, this auditorium had only three members. Not to forget one in the kitchen. That was a cheaper seat, sort of like the 'stall' seat in theatres in days gone by. Now there were only big multiplexes and no real distinction between seats, unless you counted those ridiculous lounge chairs where people lay down covered with blankets while they watched movies. If you want to lie down, sleep at home in your bed, Wadia had thought, when he had seen an advertisement for a swanky new multiplex in the newspaper that specifically laid emphasis on those 'beds.'

"Ah! Looks like we are in for a treat. So 'this' is what the emergency is about, eh? You want us to listen to another composition of the masters? Better still, something you have composed yourself?" It was Velkar. Wadia, seemingly deflated, didn't say a word. As though she could sense this, Toral asked him, "Are you okay, Rustom?"

"I'm fine. I just wanted to show you all something. I'm sorry, I realise we only met yesterday but—"

"Rustom, you are family." It was Vidya. And a surge of emotion coursed through Wadia. It felt so nice to hear Vidya refer to him as 'family.' Of course, he was not going to be adopted by the Velkars (thank God for that – the last thing he wanted was to be related to that Maharashtrian), but he knew what she meant.

And then he began to play. One minute of the most horrendous music that seemed like a torturous hour. Ramukaka had emerged from the kitchen as though he might be sleepwalking, and he now stood bang in the middle of the living room. Looks of utter disbelief crept into faces that had at first seemed to shine in eager anticipation of some really fine music. And then, right in the middle of the piece, Wadia stopped playing and looked at his guests with a sense of utter defeat.

"It was all Elise." A chill ran down Toral's spine.

"You mean the music – *all of it*? Your childhood genius?"

"Yes. I guess I'm good for nothing at all."

Velkar went over to Wadia, placed his hands firmly on his shoulders, and squeezed them. "Don't you ever say that, okay, Rustom?"

"And she's gone now?" It was Vidya.

"Yes. I think that tribute did it – the fact that her life had finally got the respect it deserved. She had been living through me all these years. All those classes... Mrs. Braganza... God! My entire life has been a lie!"

Velkar released his hands from Wadia's shoulders, and said, "No. You know what you said a few moments ago, about you not being good for anything? Let me tell you this. You're far better than you give yourself credit for. You were chosen by Elise, to live her life the way she wanted."

"Yes, but what about *me*?" And immediately Wadia thought he had said the most selfish thing. After all, the poor girl had suffered so terribly and she deserved all the happiness she could get, even if that meant using his body as her instrument. To *play* an *instrument*."

Wadia got up then, and made his way from the piano to the living room area where his guests were seated. He sank into the large emperor's chair that didn't feel like a throne any longer. Not with how small he felt.

"What an utter failure I am."

It was Toral's turn to counter Wadia. "Rustom, Velkar is right. Elise chose *you*."

"She chose me because she had no bloody choice." Wadia was angry now.

"No, she did so because she *loved* you!" It was the first time Rustom had ever seen Toral angry.

The tension in the room was palpable. Ramukaka retreated to the kitchen. His master would be all right. He was in the right company, after all, even though one of those people dropped a bit of everything he ate on the carpet in the living room. Not long ago it had been pieces of the starters that had been brought by Toral Memsab; today, it was crumbs of Marie biscuits that were served with his fine Parsi chai. He had almost sensed there might be something wrong, when the Velkars had walked into the house. After all, they had been here only yesterday. What had happened to his master? Surely one could have an off day while playing any musical instrument, but a musical rendition as warped as the one he had heard only a few moments ago?

For a long time nobody said anything. Finally Toral broke the silence.

"I'm sorry, Rustom. I never meant to say anything to upset you. I just couldn't control myself."

"It's okay," Rustom said, not looking at her. He *had* been a bit harsh on her, truth be told.

"Sorry to intervene. Did you notice any tangible change in your life after you returned from Surat, Rustom?" It was Vidya. Now why would she ask something like that? But she did have a point, now that he thought about it.

"You know, it was only after I returned from my forced sojourn in Surat, that I developed an interest in playing the piano."

"You did love the same things you loved before, too, right?" Wadia had a sense of where this conversation was headed.

"Yes. Well – I always loved fried eggs. But I never loved music, let alone playing it. It was around the time I was twelve that I suddenly demanded we have a piano in the house. My God! To think that all these years it has been Elise…"

A long silence permeated the living room; it was only confirmed now, why Wadia had been so crazy about Für Elise; why he had even *wanted* to play the piano, at all. He sighed. His entire life had been a lie.

"Well, I hope she's happy now," Wadia said, shoulders slumped. He wondered if his dad had an inkling when he were alive, that the spirit of Elise might be hiding in his son's body. Perhaps that might be the reason he had the piano sent away? In the hope Elise might leave his son for good?

"Well, I'm sure she's happy now," Toral said. "We did give her a most beautiful send-off, in a way, by paying our last respects and bequeathing her that wonderfully curated tombstone. I'm sure she's still with you, but in a different way; like watching from 'The Outside'."

Wadia sighed. It all made sense now; Miss Braganza telling him he was a natural at playing the piano. Of course he was a natural, if playing the piano came naturally to Elise. Well, perhaps not all that naturally. Elise probably made it a point to not make it all that obvious to the people around them that she were inhabiting the young boy's body, by pretending her way through piano basics.

In his study that night, Wadia wondered who it was that had experienced all those emotions when he had played Fur Elise on his record player, right from his childhood days to the present moment.

Was it him?

Or Elise?

Or perhaps the both of them?

Chapter Thirty-two
Two Lost Souls Swimming in a Fish Bowl

It had been ten long years since that fateful trip to Pardi, that Wadia found himself returning there. Jasmine had insisted he come and spend some time with her. She had been corresponding regularly with Wadia via email over the years, and while at first Rustom didn't seem to mind, over time he started taking more and more time to respond to her emails. He couldn't stand the thought that she might be even remotely interested in him. He had told the Velkars once, about this budding affection she displayed for him, and Vidya and Toral had both told him she was the sweetest woman and that he should seriously consider spending the rest of his life with her. Maybe he could even move in with her, or perhaps she could come and stay with him. That was the last time he ever brought up the subject matter with them. But now, as he was almost reaching Jasmine's home, he asked himself, 'What am I even doing here? Might this be what I truly want?'

Jasmine welcomed him with arms open wide. When he hugged her (although he did so rather half-heartedly), he felt a sense of comfort he hadn't felt in a while. He couldn't remember the last time he had been hugged like this. This was a different kind of hug; one that persisted. Awkwardly, he took his luggage and went inside. It was a Friday. He had told Jasmine he would spend a couple of nights with her (in separate bedrooms, of course, even though that was unsaid) before he went back home. He thought of Velkar's last bit of advice. He had told Rustom to kiss Jasmine the moment he saw her. That she was waiting for him to make the first move. And just for a second, after she had finally pulled away from him and stared right into his eyes before turning to go back into the house, he had felt that, yes, she had indeed been waiting for that kiss. Her body language screamed it. But he was eighty now. Too late for kissing. And so, he had just let it go. He had asked himself repeatedly as he walked into the house, 'Why are you here'?

She had given him Elise's bedroom. The little girl had spent some of the happiest moments of her life in this house, and it was only fitting he should stay in her room. Perhaps Elise's spirit was right here with him (in the room, that is, not once again in his body). He had told Jasmine he needed a few moments to refresh himself, and the first thing he did was take a long, hot shower in the spacious bathroom attached to his room. When he emerged, he slipped into his tee shirt and pyjamas. They weren't the kind of pyjamas one wore in the night. Toral had taken him shopping before he went on the trip, and she had told him that 'jammies' like this were *in*. That they had *been in* for the longest time. Never mind what that meant. Even though they were clearly not formal, they weren't overtly casual either, and since they weren't going to be leaving the house except to take a walk by the lake on occasion, she had insisted he buy at least a couple of pairs for the two evenings he would be spending there. And then he had thought, she might be a daughter to the Velkars, but she's most certainly a mother to me!

For a while Wadia was lost in the mesmerizing view of the lake through the window in the bedroom. He had always wondered why he hadn't come here all these years to visit Jasmine (because even if he weren't romantically inclined towards her, there was still a strong bond that existed between them on account of Elise, and he could surely have visited her as a friend every now and then). And then, after a decent amount of time had passed, he decided he should go downstairs. After all, his host would be waiting for him.

This time round, though, he noticed Jasmine had help. The maid who hadn't shown up the last time round, was running from the kitchen to the living room, laying the table and doing everything she possibly could so her mistress needn't lift a finger.

"You must have a fabulous cook. The food smells absolutely delicious!" he told Jasmine then, as they nursed their respective glasses of rosé.

"I have made roast chicken for you, my dear." Had she just called him *my dear*? And before he could say anything, she added, "And prawn dumplings with orange sauce and a Caesar salad. You'll have to excuse the salad though. It is purely vegetarian."

"Oh, not in the least bit. In fact, over the last few years, I have been making a conscious attempt to eat more vegetarian food. It's just, what choices do we Parsis really have, other than dhansak? Every time I eat vegetable dhansak, I feel as though something is missing."

"I know the feeling well. I'm Parsi myself, and though I enjoy my meat, I make a deliberate choice to eat more vegetables. And I have Vinita to thank for that." She gestured to her house help, standing nearby, who looked like she wanted to ask her mistress something.

"Ho Vinita?"

"Madam, mala pandhra minute dya, jevan garam karayla." Before Jasmine could translate for Wadia what Vinita had said in Marathi, into English, he gently assured her, "I'm absolutely fine with it. We can eat in fifteen minutes." And Jasmine merely nodded at Vinita and made a gesture with her hand, as though indicating to her that it was time to start getting the food onto the table.

Dinner was delicious, especially the roast chicken. The Caesar salad wasn't all that bad either. It had been a while since a vegetarian dish had made such an impact on him. Was it the rosé talking? He hadn't had a sip of wine for the longest time prior to this occasion, and it seemed to have hit him pretty hard. Not to the point where he might end up incoherent like Velkar had been that day long ago, but enough to give him a strong *buzz* (wasn't that how the kids these days described it?).

After dinner, Wadia was pleasantly surprised when Jasmine asked him if he would like some Cognac. Even though (or perhaps especially because) the effects of the rosé had most clearly not worn off, he could never say no to a glass of his favourite drink. On holiday, he could break the 'not more than three drinks a time' rule. What was even better, it was his old friend, Remy. By this time it had turned dark, but thanks to the bright lighting on Jasmine's porch, you could see the lake shimmering in the near distance. What a truly wonderful place to live in. He wondered if Jasmine might miss the sight of buildings, of civilization. After all, this wasn't the only life she had known. Before meeting Princess, she had studied in London. And she had given up her career just so she could help take care of Elise. How noble that had been.

"I was thinking of what you said on the phone to me all those years ago," Jasmine said then, looking into the distance. Wadia's mind drifted to the first time he had called Jasmine, before opting to communicate via email. He had done so because he needed to confide in her about how Elise had apparently been living inside of him all these years, and he probably wanted (or needed, rather) someone to corroborate what he was saying. He wanted to know he wasn't losing his mind. Jasmine had told him then, that he had most certainly been right about what he felt. When Elise had been alive, she had been full of curiosity about where the soul went after humans died.

It had all started with the death of her pet rabbit (they had got one for her because she loved wild rabbits that lived in the area and they knew she would take extremely good care of a pet if they got her one). Elise had broken down when she saw its lifeless body by the lake, where it had ventured to spend its final moments. It had perhaps been the first time she had encountered death, and she wanted to know where Tubby (the name of her 'once alive' rabbit) had gone. That was when they had explained to her about the afterlife. They had told her, 'Tubby has a new body now. Tubby is happy.' She went on.

"You see, Rustom, you always wondered why you felt the kind of emotions that you did when you listened to Für Elise, irrespective of whether you heard it on the radio or you had been playing it on the piano. I didn't have an answer for you then, but I think I do now."

Wadia took another sip of his Cognac. He was high as a kite now, and he hoped he would be able to walk without swaying, when the time came. Jasmine continued.

"You see, what you experienced then was exactly what Elise did. She felt pain, and you felt it too."

"Come again?"

"You see, the two of you felt the very same thing, be it pleasure or pain. The pain you felt was yours and yet, it wasn't."

Wadia mulled this over a bit. Could it really be possible, for two souls to feel pain in the very same body? He thought then of those famous lyrics of Pink Floyd's epic track 'Wish you were here'... 'Two lost souls swimming in a fish bowl... year after year." Perhaps *that* was what was meant by oneness. His body. The fishbowl. Elise and him. The two lost goldfish. He was suddenly overwhelmed with emotion.

It all came back to him; his dark childhood that had been illuminated by his love for playing the piano. That piano (or rather his playing of it) had undoubtedly got him through one of the most turbulent periods in his life. He had found himself in a terribly dark space when he returned from Surat. He thought back to the time he had spent in that city (yet another city in the state of Gujarat that he had visited, apart from Udvada, of course). That one week, largely spent in strolling through the large backyard in his aunt's palatial home. Even though he had a large, tastefully decorated room that was air-conditioned (that was the most important thing) all to himself, there was not much he could do, except read. And there were plenty of books in his aunt's well stocked library, but he was just a child and although he did attempt to read Sartre, he found himself giving up after the first few pages.

Ever since the death of his mother, something inside Rustom had changed. His father had little time for him. It would have helped if he had had friends in school, but young Rustom mostly kept to himself. He was relentlessly teased by the boys in his class for being a sissy. Not that he knew what that word really meant; all he knew was, it meant he was different from the others. It was only a matter of time before he would see 'difference' as meaning he was a cut above the rest.

The advent of the piano into his life followed shortly thereafter, and it seemed to solidify his status even more; after all, how many children grew up being addicted to the piano, and being good at it, too? However, he simply didn't care. He had found something he truly loved. And then it hit him. He hadn't saved Elise at all.

She had saved *him*.

In a world largely filled with people who strive for self-gratification and look to further their ambitions without so much as a thought for others, she had seen him through a most tumultuous time. He would have probably killed himself if she hadn't come into his life.

Rustom suddenly snapped back to reality, when he saw Jasmine scrutinizing him. He raised his glass of Cognac to her, and she raised hers to his and the glasses clinked. They sipped the rest of their drinks in silence. He wondered what she might be thinking. It was nice to be having a drink with someone. Even if no words were exchanged. And then, all of a sudden, her face lit up. She drained the remainder of her drink in one large sip, got up and said, "Come with me."

And as she led the way up the stairs, Wadia wondered what was on her mind. Surely she wasn't going to suggest they sleep together?

"May I?" she said, as she found herself outside Wadia's bedroom.

"It's your house," he said, and she chuckled and went in.

And while she played Für Elise almost as enchantingly as Elise had done (through his body, of course), he felt something.

Wadia, seated in a chair alongside Jasmine, thought, maybe, just maybe, there's something here. And even though Elise were long gone, he knew it was she that had set him up to this.

His guardian angel.

Elise Wadia.

If you enjoyed this and have not yet read *The Perfect Outside*, may we suggest you do?

In her dreams Polly is a beautiful macaw flying free in The Perfect Outside. In reality she is no more than a common green parrot, forever looking out through the bars of her cage. Beyond those bars is Fluffy, a Persian Queen of a cat, who loves her indolent, inside life — and Wadia, her eccentric, stuck-in-a-rut owner and his TV set.

Polly and Fluffy embark on an adventure and explore the meaning of being outside, of freedom and inner happiness.

Is this an allegorical tale like *Life of Pi*? A life-affirming book of self-actualisation like *Jonathan Livingston Seagull*? A parable for our times like *The Little Prince*? Or just a nice story about a parrot and a cat? We'll let you decide.

"Rohit Trilokekar writes with passion and sophistication in an era of vanilla books that say nothing! His allegorical novel raises profound questions about identity and existence, freedom and courage.... the eternal outsider/insider debate meets a fresh challenge in this delightful fable." – Shobhaa De

"Trilokekar's book is a whimsical, charismatic foray into the life of a parrot seeking freedom and a cat who has too much of it. It reads breezily, but its deep allegorical significance is never lost on the reader. The writing sparkles, and his comedic touch refreshes us constantly."

– Siddhartha Mukherjee, Pulitzer Prize winner

Milton Keynes UK
Ingram Content Group UK Ltd.
UKHW041035161123
432682UK00001B/16